HER LAST BREATH

ALSO BY TAYLOR ADAMS

The Last Word

Hairpin Bridge

No Exit

Our Last Night

Eyeshot

HER LAST BREATH

A NOVEL

TAYLOR ADAMS

wm
WILLIAM MORROW
An Imprint of HarperCollins*Publishers*

HarperCollins books may be purchased for educational, business, or sales promotional use. For information, please email the Special Markets Department at SPsales@harpercollins.com.

hc.com

FIRST EDITION

Library of Congress Cataloging-in-Publication Data has been applied for.

ISBN 978-0-06-339413-1

Printed in the United States of America

26 27 28 29 30 LBC 7 6 5 4 3

FOR NOLAN

Prologue

We're losing her.

DETECTIVE LAYLA WASHINGTON FEELS HELPLESS WAITING FOR UPdates, and this latest text message is the most ominous yet.

A young woman is trapped in a remote cave system miles inside the Cascade Range. She's injured, exhausted, and lapsing in and out of consciousness. Rescuers have managed to extract little information from her—not even a name—and at this point, questioning the victim is a waste of air and time. The team's sole priority is rescuing her before she dies. As Washington understands it, the woman is inside a limestone tunnel just a few feet high and eighteen inches wide. A cave-in sealed her inside the crawlspace sometime last night, and now she's pinned on her stomach by dense rockfall on all sides. One rescuer compared it to being stuck inside a smaller-than-average coffin.

Slowly filling with rocks.

In pitch blackness.

Alone.

For the past *eighteen hours*.

It'll be all over local televisions by six tonight. The rescue operation is now dozens strong, mostly volunteers and local experts, and will double when reinforcements arrive from Portland. The incident commander is an old fire chief from Salem, just a few years younger than Washington herself, and he runs an efficient show. An underground manager and several specialized teams—medical, rigging, litter—are currently racing to clear rock debris, hand deliver oxygen bottles, and rig a pulley system down hundreds of feet of narrow, labyrinthine tunnels. They'd found the trapped woman by the echo of her screams, but it took hours to trace her exact location and even longer to safely reach her.

Underground lifesaving operations are rare and uniquely difficult: part confined-space rescue, part firefighting, with a dash of mountaineering thrown in for good measure. Much of this particular cave can only be traversed single file, risking bottlenecks and traffic jams while equipment is passed from rescuer to rescuer like a human daisy chain. Phone and radio signals are unable to penetrate rock, limiting communication to line of sight. Every inch of progress is incremental and dangerous. The primary directive of any rescue is to not require rescuing yourself, and one team member has already been seriously injured.

Time is not on the woman's side. Each of her physical needs is a ticking clock—air, hydration, energy, body temperature—and one will inevitably run out. With every text message Washington receives, her stomach flutters with dread.

Three hours ago, there was modest hope in the old fire chief's texts: **Made contact with victim. TL can touch her fingers thru 4-inch gap in rock. Confirmed head trauma, dislocated/broken ankle, lacerations/bruising.**

Two hours ago, worry started to creep in. **Losing consciousness. Exhaustion.**

Then, finally: **We're losing her.**

And an hour of silence.

While she waits, the sixty-something detective has been doing what she does best: butt-in-chair research. The cave system is a natural formation called the Devil's Staircase, located on (and under) an isolated tract of logging forest miles from the nearest public road. The region has numerous other, more popular caves, but the Devil's Staircase seems to be the perfect carnivorous plant: remote enough to be dangerous, accessible enough to lure in amateurs. With a moderate hike and a written permit from the lumber company that owns the land, local adventurers can see stalactites the size of tree trunks and gardens of impossible rock formations growing in fungal tendrils. The photographs are undeniably striking.

However, more curious (and foolish) interlopers sometimes ignore the warning signage and explore deeper, where the lower tunnels tighten into treacherous crawlspaces and the dangers multiply. Under millions of tons of earth, a single disturbed rock can trigger a fatal collapse. Pockets of trapped carbon dioxide can become invisible death traps. Groundwater levels can rise and fall without warning. Worst of all, some of the cave's most cramped tunnel crawls—termed *squeezes* by enthusiasts—are as narrow as ten inches wide.

What would possess this unknown woman to venture to such a depth? The most inviolable rule of cave exploration is to never go alone. Either she was incredibly reckless—or she was fleeing something even deadlier.

Detective Washington hopes the woman survives to tell her story. The mountains, seen from Washington's second-floor desk in the Stevens County Sheriff's Office, look like sleeping giants cloaked in evergreens. On a drizzly afternoon like today she can barely see them at all. Somewhere out there a young woman is locked inside a vault of rock, fighting for every breath.

Keep fighting.

She's a tough gal, the incident commander had texted earlier. **She's got sisu.**

Odd word choice.

Washington had to look it up—apparently *sisu* is a Finnish

term for grit and determination in the face of hardship. There's no English-language equivalent for it, because *sisu* isn't derived from any single act of bravery. It's tireless, sustained, long term.

Worryingly, recent rainfall has also flooded the trapped woman's crawlspace with several feet of groundwater. By all estimates she should have died of hypothermia yesterday, but apparently she'd managed to lift herself up onto stacked rocks and suspend her body a few inches above the deadly cold. It couldn't have been comfortable, but it kept her alive. She'd understood that prolonged contact with the water meant death.

Sisu, Washington agreed. Whoever this woman is, she clearly has some survival skills. The detective can't help but root for her.

Keep me updated, she'd texted back. **She's a POI in a homicide.**

This was also no ordinary caving accident.

A body was discovered outside the Devil's Staircase. By the time Washington herself had hitched a tooth-rattling ATV ride up the mountain at six this morning, the site was already thoroughly contaminated by the rescue operation. It'll be a miracle if much physical evidence survives at all. But the violence of the death is unmistakable: the decedent suffered a fatal gunshot wound and stained the rocks with several liters of blood.

And the trapped woman knows what happened. According to a few fragmented communications gathered hours earlier, she'd apparently battled for her life against a killer, or even multiple killers. Maybe she'd defeated them. Maybe they're still out there, making preparations to strike again.

Keep fighting, girl. They've almost got you out.

But the rescuers are racing against uncaring physics. The woman is fading with exhaustion, her air is becoming unbreathable, and the water is rising. *Sisu* buys only so much time.

Washington checks her phone. It's already been seventy minutes since the last update.

Since: **We're losing her.**

This young survivor has already defied the odds once. Hopefully she can do it a second time. And then, once the rockfall is cleared and she's hoisted inch by inch into the blinding daylight, when she's stabilized in a hospital room, hydrated, rested, bandaged, and ready to speak, she can sit with Detective Washington and tell her story from the day's beginning. Every detail, from the moment she left her front door.

Who are you?

And what happened to you?

PART I

Tess

1

TESS DeWATER STOPPED TO HOLD HER APARTMENT DOOR BEHIND HER, hesitant to let it click shut. She worried she'd forgotten something important.

A car horn bleated down on the street, but she ignored it. Since she was young, it had always been difficult to leave her house—she had to *verify everything* and obsessively check every lock, every faucet, every potential fire hazard. Some people say Jesus is their copilot. Tess was stuck with an asshole named generalized anxiety disorder.

She held the door open, just inches now.

What am I forgetting?

Today was going to be dangerous, but her nerves would keep her sharp. Tess reminded herself that she'd accounted for everything that might go wrong, that all possibilities are finite, and that only so many things can happen—especially in a controlled environment like a cave. She pulled the door with her fingertips, just millimeters now, until the lock engaged.

Then she lifted her hand from the doorknob and made herself walk away, trying not to look back and second-guess, third-guess, as the unease lingered like moth wings inside her chest: *Something unexpected will always happen. What haven't I thought of?*

Too late now.

The apartment door was already behind her, going, going, gone, and Tess hurried down the front staircase that always smelled like urine, past the row of locked tenant mailboxes in the lobby, out the security doors, to the weedy parking lot where her best friend, Allie Merritt, idled her black Subaru Outback. A newly added bumper sticker read: *No Baby on Board, Feel Free to Crash into Me.*

Allie rolled down a window. "Get in, loser."

Tess slid into the passenger seat, and Allie floored the gas before she'd even settled. The final chorus of My Chemical Romance's "Helena" howled through brand-new speakers as Tess's safe little life vanished behind her—her bed, her laptop, her books—the brick apartment complex shrinking in Allie's rearview mirror.

It'll go fine, Tess told herself. *It'll go fine.*

Buckling her seat belt, she asked, "How often do people die in caves?"

"I guarantee more people die in cars."

"More people ride in cars. Most people don't go into caves."

Allie smirked as she accelerated through a yellow traffic light. "And today, Tess, you'll get to do both."

The morning sky was bloodred. Tess watched the fiery clouds from the passenger seat and remembered an old rhyme from elementary school. *Red sky at morning, sailor's warning.*

"How much rain does it take to flood a cave?"

"It won't rain." Allie tapped her phone. "Not until tomorrow."

Tess had never seen herself as the kind of person to go spelunking. As Saturday outings go, strapping on a helmet and a headlamp to scuttle down a damp, smelly tunnel wasn't exactly wine tasting. She didn't dislike the idea—it was the kind of adventure she'd resolved to seek more of in her otherwise sedentary life—but it's always hardest to get up and do the thing the morning of. At six a.m. on a weekend, your bed is always softest, your coffee warmest, your half-read novel the most enticing. Safety is cozy.

Allie, who had already died once before, glanced at her. "Don't be nervous."

"I'm not."

"I can literally hear your teeth grinding from here."

Next song up: the haunting piano intro of "Welcome to the Black Parade." Tess reclined the passenger seat and tried to relax, watching Allie's speedometer hover at eighty. Once you've driven on the autobahn, apparently nothing else is fast enough.

"Positive thoughts, Tess."

"*Spelunking Accident* will look cool on my headstone."

"Only dorks call it spelunking. We're going caving."

"What's the difference?"

"Cavers rescue spelunkers."

"It's a dick-measuring thing," Tess said. "Got it."

"Maybe some history on the Devil's Staircase will gird your loins."

"Leave my loins out of this."

"Imagine it's 1920." Allie swerved to change lanes, and Tess gripped the door handle with her fingernails. "And there's this prospector panning for gold in the mountains. He's had a lousy year. Nothing in the creeks but dust, fourteen hours of back-breaking work for less than a dollar a day. He's at the local bar, probably drinking his last ten cents, when he hears rumor of a newly found cave system up in the pass. Caves are formed by water, and if there's water, there's sediment. And if there's placer gold down there, he'd be the first to find it, right? So he grabs his gear and hikes up there, and soon he's wriggled far down into the earth, deeper into the Devil's Staircase than any human had ever explored. And now for some theater of the mind. Close your eyes." Allie glanced over. "Are they closed?"

"Not with your driving."

"Well, imagine you're this guy. You're slithering through a cramped two-foot tunnel on your hands and knees, sweeping your carbide lamp side to side, searching the sediment for that telltale glimmer. You didn't even notice that the crawlspace is slowly starting to tilt downward. The rock walls are smooth around you, too slippery to hold. You lose your grip, and suddenly you're sliding, uncontrolled, headfirst down a pitch-black tube—until it narrows to a width of ten inches and you stop *hard*." Allie smacked the steering wheel. "Your lamp shatters. Everything goes dark. And you're stuck."

Tess detected a subtle glee in her best friend's voice. Allie had always been a natural storyteller, and the best storytellers have a mean streak.

"You're wedged upside down in this tight space. You can't move. Your arms are extended down past your head, so you can't push yourself back up. You're panicking now, your heart is racing, and you try to thrash free, but it's solid rock on all sides. Struggling is getting you nowhere. So you focus your thoughts, ignore the adrenaline, and try to reason your way out of this dilemma—maybe, you decide, if you just calmly exhale and let the air out of your lungs, the width of your chest will contract by a few centimeters, giving you space to wriggle free. Right?"

Despite herself, Tess felt her skin tingle with goose bumps.

"So you breathe out," Allie said, "and you immediately recognize your mistake. Because you're upside down, remember? Gravity is your enemy. With your chest contracted, you slide a few inches *farther down*, deeper into the narrowing tube, and your arms are pinned, your legs are kicking uselessly somewhere above you, and now you can't even inhale a full breath because your ribs are squeezed by rock."

Her voice lowered to a whisper.

"Hundreds of feet down. In the dark. Alone."

For an uncomfortable moment the highway thrummed between them. "Welcome to the Black Parade" faded to silence, a gap in the playlist. Tess felt a tightness in her chest and realized she'd been holding her breath. "Ever since you died, you've been insufferable."

"You should try it."

"No thanks."

"Generally, we humans have a pretty good handle on the earth." Allie passed a flatbed truck with a burst of speed. "We've Google Mapped every inch of every continent, taken a zillion pictures with crisscrossing satellites, named every last mountain and waterfall on the planet. But underground? That's a ghost world, still invisible to us. Unknown."

She tapped the center console.

"And it's *right* under our feet."

Allie had visited dozens of caves around North America with her local caving group (which cutely called itself a *grotto*). She'd filmed hours of her own underground expeditions via helmet-mounted GoPro: abyssal canyons, forests of alien rock, pools of impossibly blue water. In the tighter spaces, which required elbow-crawling through glistening tunnels, Tess had observed more than once that the footage resembled a colonoscopy. For years—no, a decade now—Allie had tried to bring her oldest childhood friend along, and finally one evening, sipping cocktails at Allie's favorite rooftop bar, Tess had surprised her and given in.

You could say you "caved in," Allie had said with a boozy snort.

That was a few Saturdays ago, with two peach martinis swirling in Tess's brain. Now she sipped her lukewarm drive-through Starbucks coffee and listened to the bits and bobs of Allie's caving gear clink together in the back seat. "You know, when most people have free time they just watch TV."

"TV is bad for you."

"So is dying in a cave."

"Nerd."

"I should be studying."

"You're allowed to take a day off."

This irked Tess, but she hid it. Allie was self-employed, and if she wanted a day off, she simply made it so. In the ten years since high school, Allie's travel blog had exploded from a weekend project into a six-figure enterprise. Last year she took home two gold awards from the Society of American Travel Writers and was profiled by both NPR and *HuffPost*. Allie now hated the gimmicky wordplay of the original name—*Keep Calm and Carry-On*, a reference to airline carry-on luggage—but success can box you into a brand, and the best she could do was shorten it to *Keep Calm*. Success as an influencer also brought a lot of admin work—trafficking ads, video editing, courting sponsors—and these were all things Tess naturally excelled at. The arrangement was symbiotic: while Allie remained free to crisscross the globe to write about the mossy lava fields of Iceland and the white-sand beaches of Morocco, Tess stayed home to run the office for a (modest) part-time fee.

It's normal to be jealous of your best friend. If you aren't, congratulations on your success because your best friend is jealous of you. And Tess wasn't one to wallow. She was on her third year of part-time law school, on track to graduate next year.

"The dangerous parts are closed, even to permit holders," Allie clarified. "We'll stay in the beginner-friendly section called the Upper Vault. It's easy, safe, and the scenery is spectacular. Perfect for a first cave." She hesitated. "Still, it would've been safer to bring Ethan."

Tess bit her tongue. She'd agreed to this trip under one condition: that it would be a one-on-one outing, nobody else. Especially not Allie's boyfriend.

"He likes you, Tess."

"I'm an acquired taste. Never trust someone who likes me."

"He's also afraid of you."

"A best friend is part rottweiler."

"And I appreciate that," Allie said. "But remember, Ethan is more of a Chihuahua."

Tess laughed.

Last year on Ethan's first date with Allie, he'd suggested a spontaneous outing called a *penny date*. The rules were simple: you drive together without a destination, and at every intersection, you flip a penny. Heads means you turn right, and tails is left. After twenty coin flips, you stop and have your date wherever you are. No exceptions.

When Tess had asked Allie where they'd ended up, she'd snort-laughed: *A cemetery.*

But Ethan had been committed to the rules, and so was she. They ate picnic sandwiches among the headstones and walked the grounds. They read epitaphs. They argued about whether an afterlife existed. On the way out, they cleaned up some litter. It was the stupidest way Allie had ever spent an afternoon, but in the same breath, she'd admitted it was one of her favorite dates ever. She still had the penny.

Allie talked about Ethan often. Even today on a girls' trip deep into the mountains, *he* was still with them, his territory marked.

His sunglasses in the console.

His receipts in the door.

His cologne in the seat.

"Remember," Tess said, "Chihuahuas have a nasty bite."

Allie smirked. "So do I."

They were passing through the outskirts of Flour Gold now, a rusted-out skeleton of a mining town with more abandoned buildings than occupied ones. Tess watched as they passed a gas station, its roof sagging and moss growing on the pumps, and finally asked, "That prospector. How long was he stuck for?"

Allie sipped her coffee. "He totally died."

"Awesome."

"No one knows exactly how. Rescuers worked nonstop for days, but he was too far down, almost impossible to reach. They tried to lift him out with pulleys, but he couldn't fit. Getting desperate, they decided to break both of his legs with hammers to *make* him fit, but before they could try that, he'd slipped away."

"Suffocation?"

"Or cardiac failure. From the sustained terror."

"You're really selling this."

"Never go caving alone," Allie said. "And always establish a surface watch, someone on standby to report you missing the minute you're overdue."

"I'm guessing that's Ethan?"

Allie grinned. "Chihuahuas were bred to be sentries."

Then she swerved a hard left off the highway, and the transition from pavement to gravel rattled Tess's teeth. As the Outback's suspension jostled over potholes, she tried to sip her coffee without splashing herself and considered all the ways a cave might decide to kill you.

Crushed by rocks.

Suffocation.

Hypothermia.

Falling.

Drowning—

"We'll be safe today," Allie added. "I promise."

The next My Chem song on her playlist came up—"Famous Last Words"—and Tess couldn't help but laugh nervously.

2

IT LOOKED LIKE A GUNSHOT WOUND IN THE EARTH.

There was something unsettling about how the cave blended into the hillside of mossy rocks and knuckled tree roots. Your eye might pass over the shadowed cavity without registering its true depth. Even at a distance, Tess felt an exhaled coolness on her skin.

"That's it?"

"In all its glory." Allie slid off her backpack. "What'd you expect?"

Tess wasn't sure. Signage, maybe? The cave's entrance looked too small, too cloistered, under sticks and dead leaves. To enter, they would stoop under lichen-coated boulders and brush aside hanging green sprouts, as if trespassing into a witch's lair. The way Allie had described the Devil's Staircase—also known as the Devil's Stomach or the Devil's Throat—Tess had envisioned a majestic tunnel wide enough to drive a truck through. Not this.

"More like the Devil's Butthole," she said.

"I'm sorry, are you unimpressed?"

"I thought it'd be bigger."

"It is, on the inside."

"Is there a Minotaur?"

"Sadly, no. But plenty of bats and spiders."

Tess found herself oddly fascinated by the darkness within. Something about it looked like a special effect: a portal of absolute black on a bright morning. A creature could be staring back at them from just a few feet in and it would be fully invisible. A part of her was irrationally afraid to get any nearer—a hundred feet felt too close already—and just as irrationally, she dreaded the thought of turning her back to it.

The helmet she'd borrowed already felt like wearing a bucket, the interior chafing her sweaty scalp. It smelled like pine and cinnamon. Probably Ethan's cologne. She rubbed her arms. "These spiders. How big do they get?"

"Let's focus on the positives."

"Such as?"

"You'll be happy to know there's still cell signal out here."

Tess had researched this already but played along and checked her phone anyway. Just a bar or two on her extended network. Calls might be patchy, but it was certainly enough to contact 911. "As long as we're *outside* the cave," Tess clarified. "Right?"

"Well, yeah."

"Have they invented a phone that works underground?"

"Two hundred years ago," Allie said. "It's called a landline."

"Funny."

The forest felt prehistoric out here. There'd been no trailhead or parking lot; Allie had just pulled over and parked on the edge of the dirt road at some unremarkable spot she'd mentally landmarked. Then they'd hiked for almost an hour on a primitive horse trail over punishing switchbacks, a creek crossing, and acres of freshly logged wasteland stripped to bare soil. By then Tess's calves had burned and her throat was raw, but she'd kept pace with Allie.

Ever since they were teenagers, Tess had always been highly conscious of their different bodies and particularly their different skin. Allie's was tanned gold from hours of sun, always flecked with healing bruises and exotic insect bites from far-flung lands.

She had a white scar under her chin. Her left pinkie finger was broken once and couldn't fully curl. Her body was a record of every risk taken and lesson learned. Tess envied it not because it was pristine but because it was so well used.

Tess's skin was still new, soft, baby pale. Corpse-like in the winter months and instantly sunburned in the summer. When she was a teenager, other kids called her Wednesday, after the goth daughter in the Addams family. She had a scar of her own, too, but it was a monstrous one that embarrassed her. She wore clothing to conceal it: a massive red chemical burn stretching down the entire length of her back, from collarbone to hip. Skin grafts had been unsuccessful, and it had been infected twice. She'd had it since she was fourteen.

Allie exhaled. "Damn."

"What?"

She pointed a quarter mile down the forested valley, to a parked Jeep camouflaged in the undergrowth. From this distance it looked like a green toy car with a kayak atop its peeling roof. "I hate running into other groups," she said.

"But it's safer to have more people around, right?"

"Depends on the people."

Allie studied the faraway vehicle for a moment longer but said nothing. She seemed reluctant to comment on the more troubling fact: off-roading was prohibited out here, meaning whoever drove that vehicle was either an employee of the lumber company or a trespasser.

"Let's trog up," she finally said.

Tess unzipped her backpack and slid a battery-powered LED headlamp over her forehead, purchased on Amazon. The elastic bands squeezed her temples. She'd forgotten to wear wool socks as Allie had recommended and hoped she wouldn't notice. She clipped brand-new kneepads over her jeans, trying to act like she'd done this all before.

"Those are upside down," Allie said.

Damn it. They were.

Tess double-checked her smaller essentials: water bottle, spare batteries, Swiss Army knife, and energy bars. She'd forgotten to bring a wide-mouthed pee bottle, too. But they would be down there only a few hours, probably not long enough to worry about that, and definitely not long enough to need Allie's foil wrappers (*burrito bags*, she'd called them with a juvenile grin).

"You've got your big three, right?"

Tess patted her headlamp ("One"), her flashlight ("Two"), and her pack of emergency glowsticks ("Three"). Three sources of light are the absolute, no-excuses minimum when venturing underground. Bulbs can crack, batteries can die, and flashlights can be dropped into unreachable places. Without light, any cave can become deadly.

"Hold still." Allie clicked something to the front of Tess's helmet.

"What's that?"

"To document the day's adventure." She already had one affixed to her own helmet, too: a rectangular GoPro camera with a beady lens. "And in case we get murdered, the police will know exactly what happened to us."

"I didn't know you had two of these."

"That one is Ethan's. That's why it fits your helmet." Allie stuffed a sandwich bag containing a few spare memory cards into her pocket. Then, digging deep into her pack, she untangled a spidery mess of black belts and buckles and held the knotted thing out toward Tess. "Your harness," she said. "For descents."

Tess blinked. "Descents?"

"Yes."

"*Vertical* descents?"

"Is that okay?"

"Yeah. I just figured it was a . . ." Tess tried to sound nonchalant. "A horizontal cave."

The map she'd downloaded off the internet was hand drawn and two-dimensional. With no axis of depth, she'd assumed it was a top-down overview, and maybe it was, but the idea of rappelling down a vertical crevasse deep underground, trusting her fragile body to her own ropework, was a bit more extreme than she'd anticipated.

Ominously, different sections of the cave had been designated nicknames.

The Drainpipe.

Razor Alley.

The Chimney.

And deep within, something called *Worse Than Death*.

"Just like we practiced, you step into it." Allie guided the loops around Tess's right leg, then her left, and the harness rode smoothly up to her hips. "Like hooking up to a zip line."

She'd never zip-lined before.

"Or rock climbing."

Nope. But Tess worked up a stoic smile. "Seriously, how big do these spiders get?"

"Big enough that they can't sneak up on you."

"I hate you."

"You've got this." Allie drew the belt tightly around Tess's waist. "I know this is outside your comfort zone, and I'm happy you're doing it."

"They say to do something every day that scares you. So, *check*."

Allie held her smile, but her eyes dimmed with a faraway look. For an uneasy moment, her lip curled and she seemed on the verge of tears.

Tess stopped. "What's wrong?"

"Nothing."

She scanned her best friend's face, but Allie had always been a natural performer, skilled at controlling her emotions. Whatever it was, she'd already buried it.

"Just something with Ethan." Allie forced a shrug. "We'll talk about it later."

"Are you okay?"

"Later."

"Did he—"

"*Later.* Please." Allie pointed toward the cave. "I'm twenty-nine, and I'm alive, and I just want to forget the world and go on an adventure with my best friend. Can we do that?"

Tess nodded, dry-mouthed.

Hearing her say it aloud—*best friend*—gave her a flicker of guilt. Allie was Tess's best friend, sure, but Tess could count her friends on one hand; and she was never quite certain if she was Allie's. Allie seemed to have social contacts on every continent. She networked in her sleep.

For all their years of physical proximity, they'd never been truly close. Tess kept guarded with her secret anxieties, and Allie was seemingly too perfect to have any. They mostly spoke in humor: Allie's terrible puns versus Tess's sarcasm. The main thing they had in common was that they were both very good at making each other laugh. Making Allie explode with it—a genuine belly laugh, her tendency to snort—was a little shot of dopamine to Tess. But it was never in question who was reaching and who was settling, and in the years after high school their differences had only calcified. Letting a friendship die is easy—all you have to do is nothing—and Tess sometimes wondered why Allie hadn't yet done so.

Allie was already moving ahead, the subject purposefully

changed. "They say this cave is a portal to Hell, you know. Witches used to gather here to consult with their upper management. Hence the name."

The air grew noticeably cooler on approach. Allie's voice already seemed different, slightly tinny, like the opening in the earth swallowed sound.

Tess could feel her heartbeat in her neck, now accelerating.

It'll go fine, she reminded herself.

As for the other word Allie had used—it had been a long time since Tess had done anything that could be considered an "adventure." Over various unfulfilling jobs at law firms working for high-functioning alcoholics, three years of evening law classes, and her part-time work managing Allie's online persona, Tess's life was a blur of dull and thankless tasks. For years she'd secretly envied her best friend and her glamorous, carefree existence.

"Tess, you're sure you're okay with this? I won't be offended if you back out."

"I'm in."

"Because we can still make it a fun day if you change your mind." Allie pointed back to the trail, to the fifty-minute hike back to her car. "There's a gorgeous lake down there that Ethan and I like to camp at. Or we could drive farther, to the waterfall by—"

"I'm already wearing the girdle," Tess said. "Let's do this."

Allie laughed. She was already smiling again, that puzzling melancholy from a minute before instantly erased. The uncertainty needled under Tess's skin, and she wished she could read her best friend's thoughts. *What happened with Ethan?*

Allie wasn't telling.

"Almost forgot." She touched Tess's helmet again and then her own. "And we're live."

Tess heard two electric chirps. Both cameras were now recording.

"*Now* we can get murdered."

"Exactly," Allie said. "Take a good look at the sky. You'll never see it the same way again." And on the way inside she said something else, oddly cryptic. "And remember, Tess: the cave you entered isn't the cave you'll leave."

"What does that mean?"

"You'll see."

At first it felt like entering an unlit hallway.

The overhanging ceiling was about six feet high and dripped cold water. Daylight glowed behind them, casting distorted shadows over a floor of brown mud. It smelled like wet dirt and mildew. Stringy spiderwebs stuck to Tess's face.

"I'm proud of you," Allie said. "You're barely grinding your teeth."

"So far, so good."

Tess's eyes were adjusting to the new darkness. The interior didn't feel like an alien ecosystem, as Allie had often romanticized it—honestly, what she saw was closer to a truck stop restroom. On the rock wall to the left a gang symbol was spray-painted in red. To the right, a lopsided attempt at Homer Simpson, and farther down, a gargantuan ten-foot penis.

"I wasn't expecting vandalism," Tess said.

Allie sighed. "The dick is new."

"Does this happen a lot?"

"Too much."

A bottle clinked underfoot, startling Tess. The ground was carpeted with beer cans and soggy cardboard. Charcoal and a pool of melted plastic marked a small firepit, and beside it, a filthy sleeping bag. This caught Tess's attention—did people live here?

"Watch your step." Allie covered her mouth. "I think that's human shit over there."

They were only a few steps inside and it already reeked like a wet dumpster, food waste and sugars fermenting inside stale glass. Flies darted through the air and tickled Tess's skin. Her hiking boot landed in something conspicuously *squishy* and she tried to ignore it, staring forward down the black corridor. She focused on a silhouetted rock formation thirty feet ahead that resembled a standing figure, pulling closer in the dark. She reassured herself that if she could just get to that man-shaped rock, she'd be fine.

Twenty-five feet. She breathed through her mouth.

Twenty.

Allie pointed. "Want a certified pre-owned heroin needle?"

"Nope."

Fifteen feet.

She tried to ignore the odors and the wet squish under her boot. She knew the garbage was an important sign. As deep into the wilderness as they may have hiked, as forbidden and secret as the cave may look from the outside, it wasn't undiscovered. Humans had walked this ground before—if only to inject drugs, burn trash, and deface the walls. She kept her eyes locked on the faint shadow of that rock formation ahead, watching it gradually sharpen into clarity. Coming closer, closer.

Ten feet.

Five—

It moved. It wasn't a rock at all.

Allie breathed in a startled gasp beside her. The form had coalesced into a human figure leaning against the damp wall, casually, as if waiting for a bus. Every article of his clothing was black: pants, jacket, rubber gloves. His face was shrouded by a balaclava.

Allie recovered and smiled—"Howdy"—and the shadow raised a can in a lazy greeting. Monster Energy glinted in the faint daylight.

They passed the figure in silence, and Tess kept her eyes trained forward, trying not to make eye contact, trying not to initiate conversation. But it was already too late. His voice echoed after them: "You girls going in?"

Tess cringed.

You girls. She could sense Allie's irritation almost telepathically. Her best friend stopped and, after a deliberate pause, nodded once. "That's the idea."

"You probably saw my rig parked back there. I'm with Green Ridge." He caught up behind them, splashing mud under his boots. "I'm Jacob, by the way—"

"We have a permit," Allie said.

"No worries. Fish and Wildlife requires the company to send someone out once a year to check for signs of white-nose syndrome." He made an exaggerated aw-shucks shrug. "You're looking at the guy who drew the short straw."

Tess blinked. "'White-nose'?"

Allie nodded. "It's an infection that's—"

"Lethal to the local bat populations." Jacob's voice overpowered hers, friendly but noticeably overamped. "It looks like this gray-white fuzz growing on the animal's nose, wings, ears. Rots them alive from the inside out. It can wipe out an entire colony in a few months. And it's a fungus, so it spreads from cave to cave when spelunkers carry spores on their clothes. That's why it's incredibly important that before you enter a cave, you make sure to—"

"We've already decontaminated our gear," Allie said.

"And again, afterward."

"Of course."

"And it should go without saying, but *please* don't touch the bats."

"We'll remember that." Allie unzipped her pack and handed him a laminated permit.

Tess could tell they were sizing each other up. Behind the black mask's reinforced faceplate, Jacob's face was just a strip of tanned skin and eyes. Six feet tall and in his mid-thirties, he towered over them both with a sort of primate dominance. He barely glanced at Allie's permit before handing it back. "Which part of the cave are you two visiting?"

"The Upper Vault."

"That's good," he said. "Safer up there."

She sensed another tiny sigh from Allie. *Jesus Christ.*

Then his eyes moved to Tess and crawled down her body. He couldn't resist studying her gear: a hodgepodge of her own improvised choices (jeans, headlamp, kneepads) and borrowed gear (Ethan's helmet, Allie's harness). His eyes lingered on the front of her helmet for an extra beat, and Tess knew he'd noticed the GoPro.

"Damn," he whispered, studying the camera as it recorded him, and even through the ski mask fabric Tess could smell tartar on his breath. "What've you got there, Babygirl?"

She froze.

Allie blinked. *Babygirl?*

He seemed to recognize the strangeness of his comment and changed the subject with a burst of artificial cheer. "Hey, you girls want a cave guide?"

Allie smiled tightly. "Thanks, but we're good."

"You sure? I know where to find some amazing stuff down there. Secret places no one knows about." He took lumbering steps as he followed them. "I'm not due back to the office until four. I'd love to tag along with you."

"We're not interested."

Another big step. "Come on. I'm not so bad."

"No thanks."

"I promise, I'll stay out of your way—"

"Fuck off," Allie said.

She'd uttered it so softly, so calmly, that Tess didn't immediately comprehend what had been said. It sank in with the delayed echo of a gunshot.

Five seconds passed.

Ten.

Finally, Jacob's posture changed. He stepped back, tilted his head, and audibly licked his lips behind that strange face mask. "Your loss."

Then Tess felt Allie tug her shoulder with a hissed whisper—"Forget this guy"—and just like that, they were moving on, deeper into the cave.

She sensed the man's eyes on their backs, watching them both melt into the blackness. When they were far enough in, Tess muttered in her best friend's ear: "That was stupid. We have no idea who he might be."

"You're welcome."

"One weird comment isn't worth getting murdered over."

"It's fine." Allie grinned, all teeth. "I wouldn't have murdered him."

3

"TAKE YOUR TIME, TESS. EVERY DETAIL YOU CAN REMEMBER."

Detective Washington has interviewed more survivors of traumatic events than she can remember. Domestic violence, car accidents, suicide attempts, and even a mass shooting on a college campus. Already, she senses this young woman is somehow different.

"Honestly," she adds, "I'm amazed you're alive."

The survivor nods.

Teresa "Tess" DeWater is now awake and under observation at Sacred Heart Medical Center. Doctors have identified a concussion, a ruptured eardrum, a sprained ankle and wrist, and two bruised ribs. Her hands and elbows are torn raw, lacerations stitched on her skin like cruel hashtags. Some have needed sutures, while others have been glued and butterfly bandaged. Her flesh has swelled and darkened to a rotten purple in places. Presumably, these injuries weren't caused by the cave alone.

She'd smiled politely and held still while Washington took pictures. *Hold your wrists out, please. Lift your leg, please. Look directly at the camera, please.*

After hitting her marks like a trained seal, Tess now reclines in her hospital bed with a blanket and a pulse oximeter on her finger. She hasn't touched the Starbucks cup on the flimsy tray in front of her, although Washington had called ahead to ensure the order was exactly right. This woman survived a nightmare yesterday. Most victims would still be unconscious, but somehow she's awake and alert, ready to make a voluntary statement.

What was the incident commander's word again? *Sisu*.

An oat milk latte was the least Washington could do.

"Your age again?"

"Twenty-eight."

Washington doesn't feel old when she speaks to young people—only when she sees other old people and realizes they're younger than herself. Stevens County has one of the oldest mandatory retirement ages in the state, but with decades of service in her rearview, she's also well aware that she's past her pension's mathematical break-even point. For years now she's been essentially getting up every morning to work for free.

"You and Allie left the city at seven that morning." Washington checks to ensure her digital recorder is still running. "It's an hour drive, plus a fifty-minute hike. So that meant it was still well before noon when you'd geared up to enter the cave. And that's where you encountered this stranger for the first time."

Tess nods once.

"When he spoke to you, did his little speech sound rehearsed? Anyone can toss around a few facts. At that point, did you suspect he wasn't really a Green Ridge employee?"

"I had a bad feeling, but I couldn't confirm it."

"Did he show any kind of identification?"

"No."

"Did he have any equipment? Swabs? Dead bats in a bag?"

"Nothing we saw."

"Do you think *Jacob* was a fake name?"

"I had a bad feeling about that, too." Tess takes a breath. "I think he was waiting for us, or maybe someone *like* us. He wanted to join up with us, follow us down into the cave. In the moment

Allie thought he was just a harmless weirdo, the kind of guy she's handled before. But I think he was really sizing us up. Looking us up and down, studying our gear. Deciding if we were . . ." She looks uncomfortable. ". . . worth it, I guess."

Risk versus reward. The cold-blooded math of a human predator.

But a remote cave in lumber country, miles from the nearest access road, couldn't have been the most enticing hunting ground for a mugger or rapist. If he was waiting for his prey to come to him, he'd be waiting a hell of a long while. The Devil's Staircase is on private property, open to certified permit holders only, and the only visitors likely to come would be experienced spelunkers traveling in groups. They'd be unlikely to carry valuables, making them poor targets for a robbery. There's also just enough cell signal at the surface that potential victims would be able to call for help. All drawbacks an opportunistic predator would need to consider.

"And Allie?" Washington asks. "What did she think?"

"She told him to F off."

"I like her already."

Tess nods stiffly.

"Can you remember anything else from that first encounter? Anything else this guy said or did that can help me understand what was happening inside his brain? Anything that might explain what happened next?"

The survivor shakes her head. She's trying, but it's all she can remember.

An investigator must be careful not to overdo it here. All memory is filtered through the tissue of the beholder—in a real way, your recollection becomes a part of you—and as romantic as that may sound, it means your brain can easily overwrite the original with new memories. The human mind is the ultimate unreliable narrator, and a careless interviewer might accidentally talk a witness into remembering something they didn't see.

"What did he call you again?"

Tess grimaces, like she's smelled something rancid. "Babygirl."

"That's right."

"Something about it"—she rubs her scabbed arms—"makes me sick."

"The name?"

"The way he said it. Like property, or a toy."

Washington circles the word in her notes. She'll run it through search engines later. There are few originals in the world, and when someone says something memorably unique, it's almost always lifted from a movie. But you never know. She wonders how many women this guy might have addressed as *Babygirl* over his years—was it flirtation? An affectionate pet name? An insult? With the worst specimens out there, all three can be true at once.

"He tried to hide it, but he kept staring at the cameras on our helmets," Tess remembers. "I think he knew he was being recorded."

It's entirely possible, then, that those two GoPro cameras saved Tess's and Allie's lives in that initial encounter. The stranger may have intended to attack both women in that moment, right at the cave's daylit entrance—until he saw the two cameras and decided to adjust his plan. What did he want from them? Why was he really there?

All unknown.

"Tess, I'm sorry for what I have to ask you now." The detective takes a breath, aware she's treading sensitive ground. "Do you think there's any chance that Allie's insult . . . well, provoked the stranger into doing what he did next?"

Tess says nothing. Her lip curls, a microscopic spasm of grief.

No, not grief.

Anger.

"This was *not* Allie's fault," Washington quickly clarifies. "In no way am I trying to shift blame to the victim of a violent attack. And I'm not judging Allie, either. When people are dead, it's my job to ask every question. And what this guy said to you was wildly inappropriate—so in my view, Allie responded appropriately."

Tess half nods. Still, Washington senses the damage is done.

She doesn't trust me.

"Allie never took shit from anyone, ever," Tess says. "It's something I'd always admired about her. I was jealous of it, even. I could never do that. Whenever a situation turned confrontational, I always froze up like a deer."

"But she stood up for you?"

"Since we were kids."

"You were close?"

"Yes and no."

"How so?"

"Our friendship was complicated."

"Like sisters?"

"When I was fourteen, her family took me in," Tess says. "I lived in their guest bedroom, right next door to Allie's, for four years. So yeah, we were like sisters. Literally."

All friendships are complicated. But Washington senses there's something especially significant under the surface here.

"On our way down into the cave, I was so upset with her." Tess glances out the window, and Washington notices a ragged scab on the side of her head where it looks like a handful of her hair had been violently ripped out. "That's where Allie and I have always been so fundamentally different. If it were just me there, I probably would've let that weird Green Ridge guy walk all over me. I would've smiled and nodded and said whatever it took to de-escalate, to make him lose interest and move on. But not Allie. She didn't know any other way. She was direct to a fault. She *always* stood up for me, and that time I criticized her for it."

An uncomfortable silence. The survivor's left eye is bright red, the white entirely smothered with blood. A burst vessel.

Finally, Tess sighs. "What's the word you used?"

"*Provoke*?"

"Maybe Allie did," she admits. "Like stepping on a buried land mine."

Washington nods gently. She's reminded of her early years of traffic stops, the most statistically dangerous part of any officer's job. Rightly or wrongly, they condition you to see every interaction with a stranger as a small roulette spin. You never know who you're changing lanes beside. Saying the wrong thing to the wrong person can invite life-shattering consequences, and Tess seems to acknowledge that, too.

She adds, "You can't blame someone for stepping on a land mine."

"Of course not."

"I kept looking back," Tess says. "As we went deeper underground, I couldn't shake a gut feeling that the guy was behind us, following us down."

Although Washington was the first detective to arrive outside the Devil's Staircase this morning, she was reassigned to a support role within an hour. She'd barely had time to view the body or introduce herself to the rescue team. This was all under the pretense of utilizing her *superior information-synthesizing experience*, but she's not stupid. It's about her age. Her lieutenant was worried a woman in her sixties might break a hip on the rough terrain.

She's used to being underestimated, and she even likes it.

But not being *condescended* to.

So here she sits instead, miles away in an air-conditioned hospital room with Tess. Washington has never actually set foot inside a cave before, and at her age, she knows she likely never will. She's watched a few horror movies of varying quality and a documentary about the 2018 Thailand cave rescue, but she knows nothing can compare to the experience of the real thing. The temperature, the odors, the textures. Your body must instinctively recognize the sheer weight of millions of tons of rock and soil packed densely above your head. On some visceral level, you understand you don't belong there.

"I'm curious, Tess. What's it like inside a cave?"

She hesitates. "It's . . . hard to describe."

The highest level of the cave system is nicknamed the Upper Vault, at a depth of between twenty-five and a hundred feet. Experts on the rescue team described it as a labyrinth of spacious catacombs containing stalactites, stalagmites, and even more mystifying jargon like *coralloids* and *speleogens*. It sounded like a world from a science fiction novel. Washington tries to visualize it. "I'm assuming it was cold?"

"Yes."

"And wet?"

"Yes."

"And dark?"

"Very."

"Was it like a maze, or more linear?"

"Both, in different places."

These are all weak descriptors. Surely they can't do the physical experience justice. Washington needs more. "What are the walls like? The ceiling? The floor?"

Tess is silent for a moment. Her hair is still crusted with mud, hardened into knots. She studies the scabbed cuts on her arms, the blackened blood under her fingernails, and whispers something too faint to hear.

It sounded like: *It's not a human place.*

"I'm sorry?"

"That's what makes it so hard to describe. There are no walls or ceiling or floor." Tess stares at a point just over Washington's shoulder as she speaks, giving the detective the unsettling feeling that someone is standing silently behind her. "All of those surfaces jumble together. They're human words, a human way of understanding an interior. Underground, you have to navigate in three dimensions. There's no floor plan, no logic. You crawl and climb and twist and drop. Maps can't even prepare you for it. Caves weren't designed for humans. They couldn't care less if there's enough space for you to squeeze through. Lots of them must be impossible for a human body to fit." She takes a shivery breath. "And if you pretzel yourself deeply enough into it, far enough down, you'll stay there forever."

In the rescue operation's early hours, one of the team members had said something similarly ominous: *Not all lost cavers are recovered*. This is well-known within the caving community. Victims around the world remain wedged inside their final resting places to this day, as unreachable as the frozen bodies atop Mount Everest.

"Allie always said, *When you leave a cave, the entire world becomes new again*."

"Like a near-death experience."

"Pretty much. And the entire time, while she led me farther and farther down, a part of my brain—the paranoid control-freak part, the part that's always afraid to leave my apartment and envisions flooding faucets and burning kitchens—imagined taking a wrong turn somewhere and having to retrace my steps back. Or worse, adding to my mistake with another wrong turn, and another. Losing my way back completely."

The Devil's Staircase is a complex web of tunnels, honeycombed with multiple routes, switchbacks, and hidden passages. The idea of becoming lost inside it unsettles Washington.

She draws a line on her notepad and writes: *25 feet.*

Tess and Allie's descent began here in the Upper Vault. From this point, both women's fates were locked into a chain of events that would culminate in the region's largest underground rescue effort in decades. Boulders would be chiseled and lifted. Pulleys would be installed. And, critically, only one woman would return to the surface.

What happened down there?

"Okay, Tess." Washington leans forward. "Take a deep breath. Are you ready?"

She nods.

"What happened next?"

4

ALLIE LOOKED BACK. "THINK HE'S THE ONE WHO TOOK A SHIT BACK there?"

Tess wasn't in the mood for jokes.

The daylight drained away with every step, and the graffiti and trash seemed to be thinning out. Most of the vandalism was concentrated at the mouth of the cave, maybe because few vandals were willing to descend deeper.

"You didn't have to say that," Tess said.

"No, but it just felt right."

"I'm serious."

"So am I." Allie climbed over a car-sized boulder. "If we'd been nice to him, he would've taken it as permission to invite himself along and keep trying to flirt with you. Trust me. You can't smile your way out of some situations, because some people don't listen to *nice*. You have to learn to stand up for yourself." Allie punched Tess's shoulder, a light but precise jab. "I won't always be there to back you up."

Tess smiled, but it was too dim to see.

She'd always prided herself on having more subtle talents. Years ago, Allie's older cousins often played a drinking game called Changeling where one player was randomly selected to play the role of the secret monster. At the end of every round, the group would take a vote on the creature's identity, while that player won if they survived three votes. Whenever she was the Changeling

Tess *always* won, and the cheap beer (lake house rules: the winner shotguns a Natty Lite) somehow only amplified her devilish skills. She could feign disbelief and suspicion. She could redirect attention and play others against each other. Tess was in her element hiding in plain sight, and of everyone in that lake house, only Allie had ever had a chance of piercing her best friend's lies—and only sometimes. Everyone has things they're good at.

I may not be brave like her, she sometimes told herself. *But I'm crafty.*

Sometimes that was even better.

Allie moved on ahead, confident and agile as they left the wan gray lighting of the entrance (*the twilight zone*, she called it) and entered the dark zone. Tess had never seen such an absence of light before. The purest, darkest midnight she'd ever seen, miles from the city, had still been softened by starlight and moonlight. This darkness was absolute. It spread out to encircle them until, for a disorienting moment, Tess felt like she wasn't walking at all but floating in it.

She shivered. It was instantly colder, like swimming through a patch of chilled water.

Inhale.

Exhale.

Then Allie switched on her headlamp with a plastic snick. Tess swallowed a tremor and reached for hers, but it took several tries to find the button ("Left," Allie coached. "No, my left"). Even with both headlamps on, Tess was surprised by how small a difference they made. Their LED lights took weak bites out of the darkness and revealed hidden protrusions of pale rock, ancient slabs glistening with moisture. Look away, and it all vanished again.

Outside her circle of light, there was only that dizzying, eternal black. No peripheral vision at all. Tess felt vulnerable, like something might creep up on her from all sides.

The cave seemed to devour light.

The way forward became chaotic, the colorless walls and floor and ceiling all melting together. Allie led the way through a jumble of multi-ton boulders, some to be circumnavigated, some to be clambered over with slippery boots. Over, under, scooting, sliding. The trick to keeping your balance in such an unpredictable environment, Allie explained, was to keep three points of contact on something solid at all times.

Traversing this place was a surprising workout, assaulting muscles Tess hadn't used since elementary school. She was already sweating under her clothes, her glasses fogging. The tunnel lowered, and giraffe-like Allie had to stoop under overhangs, her headlamp sweeping low. Tess was five-two, small-framed since birth, and she navigated this world with surprising ease. *Failure to thrive,* her mother had described her infant years. It had always felt like a not-so-subtle insult to Tess, like a space shuttle stalled on the launchpad.

The odor had changed, too. The wet soil and mossy smells were far behind, replaced with something dense, bacterial, sickly sweet. The odor of decay.

Almost like . . . rotting meat?

Allie perked up as if she'd remembered something important. "By the way, Tess, if you see any giant bugs, immediately close your mouth."

"Why?"

"Just trust me."

"I *really* need to know why I should close my mouth."

"They're called *spider crickets,*" Allie said. "They can jump six feet in the air, and they have an aggressive startle reflex. That means when they see a human, they'll sometimes jump directly into your face."

Tess laughed.

"They taste awful," Allie added, "if you're curious."

"I'm not."

"On average, everyone swallows ten spiders in their sleep anyway."

"That's been disproven."

Allie froze. "Do you hear that?"

Her voice had sounded both muffled and uncomfortably loud. The silence was dense, spongy. Sound behaved strangely in this new world.

Tess stopped. "I don't hear anything."

"Just listen."

Now she sensed something. Maybe.

"Can you hear it?"

Yes. It was right at the edge of her perception. It sounded like wind: a low drone of moving air originating from somewhere deep. She could hear the vastness of the lower tunnels—were they thousands of feet across? Miles, even? As she listened, she started to detect something else, a low and guttural vibration from below.

Almost a growl. Like something was snoring.

She shivered. "What's that?"

"The Minotaur."

"Funny."

"Every cave has one."

"Seriously, what is it?"

"Caves breathe, in a way." Allie's breath misted in the glow of her headlamp. "Since warm air rises, air flows in and out consistently as the surface temperature changes. Caves are surprisingly well circulated."

"So we won't suffocate."

"Not up here."

"But?"

"But," Allie said, "farther down, carbon dioxide can sometimes sink into low spots and accumulate in pockets. It's called *foul air.* Invisible, odorless, and, when you're belly-crawling in a confined space, extremely dangerous."

"What are the signs?"

"Rapid heart rate. Difficulty breathing—"

"I mean, how do you know if the air is safe?"

Allie flicked a cigarette lighter and held it up for Tess. She had a way of making the smallest gesture look effortlessly cool. "See the nice healthy orange, with blue at the base? The weaker the flame, the worse the air you're breathing. And the faster you need to move your ass back to the surface."

"What if it doesn't ignite at all?"

She snapped it shut. "You'd already know."

At least the cave's air felt breezy and fresh, aside from the roadkill odor. The smell of decaying flesh wasn't unusual, Allie explained, because predators sometimes dragged carcasses inside caves to eat in shelter. It's not uncommon for cavers to find the ground carpeted with crunchy white bones. A naturally formed graveyard.

The tunnel split off into multiple chambers on both sides, almost like subterranean bedrooms. Tess swept her headlamp beam through these offshoots, illuminating pockets of deep shadow. Some were obvious dead ends, while others might have gone on for hundreds of feet farther. She imagined if she sliced her light fast enough she might glimpse something peering out at her from one of those bedrooms, *catch* it before it could retract its strange head.

With a quiet chill, Tess realized the ceiling was now crowded with icicle shapes, jagged and hostile. Like the spiked inside of an iron maiden. How long had she not noticed them looming overhead? They were four feet long, colored coppery red like hardened spears of dried blood. Water droplets beaded on the sharpened tips.

"Don't bump your head," Allie said. "They're fragile."

As rainwater drips through a cave, she explained, it deposits calcium carbonate. One drop at a time, these deposits gradually grow into formations of prickly stalactites. Where those same droplets land below, stalagmites form. The movement of water simultaneously erodes and accumulates, sculpting over millennia.

"Reminds me of a caving joke," Allie added.

"Let's hear it."

"You wouldn't get it. It's too deep."

"I hope you eat another spider."

All this physical exertion was making the scar tissue on Tess's back feel uncomfortably tight. Even with a shower rack full of moisturizers, her skin cracked and split apart often. Chemical burns can heal poorly, doctors told her, and hers was uniquely severe. Most burns are one-offs, but hers were accumulated over many months, several times a week, the same flesh scalded over and over just as it was starting to heal.

She reminded herself to stay focused. With every confident turn Allie took, she tried to memorize their downward route.

Right.

Left.

Right again.

Every step taken was a step farther from the surface. Every obstacle passed would be passed again from below. Tess tried to draw a mental map of the cave behind her, but the natural formations were all so chaotic. It felt like navigating a dream.

"I understand now." Her voice sounded distorted, like she was speaking near a live mic.

"What?"

"The riddle you told me. *The cave you entered isn't the cave you'll leave.*" Tess glanced back, lighting the tunnel with her weak headlamp. "It's not like walking down a hallway. In a cave, everything looks different when you're going the opposite way. So to avoid getting lost, you should periodically look back and memorize what you see."

"Exactly right," Allie said as something snapped between them like a bullet. Tess jolted, feeling a flutter of air on her cheek. The gray blur was already gone.

Just a bat.

"We won't get lost," Allie clarified. "I've got most of the cave memorized. If I had to, I could find our way back up by touch. But the most important thing I need to stress, in case we somehow get separated down here: if you see a warning sign with the Grim Reaper on it, *do not* go any farther. Not even a single step."

"Why not?"

"Just don't, okay?"

"Grim Reaper sign equals death. Got it."

"That reminds me. Want to see something cool?"

Before Tess could answer, her best friend switched off her headlamp.

Click.

Allie's circle of light disappeared, and the dirty walls dimmed around them, the chamber's illumination instantly reduced by half. Tess felt an ice pick of fear in her stomach.

"What are you doing?"

A whisper in the dark: "Turn yours off, too."

"Why?"

"Just trust me. A little tradition, and something everyone should experience at least once in their life." Allie's voice circled Tess like a ghost. "Whenever I take a group here, this is where we turn off our headlamps, our flashlights, every light source we have. And we'll all stand together in this perfect silent blackness, so black you can't even tell if your eyelids are open or shut. You lose track of your senses, your arms and legs. The dark stops being an absence of something and becomes a mass, a solid *thing* all its own, enveloping you and inches from your face. I swear, it feels soft, velvety. Almost cozy."

A grin in her voice, oddly melancholy.

"Everyone experiences it a little differently. Some people hyperventilate or have panic attacks. But to me it feels like I'm merging with the cave, like I'm a tiny creature being digested inside its giant stomach, and its enzymes are slowly breaking me down. It's like . . . it's like being dead again. If I stand still long enough, I swear I can feel myself drift apart until I'm—"

"Nope." Tess gripped her headlamp defensively, now the only light. "Mine stays on."

"Please?"

"No chance."

"Here." She reached for Tess's helmet. "I'll turn yours off for you—"

"I will *bite your hand off*."

A breathy laugh in the dark. "Fair enough."

Two years ago in Mexico, Allie died.

She'd been hiking back to her hostel from some unspecified beach when a vine dropped down to slap her head. She'd raised an arm to brush it from her hair—and felt two needles of incendiary pain in her wrist.

It wasn't a vine.

It was a fer-de-lance—an oddly whimsical name for a venomous snake—that had dropped from a palm overhead. This species is known to be a skillful tree climber, but apparently this particular snake wasn't and fell ten feet to belt Allie Merritt on the head. Even then, she'd had the presence of mind to grab her phone and snap a clear picture of the viper. A local man helped evacuate her as her wrist slowly swelled into a fleshy balloon, but through a combination of bad luck and washed-out roads, it took several hours to reach a hospital with the appropriate antivenom. It was there she died—her heart stopped for twenty seconds before being successfully restarted.

The main thing Tess remembered was Allie's perfect calmness through the whole ordeal. She'd laughed and joked over the phone on her ride to the hospital, giving woozy updates on her swelling hand and other concerning symptoms as they manifested: fever, headache, a taste of metal in her mouth. Allie hadn't even seemed concerned about losing her right hand to infection (which doctors had noted was a distinct possibility). She'd kept a stoic smile and a gallows sense of humor through the whole nightmarish week. *Keep Calm and Carry-On*, indeed.

Maybe Tess was just a coward and a control freak—well, *yes*, she knew she was both of those things—but she couldn't imagine accepting death so serenely. How could anyone? Allie was like a supernatural creature, perfect and graceful and somehow never afraid.

For years now, while Allie was working abroad, Tess often used a spare key to enter her apartment. She'd secretly rummage through Allie's closets and racks and vanity drawers, careful not to leave a trace. Sometimes she'd wear her best friend's clothes—always a little big, a little loose on her slight frame—and inhale Allie's perfume, smell her pillows and bedding. With the lights off she'd walk around the cavernous apartment in clothes that didn't quite fit, smelling like someone else. Allie never suspected it.

And maybe this was just her imagination, but Allie's living spaces had always felt curiously vacant to Tess. Like a hotel room. Allie rarely slept in her own bed, preferring to stay at Ethan's place downtown, and her shelves were bare and her countertops were empty. She owned no books or Blu-rays and only sparse trinkets for decoration. She valued space and near-military cleanliness, never indulging in guilty pleasures like trash TV or processed junk food.

But, as Tess had discovered on one of her stealthy excursions a few months ago, Allie did keep three handguns in a hard case under her bed. They were well used, rich with the candy odor of solvent. Allie had always loved plinking steel targets with her dad ever since she was a teenager, but such a hobby might not go over well among a travel influencer's main demographic of affluent, college-educated women aged eighteen to forty-nine.

Allie Merritt had her secrets, like any other mortal.

You just had to dig for them.

As for that fer-de-lance that injected her with hemotoxins and nearly sent her to the afterlife? The kindly Mexican merchant had flicked open a switchblade and cut its head off, Allie explained, to bring to the hospital and identify the appropriate antivenom.

They didn't have to hurt it, she'd grumbled. *That's why I took the damn picture.*

"Watch out." Allie grabbed her shoulder.

To Tess's surprise, the tunnel dropped into a steep vertical plunge. In the short-range glow of their lights, dangers arrived without warning.

"Careful. The rocks are wet."

Leaning over the precipice with Allie's arm braced protectively across her collarbones, she was stunned by the size of the underground crevasse. Like a hairline fissure in the earth's crust, it went on as far as their weak lights could illuminate on both sides. The width was narrow—just a few feet across—but the depth was frightening in a visceral way she couldn't articulate. Somewhere far away she heard a faint patter of trickling water.

"This is the Cascadia Subduction Zone," Allie's voice echoed through the chasm. "Someday the earthquake that'll sink Seattle into the ocean and kill us all is going to originate here, on this fault line."

"Really?"

She laughed. "Nope."

The true scale and depth of the Devil's Staircase was dawning on Tess. She remembered entire sections of her paper map had appeared stunted like lopped tree branches. They weren't dead ends, as she'd assumed; they were only unmapped, leading to undiscovered routes. It amazed her that all of this could be underground. How had it not collapsed?

"Time to catch up with your old friend." Allie pressed a metal gadget into her hand. It looked like an oversized paper clip, oblong and awkwardly shaped with a stepladder of stainless steel rungs. It looked like any number of the gadgets teenage Allie used to practice with in the tree behind her house. "Remember? It should all be muscle memory."

"I was sixteen."

"Same age you learned to drive."

"Also, you let me fall."

"I knew you'd still be butthurt about that." Allie pointed down into the black stillness. "We call this the Great Wall. It looks scary, but it's a basic descent. No overhangs, no rebelays, nothing intense. Perfect for a beginner. You'll carabiner to your harness, like this." She felt Allie's hands moving over hers in the dark, strangely intimate. "And you thread the rope through the brake bars."

The Great Wall. Tess tried to remember—had she seen that name on her map?

"Then, by squeezing the bottom two bars, you regulate friction so you'll descend as fast or as slow as you'd like. See?" Allie clicked them open and shut.

"What's the rope anchored to?"

"We use this." She looped an orange rope around a boulder the size of a fridge. It must have weighed a half ton. She patted the porous surface, as if giving it a blessing. "We call this a BFR."

"Big fucking rock?"

"Big *friendly* rock, if there's kids in the group."

"Your grotto brings kids here?"

"Haven't lost one yet." She rolled her eyes. "But I've tried."

Allie had zero patience with children. It was the closest thing she had to a character flaw, and Tess secretly enjoyed it.

Now she pointed out the anchor bolts they'd use as backups. They looked like tiny steel loops drilled into solid limestone, artifacts of explorers who came before. Cavers must always use multiple anchors on descents, Allie explained, to create redundancies if a connector fails and to keep your rope from rubbing against protruding rocks. Or else *you know what* can happen.

Tess glanced back. "What if someone cuts our rope?"

"That'd be a dick move."

"I'm serious."

"No one is going to cut our rope." Allie tossed a coil of rope over the edge and watched it unfurl. It looked like a fishing line cast out into space.

A faint thump echoed from below.

"How high is it?"

"Short enough that a fall wouldn't kill you," Allie answered, "but high enough that you'd probably wish it had."

"I hate you."

"Now watch closely." She clicked open the descender's second and fourth brake bars, threaded the rope (a "bight of rope," she called it) between the first and third bars, then closed the second. Then again below the third, shutting the fourth. She narrated every step, how she'd squeeze or spread the bars to control friction, the importance of making sure she didn't thread the rope backward (which could also result in *you know what*).

Tess listened and absorbed, but a small part of her brain fixated on the BFR behind them. That boulder, plus two anchor bolts installed years ago by strangers, would suspend their bodies above a bone-shattering drop. She tested each rope with a sharp tug, and the connections all felt reassuringly solid. Not even a millimeter of wobble.

It'll go fine, she told herself.

"Get set," Allie said.

"On rope." Tess held her hands exactly where they'd practiced and positioned herself at the edge. Instinctively she wanted to face the crevasse but couldn't. She perched eye to eye with her best friend, smelling the coffee on her breath, squinting in each other's bright headlamps. Their helmets clicked together as she hung over empty space.

"Now step off, Tess. It's easy."

She laughed. "Easy, huh?"

"Just let gravity do its thing."

"That's exactly what I'm afraid of."

"Remember, whenever you feel afraid, think of all the little things your body is doing." Allie smiled, her breath fogging in the cold air. "For example, your pupils dilate so you can see better. Your breathing becomes more efficient so you can run faster. Blood pumps to your brain and muscles, so you're stronger and more alert. Remember that being afraid doesn't make you weak. In a measurable way, it actually makes you stronger. Fear is power."

"How does crapping your pants make you stronger?"

"That's your body lightening its load."

"Gross."

"Trust me, Tess." Her eyes softened. "I'll be right here, and I promise, *no one* is going to cut your rope. If anything happens, I've got you."

It felt like they were teenagers again in Allie's backyard. Tess remembered gripping her descender with sweaty fingers—a different gadget back then, bright red—and flinching at every microscopic sway. The low creak of branches under their weight. The smell of tree sap. And Alma herself—yes, hard to believe her name was Alma way back then, before she changed it to Allie—a wild-eyed teenager with her blond hair tied in a bun and an oily red pimple on her chin that must've ached like hell, squeezing her wrist and telling her: *You've got this, Tess.*

You're a survivor.

Now that strange melancholy was back in Allie's eyes. Tess could see it again. Whatever this problem was, it weighed on her. She wanted to ask her best friend directly: What *really* happened between her and Ethan?

"You've got this," Allie whispered. "You're a survivor."

Past and present aligned, like déjà vu, and it gave Tess a chill. God, she wished they could be those kids again. Their adult lives were messy and complicated. Back in that tree, they were both still new. Unformed.

Repeat after me, Allie had whispered. *I can do it.*

I can do it.

Say it again.

I can—

Then sixteen-year-old Allie pushed her ass out of the tree.

Tess tipped over the edge, and for a stomach-turning instant she was in free fall—but then the equipment took over and the harness tugged her pelvis. She lurched, her feet kicking empty air. She gasped embarrassingly loud, and the GoPro surely recorded it.

The rope creaked in her neoprene gloves, as taut as wire.

But it held.

"Perfect." Allie's voice was several feet above. "Now spread the bars to descend."

With numb fingers, Tess pulled the bars apart as instructed. The orange rope snarled through startlingly fast, spraying flecks of mud. *Oops.*

One small movement at a time, then.

Slow and controlled.

"There you go," Allie called. "Like that, all the way down."

Tess wasn't listening. She appreciated Allie's support, but she was deep inside her own head, concentrating on her senses: her hiking boots wall-walking down slippery stone, the harness snug around her waist, the prehistoric air in her throat. The only thing suspending her above a near-fatal drop was a rope and the gadget in her sweaty fingers.

She was really doing this. It was a Saturday morning, and Tess DeWater was rappelling down an underground ravine, suspended in total darkness. Ice-cold water trickled down on her from above, running down the back of her shirt.

She coughed on a laugh. It echoed back, distorted.

Above, Allie was smiling like a proud parent. "Say it again."

"I can do it."

"I've missed you, Tess."

I've missed you, too, she was about to say when a bolt of incendiary pain pierced her skull. It filled her mind, crowded out every other thought, and her body lurched to a stop.

5

"TESS?" ALLIE SHOUTED FROM ABOVE. "WHAT HAPPENED?"

She didn't know.

"*Tess.*"

Her neck was twisted, forced into an awkward angle. She tried to turn her head—she couldn't—and felt another flare of eye-watering pain.

My hair.

It's tangled in the descender.

At the edge of her blurring vision, she could just barely see it: a black hairball gnarled up tightly between the rope and the metal racks. Impossible to untangle. She felt spreading warmth under her helmet and knew her scalp was bleeding.

"Are you okay?"

She choked on embarrassment. She'd tied her hair up into a tight bun as Allie had instructed, but that had been hours ago. At some point in all her physical exertions the knot had loosened, and now a lock of her hair was snarled through the muddy gadget.

She couldn't go up. Or down.

Her boots kicked over the void. She was swinging now, side to side like a pendulum. The rope creaked again with tension, and this time she felt the vibration through her tangled hair, in her scalp. She couldn't turn her head to look down. Below was a blind drop, and it could be into mud, or water, or a bed of spear-edged rocks.

"It's okay," Allie called down. "This is a minor hiccup."

"Feels pretty major."

"Stay calm."

"I am."

"And don't move." She heard scuffling movement, Allie's gear rattling somewhere above. "This kind of thing happens. I'm going to rope down to you for a closer look, okay?"

"Okay."

"Just *hang out* until I get there."

"Funny."

With every passing second she felt more vulnerable. The pain in her scalp was growing. A handful of her hair had been sucked up, locking her face sideways. She couldn't move her neck a centimeter. It was a strangely volatile position: the thing holding her head hostage was also the thing holding her to her rope.

And disconnecting? Not an option.

Inhale.

Exhale.

"Remember, fear is power."

"Yeah? I feel like lightening my load right about now."

Allie laughed, but her voice sounded strangely distant.

Warm liquid dripped into Tess's eyes. Blood? She tried to blink it away. She held the rope with both gloved hands, as tightly as she could squeeze. The rope creaked again, and the sound reminded her of brittle glass under pressure. She struggled to brace her feet against the wall, but the wet rock was too slick.

"Don't do anything stupid, like detaching," Allie called from the ledge above. "This is perfectly fine. I'll be down in two minutes."

"*Okay,*" she croaked without air. Breathing was becoming difficult, like she was inhaling water. It was vaguely humiliating, swinging in a harness with her neck bent sideways, her hair tangled in her own equipment. She wondered what was taking Allie so long up there—would she attach to the same rope and descend to help? Was that even safe to do?

Until then, she was on her own. And, Tess was realizing, she was tired of being rescued.

I'll figure this out myself.

With her free hand, she patted down her jeans pocket until she found her Swiss Army knife. For a heart-fluttering moment, it nearly dropped between her fingers.

"Tess?" Allie noticed. "What are you doing?"

Not killing myself, I hope.

Raising it to her face, careful not to drop it down the abyss, Tess bit the knife open with her front teeth. She tasted cold metal. The two-inch blade clicked into position.

"Careful, Tess. Maybe wait for me, yeah?"

"I've got it."

"Whatever you do, don't cut the rope."

"I won't." She bit the glove off her right hand. She'd need full sensation in her fingers. Then she took a breath and raised the blade behind her left ear, out of her view. She found the lock of hair, taut as a violin string. Definitely not the rope. She touched it with her bare fingers several times, to make absolutely *certain*. Then she started to cut in a slow, sawing motion.

Come on.

The knife's edge was blunt. The motion made her entire body swing.

Come on, come on—

Her hair snapped suddenly, quicker than she'd expected.

Without resistance the knife sliced forward, out of her control—but cut only empty air. The rope was undamaged.

And she was free.

She exhaled through shivering teeth and stretched her neck, finally able to move it again. She squinted up into the glare of Allie's headlamp. "I'm good," she shouted. "I handled it."

"Badass." Her best friend was impressed.

Tess wanted to cheer. She picked hair from the descender bars to clear the jam. The warmth trickled down her cheek, tickling her bare skin. Was it more blood? Sweat? It didn't matter. She ignored it all and laughed with a raw throat, a new voice she'd never heard before echoing off the crevasse walls as she dangled.

Allie grinned above. "Fun shit, right?"

"*Hell* yeah."

At the bottom Tess stood on reassuringly solid ground, every tensed muscle in her body now relaxing. Allie was demonstrating ascent techniques, but she was barely listening.

Now buzzing with adrenaline, Tess relished the chance to do it all over again. Hell, an even higher drop. A hundred feet? Bring it on. She didn't feel embarrassed anymore; she was empowered. Shit happens. Hair buns come undone. She'd handled it.

Allie was halfway through showing how to tie something called a Prusik hitch when she froze. She dropped the rope, the lesson instantly forgotten. "Tess. Do you see that?"

"See what?"

Allie raised a finger to her lips. *Shh.* As if someone might hear them.

Then she pointed up.

"Just look." She stared up the crevasse, at the steep ledge they'd rappelled from. It was now pitch-black. Their lights couldn't reach the ceiling of sharp stalactites, but Allie covered her headlamp with her palm anyway.

"Cover yours, too," she whispered. "Do you see it?"

6

"WHAT SCARED HER?" WASHINGTON ASKS.

"Above us," Tess says, "at the top of the Great Wall, the ledge where our rope was anchored . . . the ceiling seemed to glow."

"From someone else's flashlight?"

"Not exactly."

"Why not?"

"Because . . ." Tess hesitates. "The glow was *red*."

A sharp knock at the door.

The survivor jolts in her bed, but it's just a nurse coming in to check vitals. Washington pauses her recorder and waits politely as the woman logs Tess's blood pressure, heart rate, and oxygen levels. Her work finished, she smiles and ducks out.

The room feels a little colder now.

"Just this faint red glow. I don't know how else to describe it." Tess takes a breath and listens to the woman's Crocs squeak down the hall. "Whatever . . . whatever generated it must have been hovering just behind the cliff, just out of our view. It was right at the edge of my perception, there but not there, like an optical illusion."

Washington taps her pen against her thigh, a thoughtful tic.

In the late twentieth century, legend goes, Soviet engineers once tried to dig the deepest hole on Earth someplace under remote Siberia. Nine miles down, their drill head broke through to an unexpected hollow cavity. In this impossible space the unmanned apparatus measured a temperature of two thousand degrees Fahrenheit, hot enough to melt cast iron. Puzzled and curious, the engineers lowered a microphone and recorded several seconds of staticky audio: a chorus of wailing human screams. The cries of the damned, if you believe that sort of thing.

Washington sure doesn't. "How long did this red glow last?"

"About five, ten seconds."

"Then it faded?"

"It was so subtle, I honestly couldn't say if it was ever really there at all or if I'd just imagined it because Allie saw it first. I was creeped out, but I tried to act calm. We both stared up into the dark and waited for a few minutes, but it never came back."

"Did you want to leave the cave?"

"Honestly, yes."

"Did you suggest it to Allie?"

She shakes her head.

"Why not?"

"I didn't want her to think I was a coward." Tess hesitates, reconsidering. "But the main reason . . . to turn around and go back, we would have to go *toward* it."

Washington nods. In effect, the bizarre sighting had cornered them.

She draws on her notepad and writes a new depth: *90 feet*. According to the rescue team, the bottom of the fissure dubbed the Great Wall is approximately nine stories underground. At this point, Tess and Allie were farther down than most of the New York City subway system, far beyond any radio or cell signal, and now they were faced with a troubling dilemma—continue deeper underground, or face the unknown glow head-on?

"What did Allie think?"

"I'd never seen her scared before," Tess says. "But I think she was more concerned than she was letting on. To make me feel better—and maybe herself, too—she climbed back up the rope to check it out, to see what it was."

"She went alone?"

Tess sighs. "She was always the brave one."

"THERE'S NOTHING UP THERE," ALLIE ANNOUNCED WHEN SHE RE-turned, tugging rope through her descender. "I didn't mean to scare you."

Tess studied the space above.

"It was probably another group passing by," she added. "Cavers bump into each other all the time. It can be spooky when you see unexplained lights."

"Why was it red?"

"Light dims as it bounces down tunnel walls." Allie shrugged. "Or maybe for the first time in caving history, two people saw the same bogey."

"The same what?"

"A *bogey*. A cave hallucination." She packed up her ropes and slings in her bag. "It's normal for your eyes to play tricks on you down here. Sooner or later, everyone in the group sees inexplicable things in the dark. So we just call them bogeys."

"Everyone sees them?"

"Everyone."

"How do you know they're not real, then?"

"It's a type of dissociative identity effect, I think. Spend enough time in darkness staring at deep pools of nothing, and the part of your brain that recognizes faces and patterns goes haywire. Your mind insists on seeing *something*."

Tess had heard of this before. The common, but poorly understood, psychological effect is what makes the Bloody Mary myth so enduring. If you stare long enough at your reflection in a dimmed mirror, you'll experience a similar thing. The human brain isn't designed to repeatedly receive the same information for a prolonged time. After a few minutes, it'll begin to misfire. Some people see gruesome deformations in their own reflection; others see animal visages or dead family members or worse. Allie claimed she'd seen her own face melt like clay.

For some reason, teenage Tess never saw anything in the mirror. No matter how long she waited, she saw only her own unimpressed face, underlit by wavering candlelight.

Maybe you're already a monster, Allie had teased.

Tess always was the best Changeling, after all.

As they ventured deeper their surroundings changed. The rock surfaces were smoother and cleaner down here, rippled with wavelike patterns. Some were sculpted into surreal curtains and frozen waterfalls, reminding her of melted candle wax or even hardened snot. This alien material was red brown in some places, sulfurous yellow in others ("Flowstone," Allie called it). In a shallow pool of clear water, she pointed out clusters of pale white orbs resembling amphibian eggs ("Cave pearls," she said). The stalactites and stalagmites were growing larger, too—some joined into columns as thick as tree trunks. The two women sidestepped between them, like they were exploring an underground forest.

"I have a surprise for you farther down," Allie said, shifting her pack to fit through. "When you go deep enough underground, the laws of physics don't quite work."

"How so?"

She flashed a devilish smile. "It's a surprise."

The strangeness of this environment unsettled Tess. It was all dead rock, but somehow it was also alive in a perverted way, always changing, silently twisting and rearranging itself in the dark, only freeze-framed by their lights.

"Now I need to know what this surprise is."

"Be patient."

"Am I being murdered?"

"Don't give me ideas."

The walls, too, were studded with strange, warty nodules. They looked oddly painful to Tess, like hives or blisters. She was afraid to touch them. This speleological formation, according to Allie, was called *cave popcorn*.

"Or *cave syphilis*, if you prefer."

"Gross."

"Good luck unseeing it now."

Even this far into the underworld, there were still faint signs of human exploration. Anchor bolts glimmered in the rock faces, but much rustier than the ones on the Great Wall. Decades older, maybe. Tess wasn't sure she would trust her weight to them. On the sandy sediment floor, her headlamp found silver energy bar wrappers and corroded aluminum cans, but now the cans were much older. She realized she hadn't seen that particular Pepsi logo since she was a child. There it was on the ground, as if manifested into existence.

"If everyone sees bogeys in caves," she said, "what have you seen?"

"If I focus my eyes for a while?" Allie shrugged. "I'll see something like a light show. Colors melting together like a big churning cauldron of paint."

Tess had never tried staring into the darkness before. Not consciously. She wondered what she would see if she kept looking.

"Sometimes," Allie continued, creeping behind her, "I think I can see reaching appendages in the dark. Like something big and intelligent is right in front of me, just out of sight. If I had a night vision camera, I'd see it. But I don't. So I can only sense its form. It's a shadow of a shadow, always a few inches beyond my perception, and I can't hear it or touch it. The closer I step toward it, the farther it shrinks away, like our cautious little dance."

Tess felt breath on the back of her neck. "You're trying to scare me again."

"Is it working?"

She ignored her and stooped under low stalactites, accidentally scraping Ethan's expensive helmet anyway, and tried to visualize ten stories of solid earth overhead. All those millions of tons of bedrock and boulders and dirt, densely compacted. No wonder phones and radios didn't work down here. And every step took them deeper.

Allie helped her navigate a sharp drop. "It's good to reconnect, Tess."

"It is."

"I feel like I don't know you anymore. Like we've become strangers."

Tess avoided eye contact. "Life is busy."

"It's also short."

"You're in a reflective mood."

"Yes." Allie smiled sadly, studying the way ahead. "I am."

Tess thought about the two GoPro cameras silently recording on their helmets and her best friend's macabre joke: *In case we get murdered*.

An odd thing to say, given the circumstances.

There were many things about Tess's life that Allie (hopefully) didn't know, and she had to assume the same was true of Allie's. If good fences make good neighbors, the same must be true of friendships. Two weeks ago, Allie flew to Costa Rica on what was supposed to be a ten-day trip, but on day five, she'd inexplicably called Tess early in the morning and asked for her help in organizing a last-minute flight home from the nearest international airport in Liberia. Her voice had sounded scratchy and congested, like she'd been crying. Whatever had happened was somehow worse than the viper bite in Mexico, the time she'd literally died. What could scare Allie Merritt worse than death? She'd never told Tess. She never wrote the contracted pieces, either, which surely burned a few bridges with her sponsors.

All of it—Allie's mysterious incident in Costa Rica, her recent trouble with her boyfriend—felt connected somehow. Maybe true friends would've readily spilled their guts to each other, but theirs was a more complex and guarded relationship. Tess couldn't ask directly, so she dropped his name to see what she said: "If Ethan is our surface watch, he knows exactly where we are, right?"

"He'd be a crappy surface watch if he didn't."

Just more jokes, smirking half-answers, their shared language. Allie had never been easy to read. Tess was getting frustrated.

And what aren't you telling me?

On the way down their headlamps illuminated the final graffiti at the lowest depth, spray-painted by the most intrepid vandal: a faded red pentagram.

"This is where we usually sacrifice a goat," Allie said.

"Bummer we didn't bring one."

That wicked smile again. "Why do you think you're here, Tess?"

7

"I HEARD FOOTSTEPS BEHIND US," TESS SAYS.

The detective stops writing notes and looks up.

"The noise was faint. But I *knew* someone was following us. I could hear shuffling down the tunnel behind us, boots and gloves on muddy rock."

"Did Allie hear it?"

"When I told her to stop, the footsteps went quiet, too." She hesitates. "It was almost supernatural how perfectly they'd matched our pace. I watched behind us with my flashlight. We listened to the silence for a long time, just waiting for it to move again."

Of course, Washington knows, this would have been an inconclusive test. A stalker would know better than to reveal himself. "If the Green Ridge guy was secretly following you down the tunnel and he heard you both stop walking suddenly, he'd stop, too, wouldn't he?"

"That's exactly what I told Allie."

"She wasn't afraid?"

"She had an explanation for everything." Tess shrugs with an emotion the detective can't quite pinpoint. Annoyance? Sadness? Something else?

"How'd she explain it?"

"She just smirked at me, like it was all a joke. She said she was sorry, she'd forgotten to show me something. She said, *Watch this*. Then she raised her foot and took a loud step."

"And?"

"And that same step echoed from the dark behind us," Tess remembers. "She took another, and I heard another matching echo. That part of the Devil's Staircase is weird, apparently. I forget the word she used, but something about the shape of the tunnel bounces sounds right back at you. Like an echo, but perfectly preserved."

Another human sense corrupted by this strange underworld. Last year in London, Washington experienced a similar acoustic phenomenon called a *whispering gallery* in St. Paul's Cathedral. By standing in just the right place, you can whisper to someone standing fifty feet away, and they can hear you with startling clarity. She'd learned of this only when she heard her husband's breathy, disembodied voice inches behind her ear: *Hello, Layla*.

"So," Tess says, "I stomped to test it myself."

"And?"

"Sure enough, a duplicate echo came back."

At this point, Washington knows the two women were standing just a few feet from the site of the attack. Tess and Allie were right at the precipice of a life-altering act of violence. They had no idea what awaited them.

Except—maybe Tess did.

"I worried that someone was just using the audio trick to get closer to us," Tess says. "Taking advantage of the tunnel's weird acoustics. He could be following behind us, letting the crisscrossing echoes mask his footsteps."

An admittedly cunning strategy for a stalking killer. Anywhere else in the cave's tomblike quiet, the slightest human movement would stand out and be easy to track. Anywhere except *there*, in that particular tunnel.

This man knew what he was doing.

"And . . ." Tess's voice weakens. "Allie thought I was being paranoid."

It's only paranoia until you're right. Most rational people would see ordinary events in the blur of daily life: an inappropriate remark from a lumber worker, an optical illusion, a known auditory phenomenon. The greater picture forms only after the tragedy, after people are dead. But this young woman, in her intuition, managed to sense the danger before it chose to reveal itself. Tess was an intelligent woman, canny and perceptive.

"You're good with details, Tess."

"I've always been a bit of a control freak."

"How so?"

"I've never been comfortable being a passenger in other people's cars, or flying, or even getting on a roller coaster. The sensation of being powerless . . . bothers me."

"Where'd it come from?"

She shrugs. "A survival tactic, I think."

"Bad home?"

She nods.

"How bad?"

"I never met my dad, and my mom had a drug problem." Tess sits upright in her bed. "She'd . . . convinced herself that I was possessed by the devil. When I was little, I even believed it, too. She told me over and over that I was different from the other kids, that I didn't have a soul. She said I had the devil's yellow eyes, what she called *deceiver's eyes*. She said I was his baby, not hers, and that I had a forked tongue. She made me pray dozens of times a day. Walking around that tiny house was like navigating a minefield. I learned to say the right things and avoided saying the wrong things." Her eyes flick to the floor, embarrassed. "I still catch myself lying about things I don't need to lie about, like what I had for breakfast."

Compulsive white lies are a common reflex among survivors of domestic childhood abuse. When pain or punishment can come at any moment, you learn to adapt.

"And . . . if you said the wrong thing?"

Tess takes a breath. Then she lowers her hospital gown to expose her bare shoulder. Under the fresh cuts and bruises, the skin on her back is blotchy red with scar tissue. Her flesh is hard and almost shiny, like plastic. Candle wax, even.

It's a burn, but no ordinary one.

Washington's stomach turns. "Acid?"

"Bleach," Tess says. "To burn away the devil."

"I missed that part of the Bible."

"So did my mom."

"I'm sorry, Tess. That's terrible."

"For months and months, as bad as it got, she kept threatening that if I ever told anyone about it, she'd throw my cat into boiling water." Tess covers up again. "It was Allie who convinced me to be strong and tell the police anyway."

"And your cat?"

"I snuck her out of the house in my backpack."

Clever.

"Allie's family took me in during the criminal investigation. Her parents are lovely people. I owe them everything. I ended up living in their guest bedroom for most of high school. Allie and I were basically sisters for a while."

"And your mother . . . still in prison?"

"Never convicted."

"Why not?"

"Bungled prosecution. Mishandled evidence. It just never came together, somehow, and the judge had no choice but to dismiss it." Remarkably, she doesn't seem bitter about this. "Seeing how the system can fail from the inside . . . it's why I decided to go to law school."

"To do it right?"

Tess nods. "It took me years to be brave enough to speak up

about what was happening to me. And I only found the courage because I had a friend like Allie. If she hadn't been there, I would've kept avoiding confrontation at all costs and stayed in that house until she killed me." Her eyes harden. "I want to do right for the next kid."

Now, Tess is just a year away from taking the state bar exam. Good for her. Most of the law students Washington has met are in it for the money, her nephew included. Often they know just enough to be dangerous, like a toddler with a firearm.

Tess is clearly different.

"I wish we'd turned around," she whispers. "I wish I'd listened to my gut and not trusted Allie's word that everything was normal. I sensed something was wrong, I could feel it, but I was too timid to speak up about it."

"What happened isn't your fault."

"I could've stopped her."

"If Allie was as stubborn as you say, I doubt it."

"I could have. If I pushed harder."

"Let me propose an alternative version of the day, then." Washington sets her notepad down and interlocks her fingers. "Let's say that after you encountered that Green Ridge employee, who we now know wasn't really a Green Ridge employee, you'd both decided to leave the cave. The whole trip canceled due to a bad feeling. You and Allie would have been alone in the woods on the long hike back to her car, with no cover, no weapons, miles from help. He would've killed you both."

Tess nods, unconvinced.

"Another alternative: had you and Allie turned around and left the cave at any point—after seeing the phantom red glow, after your suspicion about the footsteps—you'd still have had to go right through him to reach the surface. Again, you'd both be dead."

"What are you saying?"

"As I see it, you and Allie were already in this man's fatal trap the moment you set foot in the Devil's Staircase. You couldn't feel it, but his snare was already around your necks. And you both made the best choice for your own survival, maybe even the only thing that saved you: you *kept going* deeper into the cave. You stayed ahead of him, out of his reach. That's what kept you alive that day. It's why you're here in this hospital, Tess."

The survivor nods reluctantly.

It's impossible to ask her now, but Washington suspects Allie might have figured this, too. As tough and worldly as this young woman seemed to be, she might have been concealing her true suspicions from Tess. The Devil's Staircase is full of hidden dangers, and an experienced caver like Allie might have planned to use them to elude a dangerous enemy or force him to lose interest and move on.

Or maybe she even knew a *lot* more. As Tess described it, throughout the day she'd seemed almost willful in ignoring and minimizing her best friend's fears. Did Allie have a secret motive?

"I tried to take unpredictable steps," Tess said, "daring whoever might be following us to screw up, mistime a step, and reveal himself."

"Any luck?"

She shakes her head. "Every time, the echo was a perfect copy."

AS TESS FOLLOWED ALLIE DEEPER UNDERGROUND, THE LANDSCAPE seemed to morph around them. Now there were fewer labyrinthine alternate routes or side chambers to memorize. Tess could sense their surroundings narrowing, funneling them until no other options existed and there was only one direction to go. *Down.*

Tess asked again, "What's the surprise?"

"You'll see."

At this depth, all forms of life seemed eradicated. No more spiders or crickets, no more streaks of bat guano. Even the oldest Pepsi cans were gone. Only varying textures of lead-gray rock, as lifeless as the interior of an asteroid. She wondered if they were entering some new phase Allie hadn't yet explained, somewhere deeper than even the dark zone.

The tunnel kept shrinking like fun-house walls, crowding them single file. Tess had to walk directly behind Allie to fit, her headlamp's circular beam fixed on the woman's back, and the surroundings tightened further until they were sidestepping between ancient formations. Finally it tapered to nothing at all, and they stood together in a small pocket of the earth as cramped as a janitor's closet.

A dead end.

And a strangely anticlimactic one.

This didn't match the planned route. Tess worried she'd misread the map—or could Allie be lost? On paper, the Devil's Staircase had looked like a giant ant colony, snarled with entwined tunnels. So where *was* all of it?

"Now"—her best friend grinned—"the fun part."

8

TESS SAW IT NOW.

It wasn't a dead end at all. Whatever prehistoric underground stream carved this passage had changed direction here and drained straight down, through a small cavity at their feet. It was ringed with shiny brown sludge, like an open orifice.

Allie nudged her. "Guess what it's called."

Tess could only stare. They were already deep underground, but this felt like gazing into an entirely new tunnel: a cave inside a cave. It was too small to walk through. A human would need to *crawl* inside it. She tried to remember the named areas on the map she'd studied—some descriptive, some darkly humorous—until finally it surfaced in her mind.

The Drainpipe.

She must have whispered it, because Allie nodded. "Bingo."

"We're going into that?"

"Through it, yes."

"Really?"

"Really." Allie's enthusiasm was almost evil. "It's a bit of a squeeze."

"No *shit.*" Tess knelt on her kneepads and peered down the tiny chute, her borrowed helmet scraping rock. The crawlspace was a little over two feet wide, barely enough space for a human to fit through on their elbows and knees. The tight corridor was studded with protruding rocks, some sharp-looking. Tess was reminded of the interior rows of a shark's teeth, layers of crooked fangs, like they were gazing inside a mouth. Or a meat grinder. Even with her flashlight, the darkness within felt thick and powerful. "What if I get stuck?"

"The biggest caver always crawls first," Allie said. "That's me."

"What if *you* get stuck?"

"I won't."

Allie had described these kinds of claustrophobic passages before, but Tess had always assumed there was some exaggeration at play. Even her GoPro footage had been misleading. Now that Tess was underground herself, she understood that first-person video could never convey the oppressive darkness of a cave, the closeness, the *pressure* of it. Nothing compares to the physical, full-body experience of being there.

And it was about to get significantly worse.

"Ethan calls it Bishop's Crawl," Allie said.

"Why?"

"Remember the part in *Aliens* when Lance Henriksen's character has to crawl a mile down that long, narrow pipe?"

"Your boyfriend is weird."

"I usually scoot in feetfirst," Allie said, lowering one muddy boot inside to demonstrate. It looked like she was feeding herself down the throat of a python. "About fifteen feet down, there's a few extra inches of overhead space where you can turn your body around. It's a long tunnel. Really long. I know this is breaking the rules, but I always tell people to crawl headfirst the rest of the way, so you can use your headlamp to see where you're going."

Above the opening, something glimmered in Tess's light: a metal sign bolted into rock, rust-eaten and slimy. She palmed away mud to reveal a black stencil.

ENTRAPMENT HAZARD
Proceed at Your Own Risk

"We've already passed two of those," Allie said. "That's just the lumber company covering their asses. Remember: as long as there's no Grim Reaper, we'll be fine."

"Great."

Tess knew Allie was trying to make her feel better in her clumsy way. And it was reassuring nonetheless to find more evidence that humans had been down there. She'd never imagined she'd miss the graffiti and Pepsi cans.

She realized she'd never actually asked Allie how deeply she'd explored this place. She led a group here at least twice a year. Had she traversed the entire system? The cramped lower reaches where that prospector died over a hundred years ago? She imagined acres of narrow tunnels under their boots, all hundreds of feet farther down.

So far down, the only way to rescue the trapped man had been to *break his legs*.

And it hadn't even worked.

"Trust me," Allie said. "This is why you wore kneepads."

She nodded weakly.

"Everyone does Bishop's Crawl a little differently. You either baby crawl on your hands and knees or go flat for a full-on belly crawl. Whichever is more comfortable. And watch out for sharp rocks. When it gets tighter—and it will, in a few spots—you'll want to roll over and squeeze through on your back so you can breathe easier. Keep one arm forward and one arm trailing your body, so you don't get bunched up in a spot you can't escape from. Remember, you're smaller than me, so if my ass can fit, so can yours."

"If I get caught on something, what do I do?"

"You won't. But if you do, I'll guide you out of it. The most important thing to remember is to stay calm. If you hyperventilate, your blood vessels swell and your body actually gets a few millimeters bigger, which won't help. And don't thrash or panic, because all you'll do is bruise yourself. Remember: the cave will always stay the same shape."

"Unless it collapses."

"Let's not jinx ourselves." Allie patted smooth rock. "The bogeys are listening."

As Tess studied the cramped tunnel, she felt a faint breeze on her cheek, like the exhaled breath of something waiting at the bottom.

"Feel that?" Allie pulled off a glove and held out her bare palm. "If it blows, it goes. If there's an air current, there's more cave."

"I'm guessing my surprise is at the bottom?"

She grinned. "Sure is."

"That doesn't sound sinister at all."

"I promise, Tess, what's down there is *amazing*. It's a thousand times cooler than anything you've seen so far. It's a long, tight crawl to get there, but it's worth it."

Tess said nothing. Like the presence of the cameras, she hadn't expected this. She was sensing a hidden motive under Allie's words. Why change the plan now?

Why didn't you mention this before?

"We were supposed to stay in the Upper Vault," Tess said.

"That was it. The real cave, ninety percent of it, is still down there." Allie hesitated, suddenly vulnerable. "I'd planned on making it a quick day, but watching how you handled the problem with your descender . . . I thought maybe you'd be up for more of an adventure. Seeing more of the cave with me."

With me. There was a hopefulness in her voice that broke Tess's heart.

"Well? What do you say?"

"DESCRIBE THE NEXT FEW MINUTES CAREFULLY, TESS. TRY TO REMEMber every detail." At this point, Washington knows, the two women were standing where it happened.

The long, cramped tube known as the Drainpipe—or Bishop's Crawl (to Allie and her grotto)—is the first truly challenging section of the cave. Rescue crews described the crawlway as between two and three feet high and sloping thirty degrees downward, crowded with loose cobble and pools of sandy mud. There's no room to stand up or even crouch. Not everyone is psychologically capable of entering such a space.

It made Washington think of an iron lung—the antiquated mechanical breathing apparatus. Some polio victims had to live inside them.

"Why do you think Allie wanted you to go down there so badly?"

"I don't know."

"Did she try to guilt you?"

"Of course not."

"Do you have a guess? A feeling?"

"Allie always looked out for me. I think she wanted to give me the opportunity to face something that scared me and defeat it." She tugs her gown to hide the scarred flesh on her back. "So I'd be reminded that I could."

"And?"

"I couldn't do it," Tess says. "I kept thinking back to her story from that morning. The guy who crawled down a cramped little tunnel like that one, how he slid into a narrowing squeeze until he couldn't move or breathe. And I just . . . my throat closed up. I couldn't."

Honestly, Washington can't say if she'd have done any better herself, even if her joints were up to it. It's not fear or weakness that holds most people back from entering such dangerously confined spaces, but simple evolved instinct. Like jumping off a building or inhaling water, your body just *knows* it's a bad idea and fights you if you try it.

"Was Allie disappointed?"

"She understood, I think. She told me I didn't have to do anything I didn't want to, which only made me feel worse. But the truth was . . ."

"You *wanted* to go down there."

Tess nods.

Then she forms a wistful, genuine smile. "The day had been exhilarating, honestly the most fun I'd had in years. I can't describe it, but being scared is kind of addictive, you know? Hooking up and trusting my life to a rope and a harness, cutting my hair out of a descender with a crappy knife. I was starting to feel like a badass, like I could handle myself the way Allie always could." She breathes out, deflating. "But then, looking at this new challenge, it was like I'd leveled all the way back down to my old self. The longer I stared down the Drainpipe, the more my throat tightened and I felt sick. I had to close my eyes. I couldn't follow Allie down there, and I hated myself for it."

She looks up, and the fluorescent lights shadow her face harshly, making her eye sockets appear dark and hollowed.

"And then it was over, just like that. I could already feel the adrenaline leaving my body, half relief and half disappointment. The whole day ended early because of me." She hesitates, a slow acceptance. "It cuts both ways, you know."

"What does?"

"The thing you told me earlier, to make me feel better." Tess glances at the digital recorder on the table, still listening. "Because we know now that he was stalking us. If Allie and I had hiked back to the car, we would've been killed. And if we'd turned around inside the cave, we would've been killed, too. Moving *forward* was what kept us both alive, right?"

Washington nods.

Tess exhales, her shoulders heavy. "Until that moment, when I made us stop."

"WE CAN ALWAYS COME BACK SOMETIME," ALLIE SAID WARMLY, WITHout a trace of disappointment. "You did amazing, Tess."

Her mouth was dry. "Thanks."

"I wasn't trying to spring the Drainpipe on you. I just . . . I've really had fun with you today, Tess. It felt like we were kids again." She looked away and kept nodding, as if building herself up to say something. "And honestly, I think I've been trying to distract myself, too. Something has been bothering me."

"What?"

"I . . ." Allie stared up at the stalactites, at the sharpened fang-like points beading with water. When she looked back, her eyes glimmered with tears. "I'm sorry I waited so long to tell you this. I've been in denial, I guess."

Tess touched her arm. "What happened?"

"Ethan and I . . ."

She trailed off and said nothing. It took Tess a few confused heartbeats to realize Allie had frozen, the words caught in her throat.

She turned and saw it, too.

Up the tunnel, the red glow had returned. Now it was closer, brighter, impossible to deny, hovering six feet off the ground like a ball of incendiary plasma.

9

"*PLEASE* TELL ME YOU SEE IT, TOO."

"I see it," Tess said.

The light reflected down the corridor of limestone, glinting off rivulets of trickling water, replacing every color with red. The tunnel suddenly felt like a photographer's darkroom. She heard a sharp intake of air beside her and realized the unbreakable Allie Merritt, the woman who'd already died once before, was finally afraid.

Still, she stepped forward.

"Who's there?" Allie's shout was startlingly loud in the limited space. It echoed strangely, and Tess heard a disembodied mimic of her best friend's voice—*Who's there?*—as the tunnel's sonic trickery did its thing.

Her voice rebounded to silence.

No answer.

The red light didn't move. Every shadow held still.

"I . . ." She glanced back at Tess—just a blink of uncertainty—and then hardened again. "Whoever you are, you need to back off. I have a gun."

I have a gun.

I have a gun.

I have a gun. The cave mocked her bluff.

Tess knew Allie practiced at an indoor range twice a month and owned three target pistols. She also knew for a fact that none of the three was here.

This part of the tunnel was linear: one way forward and one way back. There were no formations to hide behind, no alternate routes to skirt. The hovering red light saturated the entire world, turning the rock, the dripping water, Allie's skin, all red. Everything livid, arterial red.

"That's the only way back," Allie whispered.

Past the red light.

"What is it?"

"I don't know."

Then it moved—Allie shivered with a jolt—and it seemed to levitate closer to them, throwing new shadows. Red light and blacks swirled, the tunnel a giant kaleidoscope.

"Tess," Allie whispered. "Stand behind me."

She did.

The ball of fiery light intensified, and a new form separated from the darkness: a human figure wearing a red headlamp. As it strode closer, Tess kept her eyes locked on the sandy floor. She didn't need to see his face. She already knew who it was and what was about to happen.

A familiar voice echoed: "Nice to see you girls again."

Allie said nothing.

"How's the cave?" His red beam spotlighted her. "Spectacular, right?"

She took a step back—nudging Tess, too—but there was nowhere to retreat to. The rock walls were suffocating; cold stone enclosed them on all sides. The figure's wide shoulders blocked the tunnel. Tess felt her best friend's neoprene-gloved fingertips press her collarbone, holding her back. And in Allie's other hand, something glinted. Held low, concealed purposefully behind her hip.

Her survival knife.

Shielded from the man's view, Allie thumbed the blade open with a soft *tick*.

"So, I need to get something off my chest." Jacob strode closer, his face still obscured behind that balaclava. "When I introduced myself back there, I lied about being affiliated with Green Ridge. The truth is I'm more of a private contractor working in the area."

Allie's voice was brittle. "What do you want?"

"Just to talk."

"We're talking now."

"And I understand how this looks, but please let me reassure you: I have no bad intentions here. Cross my heart." He patted a hand to his barrel chest. "To be honest, what you said to me back there hurt my feelings. So I figured I'd follow you two down here. Maybe, I figured, after some time to think about your nasty words, you might take this opportunity to apologize to me."

Allie's grip tightened on her hidden knife. "You came here for an apology."

"Yes."

"That's all?"

"Yes."

"And after I apologize, you'll just leave?"

"Yes." He straightened a glove.

"I don't believe you."

"Cross my heart," he repeated in a gentle and pleasant voice. "But I'd need to get closer to properly hear this apology. I believe in mutual respect, and apologies are best done face-to-face. So I can safely get close to you, I'll have to ask that you both kindly take a few precautions."

He tossed something down the tunnel. It splashed into a puddle at their feet, and Allie's headlamp illuminated it.

A bundle of white zip ties.

"It's strictly for my own safety," he clarified, his voice muffled by fabric. "Please understand. If I'm going to get close enough to hear your apology, I have to make sure I'm not making myself vulnerable. You've already shown hostility toward me today, so I'd say some caution on my part is warranted, don't you? You never know who you're meeting in the woods."

His red glow flicked down to the zip ties.

"So," he added, "I have to kindly ask you both to tie your wrists, please."

Allie glanced back at Tess with wide eyes and shook her head once. The motion was both furtive and sharp, the message clear.

Don't do it.

"Sorry. I know it's awkward." He stretched his shoulders, lazy and catlike. "You don't even have to put your hands behind your backs. They're not handcuffs, and I'm not a cop. Just loop the cable around your wrists, thread the edge through the little square, bite with your teeth, and pull. It's surprisingly easy."

Allie said nothing. She was a coiled rattlesnake, every muscle tense.

"I've been very polite so far," he added. "Wouldn't you agree, Allie Merritt?"

Tess felt a change in her best friend's stance. She could sense the woman's thoughts, a stab of crystalline terror: *He knows my name.*

How does he know my name?

"I'll make you a counteroffer," Allie responded, her voice surprisingly controlled. "I have almost fifty thousand dollars in my bank account. If you let us both leave this cave, right now, I'll give you my debit card."

He snorted. "I'd just take it anyway—"

"And my PIN."

Silence.

Jacob's face was unreadable behind the black ski mask. But he tilted his head with a creak of rubber and fabric, as if considering the offer, and the headlamp's red light shifted slightly. With her free hand, Allie unzipped her side pack and tossed her wallet.

It splashed near his boots. He didn't pick it up.

"Here's the deal." Allie's tone was low and measured. "We'll all leave this cave peacefully. First, you'll let my friend go to the surface. Your problem is with me, not her."

His gaze flicked to Tess, then back.

"I'll wait here with you for a few minutes, so I know Tess is safe, and then I'll go, too," Allie said. "I'll give you my PIN, plus whatever bank information you need. Then we'll all three go our separate ways. No one has to tie themselves up, and no one gets hurt. Deal?"

He made a slurping noise, as if sucking on his lip. "Tempting."

"Is it a deal?"

"You'll just report your card stolen."

"Twenty-four hours."

"And I'm supposed to trust you?"

"Cross my heart." Allie didn't blink. "Or whatever dumb shit you said."

For a few seconds, neither side spoke. Then he shifted his weight, and Tess saw something Allie didn't: the faint outline of a handgun concealed in the man's pants, its barrel resting somewhere above his testicles.

"You're a badass, Allie Merritt. I'm starting to admire that about you." He sighed, his hand resting on his belt. "But it seems we've reached an impasse."

TWENTY-EIGHT HOURS LATER, IN A RECOVERY ROOM AT SACRED HEART Medical Center, Tess has to stop. Whatever happened next, she's not sure if she can say. Her cheeks flush and tears glisten under fluorescent lights. On a monitor, her heart rate is accelerating. She squeezes her hands into fists and breathes. Then she looks up at the detective with haunted eyes, the burst blood vessel a vivid red butterfly.

"He . . . shot Allie in the head."

10

"I'M SO SORRY, TESS."

Nothing you say can help. Washington learned that decades ago. But you say things anyway because saying nothing is worse.

There's something uniquely upsetting about witnessing death by gun violence, something only the initiated can understand. The movies lie. Getting shot isn't a sanitized off switch. The physics of a fast-moving projectile penetrating skin, tissue, and bone are frankly horrifying. Even if shot fatally in the head, the human body takes a few seconds to fully die, and those seconds can be sickening and messy: intact parts of the brain often struggle to reboot, lower functions of the body reflexively cling to life, the eyes, nose, and mouth leak blood. Air wheezes out of slackening lungs in the victim's recognizable voice.

Just by standing near the gunshot, Tess herself suffered a ruptured eardrum. This was to be expected after the killer fired a handgun inside a cramped tunnel. Rock walls on all sides would have magnified the blast to an earsplitting volume. The survivor likely doesn't realize how fortunate she is to have received only minor hearing damage. If it could be any consolation, the killer almost certainly blew out his eardrums, too.

By Tess's account, this ski-masked stranger posing as a Green Ridge employee—"Jacob"—had followed the two women, eavesdropped on their private conversations, and finally, once deep enough underground and beyond help, chose his moment to attack.

From here on, every word matters.

Every detail.

Washington turns to a new page on her notepad and checks to ensure her digital recorder is still running. "Are you okay, Tess?"

The survivor's face is bloodless. She studies the tile floor. "It's my fault."

"Look at me."

"If I'd been faster, if I hadn't frozen up like I always do, we could've both fought back and maybe we'd—"

"Look at me, Tess." She slides her chair forward and meets the woman's gaze. "If you'd tried to fight him he would have killed you, too. Full stop. He had a gun. You had a pocketknife. The only person responsible for what happened to Allie is the man who pulled the trigger."

She says nothing.

"And this wasn't a robbery, either. This guy wasn't here for anyone's PIN. He brought zip ties. He was there to make you both *disappear.*"

Tess wipes her eye.

"And Allie saved you. She bought you a few seconds to escape. That's her gift to you." The detective reaches out to squeeze Tess's thin wrist. "Your best friend loved you, and in that terrible moment she proved it. She's a hero. Don't take that away from her by blaming yourself."

She keeps her voice low and comforting, but her mind races with new questions. The story has taken a hairpin turn, and the real work begins now.

"Tess." She leans in closer, her fingers interlocked. "I can't even imagine how difficult this must be for you and how painful it must be to relive the experience. But you have to understand, I can't do this without you. I need your help. I need you to describe exactly what happened next. After this stranger shot Allie in the head, how did you escape?"

"I was cornered." Tess rubs her eyes. "I couldn't hide or fight. All I could do was run."

"Run where?"

"*Down.*"

The detective draws a line on her notepad to mark a new depth, the point where the Devil's Staircase becomes truly dangerous.

"He shot at me," Tess says, "but I hurled myself down the tiny opening."

A blind plunge.

Headfirst.

The Drainpipe, Washington writes. The winding, narrow crawlspace that Tess had been too frightened to enter before, now only the second-scariest thing in her world.

11

"I LANDED HARD ON MY STOMACH," TESS REMEMBERS. "THERE WAS no space to turn around. Just solid rock, inches from my face."

Just imagining it gives Washington a chill.

"I tried to push myself up into a crawling position, but the ceiling scraped my back. I couldn't stretch my arms." She steadies her voice. "I blinked, but my eyes were full of mud. It was cold, wet, pitch-black. I didn't know how long the Drainpipe was, or how far I'd slid, or how close he was behind me. My ears were ringing, but I could hear him moving somewhere above me, his boots stomping. He was screaming, swearing, pissed that I'd gotten away. I think I'd landed maybe five or six feet down, just out of his view."

A few hard-fought seconds of safety.

But Tess would've also been helpless, wedged upside down inside the chute. She was sealed in on all sides by rock. From such a vulnerable position she would've been unable to fight back or even see his attack coming.

"I couldn't breathe. I cried out, and my own voice sounded deafening, trapped inside the tiny space with me. I screamed and screamed, breathing my own reused air, on and on until my throat was raw. It felt like drowning, but it never ended. I remember wanting to die."

The survivor hesitates.

"And then . . . I saw that red glow again. Lighting up the

walls around me, getting brighter. And I heard shuffling, scraping sounds. I knew he was cramming himself down the tunnel after me, following me down. I couldn't see him, but he was close."

She shudders, reliving the nightmare in tactile detail.

"I felt a breeze on my bare ankle, just above my sock—he was right there, *right there*, crawling behind me—and I kicked at him. I had to go deeper. I threw myself down the narrow tunnel, fighting to stay ahead of him, using big rocks as handholds and footholds to pull myself through. They cut me on all sides, tugged my harness, bumped my helmet, caught on my clothes. I didn't even have room to look back. But I could hear his breaths, these huffing pants like an attack dog. I could smell his sweat." She hesitates, as if afraid to say it. "And I heard . . . something else. This weird metal ticking noise, right behind me."

The detective furrows her brow. "Can you elaborate?"

"Like this." Tess raps her knuckle on the hospital tray, as steady as a heartbeat.

Click.

Click.

Click.

Washington's stomach twists. She knows what Tess was hearing. She already saw it this morning: a seven-inch KA-BAR combat knife with a grooved metal handle. The official fighting knife of the US Marine Corps. The killer had carried it in his fist as he chased her on hands and knees—and with every lurching motion, steel clicked on rock.

"I kept crawling," she whispers, "trying to stay ahead of that sound."

Wedged inside the tunnel, Tess would have had no defense against the killer and his knife. If he'd caught her, she could have only kicked blindly, her face and vital organs out of his reach, but her lower body vulnerable as he stabbed and slashed, severing arteries in her ankles, inflicting enough damage to ensure she bled to death in the confined space. A truly miserable way to die.

He had a gun, of course, but he'd made the decision to switch to his knife. He'd probably (painfully) learned that a firearm was near useless in a cave. Fired in open air, a .45-caliber report is over 160 decibels, loud enough to damage unprotected ears. Indoors, sound bounces off walls and its power amplifies. The Drainpipe made this a thousand times worse: firing a gun inside a shoulder-width crawlspace inches from your face would all but guarantee permanent hearing loss. Then there's the risk of a fatal ricochet. A single bullet could shatter into lethal bouncing fragments, turning the narrow tunnel into a meat grinder. In all likelihood, he'd never planned to fire the pistol that day at all, carrying it as a backup and relying on his own physical threat—until Allie and Tess refused to zip-tie themselves. Until they put him at an *impasse*, in his own words.

The killer's gear was unconventional, but there was clear intent behind every choice. The rubber gloves, the reinforced balaclava. Even that surreal colored headlamp, like something from a nightmare.

"Tess, why do you think his headlamp was red?"

"I didn't ask him."

"Well, it reminds me of something I honestly haven't thought about for years," Washington says, and shrugs. "I have an educated guess."

Tess glances up, curious.

"Back in the army, we trained for night patrols, walking in pairs through the forest, and we didn't use regular lights. We used special red flashlights."

"Why?"

"Normal light causes your pupils to contract, letting less light in and erasing your night vision. But the human eye is much less sensitive to light on the red spectrum. So if you patrol with a red flashlight, your natural night vision stays intact, and your light signature is tougher for the enemy to spot."

"Win-win," Tess says.

"Exactly."

This ambush had been intelligently planned, and the killer would know he couldn't pursue Tess forever. An unwitting third party—cavers, trespassers, an *actual* Green Ridge employee—could stumble across the dangerous scene at any moment. And the longer he remained at the Devil's Staircase, the more likely he'd unwittingly leave evidence connecting himself to the crime. Hair. Skin. Clothing fibers.

His time was limited, too. He knew it.

"I kept crawling deeper," Tess says, "fighting to stay ahead of his red light. I was getting exhausted. I could feel him right behind me."

She was cornered inside a tiny tube, chased by a monster. That steel blade scraping rock behind her hiking boots, seconds from plunging into her unprotected ankle.

Click.

Click.

"My hands were getting sliced up as I crawled. My helmet kept bumping. I was getting stuck on things, and I realized the tunnel was narrowing around me, getting tighter and crowded with loose rocks. Some I could push away. Some were too heavy. I tried to arch my back and squeeze between them, but I was running out of space. Ahead, with my headlamp turned sideways, I could see the way forward was blocked."

She takes a shivering breath.

"It was a dead end."

12

THE CAVE-IN, THE INCIDENT COMMANDER HAD CALLED IT.

Ceiling collapses are part of a cave's natural life cycle, Washington quickly learned. In this part of the Drainpipe, the crawlspace is crowded with rock debris from one such recent collapse. The blockage is mostly football-sized rocks, but the largest obstacle is a sandstone boulder roughly the size of a beach ball, perhaps four hundred pounds, that dislodged from above and settled between two slanted walls.

To reach the trapped woman, rescuers had to negotiate several of these unstable areas. In the early hours of the search, one member of the first team unwittingly nudged a boulder that happened to be load bearing. They'd been evacuating him from the cave entrance when Washington first stepped off the ATV this morning, and she'd only glimpsed it: a sharp spear of gray white protruding from the man's bent forearm, oddly clean-looking under the blood-soaked bandages. This was a new world with new rules, and under millions of tons of rock, human bones don't stand a chance. All it takes is a little pressure in the wrong place.

This dangerous landmark put Tess halfway down the Drainpipe. *130 feet,* the detective writes.

In total darkness.

With a killer on her tail.

"There was a little gap underneath where the boulder had settled," Tess says, demonstrating with her scabbed hands. "With my headlamp, I saw more space, more tunnel, on the other side. And I knew that if I squeezed just right, I might fit through."

"How wide was the gap?"

"Maybe a foot."

Jesus.

"I wasn't sure if I could fit." A wincing smile. "But I knew *he* couldn't."

The killer was broad shouldered, a muscular two hundred pounds, much bigger than Tess. As physically strong as he likely was, he wasn't built for tight squeezes. Certainly not twelve inches between slabs of solid rock.

This would be an advantage—if it worked.

"Thinking of what I'd have to do . . . it made me want to throw up."

"Hell, it makes *me* want to puke."

It would have been a nerve-racking test, to wriggle under the suspended block. Like all loose cave debris, it could've been unstable. If it shifted only an inch, it could pin Tess in place and crush her lungs inside her rib cage—another truly miserable way to die.

But the death that followed her was even worse.

"The red glow was brightening around me. He was catching up fast, crawling just a few feet behind me. I knew that if he touched me, I was dead."

His Marine Corps KA-BAR knife would plunge into the soft flesh of her legs, raking through tissue, severing arteries, and scraping bone . . .

"I couldn't fit through with all my gear," Tess says. "So I took off my side pack and pushed it through. Then I rolled my water bottle through. I had to slide everything through the tiny gap, as fast as I could."

Go, Tess.

"My helmet, too. I pulled it off, pushed it sideways so it would fit."

Go-go-go—

"Last, myself." She steadies her voice. "I remembered what Allie told me. I flattened down to my stomach, exhaled all the air from my lungs, and squeezed in."

"I got stuck."

She swallows.

"But I kicked and pushed hard—I had to stretch one arm out and twist my head sideways, scraping my ears against rock—and I slithered through. On the other side, I tucked my feet out of his reach. There was just barely enough space to turn around, so I reoriented my body and faced him through the gap. I realized how *close* he'd been."

That ski-masked face, now stymied.

Her voice hardens. "And I realized . . . I had the advantage."

The killer couldn't reach her through the rockfall. What could he do now? By the skin of her teeth, Tess had outraced him and ventured too deep underground to follow. She'd used the cave's hostile geography against him.

"Good job," Washington says. "You'd made yourself unreachable."

"No. Not just that."

"What?"

"He wasn't staring at me. I realized he was staring at my helmet," Tess says. "At first, I didn't understand. Then I touched it, and I felt the plastic mount on the front. Allie's GoPro."

Still recording.

Her voice shivers with adrenaline. "It had been recording the entire time."

Ever since Tess and Allie had first entered the Devil's Staircase that morning, every word, every breath, every detail Tess had craned her neck to see, the waterproof action camera had seen, too. By her account she'd filmed glistening formations and abyssal drops, her mishap on the rope, her unresolved final words with Allie.

And the moment this man shot her.

In high definition.

Now Washington understands the true depth of the killer's dilemma. According to Tess, she hadn't just witnessed her best friend's murder—she'd unwittingly *filmed* it.

And she was wearing the recorded video footage on her helmet. No wonder this man chased her so aggressively down the Drainpipe—he had no choice. He was locked into this high-stakes situation as surely as Tess was, and now he couldn't reach her behind the cave-in. Even if he fired his pistol through the narrow gap and shot the woman in the head (at the cost of his own permanent hearing loss), the camera and its damning footage would still be unreachable on her body.

"I stared back at him," Tess says. "I tried not to think about Allie. I told myself I'd grieve for her later, when no one was looking. Face-to-face with her killer, I had to be strong."

"Did you speak to him?"

"I told him . . . I'd filmed what he did to Allie. Every minute, every second, was on the record." Her voice lowers. "I told him that whatever happened, I'd make sure he went to prison."

In a heartbeat, the terrified survivor transitioned from prey to hunter. She'd outwitted this dangerous man, captured him on video committing murder, and the footage was right there on her helmet, *just* out of his reach. Washington can't help but enjoy the woman's victory, as tenuous as it may have been.

Tess only nods in slow, robotic motions. A tear rolls down her cheek.

For Allie.

Grief has aftershocks, Washington knows. They hit unpredictably when your guard is down. It can feel like a form of torture, rediscovering your loved one's absence from every tedious angle—when you find their favorite coffee creamer spoiled and forgotten in the back of the fridge, when you realize you should probably delete their number from your phone. She can see it rippling through Tess now, the same soul-deep shocks that would have first hit her in that tunnel: her best friend of sixteen years was dead. The girl whose family took her in, the restless spirit who lived to explore the world and the places underneath it, the larger-than-life, enigmatic Allie Merritt was gone forever.

"She'd be proud of you, Tess."

She wipes her eye with her thumb. "I hope so."

13

"WHAT DID ALLIE'S KILLER SAY?"

"Nothing."

"Did he seem upset?"

"I couldn't see his face behind the ski mask," Tess says. "But he seemed calm, almost methodical. Like he'd considered this as a possibility, and he was prepared for it. I could hear him moving on the other side of the boulder, scrapes and thumps. He was rummaging around, maybe looking for any gear I'd left behind. Then . . . he left."

"Back to the surface?"

"He had to crawl backward like a big python. I watched his headlamp disappear up the tunnel. Eventually it was just that red glow, slowly fading."

"You beat him."

"Barely."

"How'd it feel?"

"I wanted to laugh and cry and scream and throw up, all at once." The survivor takes a breath. "It didn't feel real. I couldn't believe I was still alive."

But Tess would have only bought herself time, and not much of it. She'd outwitted this dangerous man and made herself unreachable—but now she was wedged deep underground, far from help. Allie's killer knew he couldn't leave a witness alive, let alone a witness with incriminating video footage of the whole thing. He couldn't allow her to leave.

His next step would be to guard the cave's entrance and keep her imprisoned inside. He was already well equipped to outlast her. By her own account, Tess had packed for only an afternoon outing—just a few granola bars, spare batteries, and a water bottle. Soon she would be hungry and thirsty. Eventually her headlamp would die.

"I wished I could stand up and stretch my legs. I couldn't even sit up without my helmet hitting the ceiling."

Tess was still only a fraction into the cave's true depths. She was still hundreds of feet from where the rescue operation would concentrate its efforts.

"The red glow from his headlamp had disappeared." She lets out a breath. "He was gone. Now it was just me, lying on my stomach in the dark. The mud was freezing cold. And maybe it was just the adrenaline, but all my senses felt so weirdly acute. I hadn't noticed how humid the cave's air was. Or all the little smells. I could hear the falling water droplets with perfect clarity, my breaths, my heartbeat. And I wondered if this was the experience Allie had told me about, like coming apart on a molecular level. Losing yourself."

Like I'm a tiny creature being digested in a giant stomach.

She hesitates, as if embarrassed to say it. "And a part of me actually wished he'd come back," she admits. "Somehow, being alone down there was even worse."

Our own brains can sabotage us.

Six months ago Washington was driving alone on the freeway late at night and suddenly couldn't remember where she was going. It felt like she'd woken up from sleepwalking. The disorientation was terrifying, a jolt of animal fight-or-flight. She had to pull over onto the shoulder, her heart pounding in her ears. She never told a soul about the episode, and she never even determined where or why she'd been driving. It was as if something had hijacked her body for its own purposes and then relinquished control without warning at seventy miles per hour. Sleep deprivation and long hours were at least partially to blame, but it was part of a troubling pattern of missed appointments and lost thoughts.

She researched it, like any detective, and reassured herself that a certain amount of spaciness is just an inevitable part of aging. All cells in the body break down over time. Inside the brain, the mechanisms that convert glucose to energy and dispose of waste are often the first to fail. Cerebral debris accumulates and neural processes slow down, congested by cellular crap. Individuals with higher IQs are more likely to notice the signs because they simply have further to fall. It's only something to worry about if other people notice your mental glitches. At the time, this made her feel better.

But that's the thing. Maybe other people *have* noticed.

She's felt the sympathetic eyes on her while she grasps for a word for just a second too long. She's sensed the polite pauses, the moments a conversation shifts gears to accommodate her. Once that seed is planted, even normal brain farts become further evidence of neurological decline. You can't win against confirmation bias. Last week, her lieutenant had quietly taken her into his office and recommended she subject herself to a cognitive assessment.

No disrespect, he'd assured her.

Of course.

But Washington knows she's here at the hospital because of her perceived frailty—and not just her body. She's been sidelined, seated indoors to question Tess and take notes, while the real work happens miles away.

A cave is a uniquely challenging crime scene to process. Because the interior environment is protected from rain, wind, and most predatory animals, physical evidence can stay intact for years. This is not a good thing. It means the sprawling tunnels have already been contaminated by thousands of prior humans, each leaving behind their own perfectly preserved footprints and handprints. Add in all the stray hairs, clothing fibers, and general waste, and the Devil's Staircase is a daunting trash heap of unrelated leads to sort and eliminate. Then throw in a day-long rescue effort *on top of that*, with rock chisels and oxygen bottles and scores of boots and gloves touching and moving everything. The incident commander had already assured the sheriff's department—twice—that his people were being mindful of the parallel criminal investigation, but saving the trapped woman had to take priority. It's impossible to safely navigate dangerous crawlways without also obliterating evidence. It'll be a miracle if much can be recovered at all.

This means determining what really happened that day will depend less on analyzing the scene of the attack and more on firsthand accounts like Tess's. Things seen and heard, gathered by careful interrogation. Old-fashioned police work. It's amusing, then, that the powers that be may have unwittingly reassigned Washington to the most crucial role in the entire investigation. This is an opportunity. And a risk.

Don't blow it.

If she does, she might find herself facing more than a cognitive test.

"It's important that we establish a timeline," Washington tells the survivor. "Do you know how long you waited behind the cave-in?"

Tess shakes her head.

This is to be expected. Since the moment Tess and Allie took their first steps underground, their bodies' circadian rhythms began to unravel. Without a sun to track across the sky, without electronic devices, measuring time becomes subjective and unreliable.

She prompts: "An hour?"

"Maybe."

"Two hours?"

"Enough time passed that I started to worry about my batteries. The idea of being in complete darkness without light terrified me, but I needed to plan ahead. I kept my headlamp off. I avoided using my flashlight. I checked Allie's GoPro, still recording—the battery was twenty percent, I think. It would die soon."

"Did you . . . watch the footage?"

She shakes her head. Seeing it happen once was enough.

Then she rotates her shoulders and stretches her sore arms in her hospital bed, clearly grateful to be free from the confined space. "Lying on my stomach was getting uncomfortable. My elbows and knees went numb at first, and it gradually turned into pain. Eventually it was unbearable, like a full-body hernia. I wished I could stand up, so badly. My body needed space."

"Could you hear the killer?"

"I kept holding my breath and listening for him. Every now and then I heard scrapes and scratches in the dark. Like something heavy being dragged. Weird noises, echoing down the tunnel. Maybe my senses were playing tricks on me."

What had Allie called them?

Bogeys.

The longer a person remains wedged in this sensory-deprived state, Washington knows, the less reliable their firsthand experience becomes. It's a situation the human psyche simply isn't designed for. When subjects are left alone in an unlit room for long enough, a psychological phenomenon called the *prisoner's cinema* can develop. Some see light shows, as Allie herself described, while others claim to see strange colors or even ghosts and demons, until it becomes impossible to untangle memory from hallucination. In ancient times, followers of Pythagoras ventured into caves to receive visions from the gods. No drugs required. Even before facing the prospect of her own cognitive decline, Washington has always found it disturbing how little it actually takes to unravel our minds—merely darkness and quiet.

During this stretch of missing time, the male suspect, "Jacob," was surely in damage control mode. His highest priority would be keeping his second victim contained in the cave.

"I knew I had to wait," Tess whispers. "No matter how uncomfortable it got. If I crawled back up to the surface, he would be there, waiting for me."

He couldn't leave the cave. He was locked into this life-and-death standoff with Tess, a meek and petite woman he'd presumably judged to be easy prey, and under no circumstances could he allow her to escape with the GoPro footage. He was probably hiding somewhere just outside the Drainpipe in silent ambush, hoping to lure Tess out so he could cut her throat. She was wise to stay prone down there inside the narrow tunnel, as painful as it must have been.

"I knew he was on a ticking clock, too," Tess says. "He couldn't wait forever."

"How so?"

"Allie and I couldn't just disappear in the mountains. I work Mondays and Thursdays at a law office, and if I was a no-show, my boss would look for me."

"Eventually."

"And even better: Allie had set up a surface watch, remember? A responsible person who wouldn't be present on the trip but who'd know everything—where we went, where we parked, when we were due back. I knew that when Allie failed to check in with him in the next few hours, he'd take the appropriate steps and report us missing."

His name remains unspoken, like she doesn't want to say it.

Washington writes: *Ethan Ramirez*.

Allie's boyfriend of a little over a year. Physician on his second year of pediatric residency, hiking enthusiast, frequently credited on *Keep Calm* as Allie's photographer and travel partner. At first glance, an uninvolved party to the attack.

"Ethan would report us missing," Tess whispers. "All I had to do was stay alive long enough."

"Were you and Ethan on good terms?"

"Sure."

"Can you describe him?"

"Just under six feet tall. Black hair—"

"I know what he looks like. What kind of person is he?"

"He's . . ." Tess licks her lips, like she's trying to think of something nice to say. "Ethan always seemed like a decent guy."

"Decent?"

"A good person. A gentle person. He was always kind to Allie."

Good. Gentle. Tess is being surprisingly vague about Allie's boyfriend, someone she should have strong opinions about. There's always tension between a best friend and a romantic interest, between the one who knows you best and the one who's trying to. Washington studies the survivor for signs of discomfort. *Why are you evading?*

What are you holding back?

"You didn't trust him?"

"It wasn't that I didn't trust Ethan, or suspected he was secretly dangerous or anything like that. I just thought he was . . ." Tess hesitates, as if searching for the right word. "To be honest, a bit of an airhead."

Washington laughs. "Dumb?"

"Simple. Like a puppy."

"People love puppies."

"I'm more of a cat person."

"Were they happy together?"

"From everything I saw they seemed like a perfect couple," Tess says. "But Ethan was always so . . . guarded around me. Like he was afraid of me. Whoever he really was, I felt like I never actually knew him."

"I need specifics, Tess."

She nods, trying to remember.

"Okay." She studies her Starbucks cup on the hospital tray, still untouched. "Allie told me this once. Last year, she took him to a conference in New York to accept one of her awards. They were out to dinner, and Ethan was just stepping out of their Uber or something, and he froze suddenly and pointed down at the sidewalk. *Look at this,* he said to her. It sounded important, urgent even, so Allie scrambled over to him so fast she almost tore something on her dress, certain it was something terrible on the concrete."

"What was it?"

"A flosser."

Washington blinks.

"One of those little plastic dental flossers, used by some stranger to scrape crap off their teeth, discarded on the sidewalk. And Ethan looked up at her, straight-faced, dead serious, and said, *I think we can use this*." Her lips curl into a wincing smile. "It became their running joke. Whenever he found one, he'd take a picture and text it to Allie out of the blue. *Think we can use this?* She actually kept an album of them on her phone, all these photos of used plastic flossers in different colors, different cities."

"Gross."

"They're everywhere. Once you start noticing them, you can't stop."

"Not sure I get the joke."

"Honestly, I didn't, either." Tess's smile slowly dims. "But you wanted an example of who Ethan was, right? That was him. He could make Allie laugh so hard she snorted. In just a year he'd figured her out somehow, unlocked all her secret codes. It felt like he already knew her better than I did." She's about to say something else but stops herself.

Washington is detecting jealousy.

On *Keep Calm*'s social media, Allie and Ethan appear almost insufferably privileged as they tour the world on their six-figure incomes, whiskey tasting in front of a mossy Scottish castle, giggling on a beach in Thailand, snuggling up with a bottle of wine and watching the northern lights over Reykjavík. Who wouldn't be jealous of that life?

She pushes a little harder. "Any trouble in paradise?"

"That morning, I'd sensed something was bothering Allie."

"What?"

"I don't know. It had something to do with Ethan, though." Tess shrugs emptily. "They'd had fights before, but this was different. Something serious was weighing on Allie. And she never had a chance to tell me what it was."

Washington underlines his name.

No relationship is perfect, and the ones that appear so are often hiding the most rot. Right now the young physician is at Providence Portland, a much larger hospital than this one. When he's questioned, what might he have to say?

Who are you really, Ethan?

"In that moment, it gave me hope," Tess says. "Back home, Ethan knew exactly where Allie and I were, and he was waiting for us to check in. He was familiar with the cave and the area." Her voice creaks with sadness. "And . . . he had no idea his girlfriend was dead."

The detective nods gently.

"Once Ethan reported us missing, I knew the killer would have no choice but to run. That hope kept me alive, kept me focused in all that cold and pressure and blackness. I couldn't wait to see the look on the asshole's face when it happened."

When search parties arrived at the Devil's Staircase, the situation would change. The killer's best chance to avoid arrest, his only chance, would be to flee the scene. And when there's video footage involved, runners don't often make it far.

"All I had to do was wait," Tess says. "Just stay crammed inside that little crawlspace for as long as the air lasted. It was unpleasant, but it was survivable. Just a few more hours until Ethan realized Allie's text was overdue. Help was coming."

It was a waiting game, then.

"Until"—Tess sighs—"I remembered our valuables were all in Allie's main pack."

Back in the Upper Vault.

With her body.

"Meaning, the killer had access to our *phones*."

14

"THAT'S UNFORTUNATELY CORRECT," WASHINGTON SAYS. "INSIDE THE suspect's vehicle, we found your phone and Allie's, both smashed to bits. But first, he'd used them to send these two text messages."

She slides a piece of printer paper across the tray table. Tess reads it, then looks away in revulsion. *Bastard*.

With his prey cornered inside the cave, the killer would need to buy himself more time. After (presumably) studying the women's phones and learning about each of their lives, he'd texted Ethan from Allie's phone and Tess's manager, Sandra, from her own. The cover stories were tailored for each: Ethan was told that Allie and Tess's caving trip had morphed into an impromptu camping trip at Blue Lake (where cell signal is of course nonexistent). Tess's manager, meanwhile, was told that Tess had contracted a nasty stomach flu and would be absent for the next few days.

It's disturbing how capably he'd managed to mimic the women's individual voices. Allie's text to her boyfriend was cutesy and funny, while Tess's message to her boss was terse and professional. This killer was diabolically intelligent.

In fact, he was *too* intelligent.

No random stranger should have known so much about Tess and Allie both—the passwords to their phones, their mannerisms, the people in their lives—to act out such a convincing deception. Her gut tells her there's another layer here.

Over three decades, nearly every criminal Detective Washington has tracked has turned out to be disappointingly stupid. There's always an inconvenient cell tower ping, or a stray fingerprint, or a surprise cameo on a traffic camera. Force a liar to repeat their story and cracks will show. Pick at those flaws long enough and the whole thing will collapse. TV dramas love to show detectives cornering their prey in big, cinematic moments of revelation, but it's really a thousand smaller moments accumulated gradually by the steady grind of procedure, examining conflicting statements from all sides, ruling out every dead end. That's the true discipline: a long, steady feat of patience and endurance.

Her old partner used to quote Elvis: *Truth is like the sun. You can shut it out for a time, but it ain't going away.*

"This guy was a step up," Washington says. "He wasn't acting on impulse. He planned ahead. He made preparations. And when you turned out to be more difficult to kill than he'd expected, he proved he could improvise, too."

With two clever text messages, he'd bought himself at least several days before anyone noticed the two women were missing. He was back in control.

"While I waited in the tunnel, I imagined Allie's voice in my head, encouraging me, guiding me." Tess flashes a pained smile. "I swore she was still with me, somehow."

With her index finger, she's tracing something on the hospital tray table. Three repetitive motions, three sides. A triangle.

"I know I'm just being wishful." Her smile wilts. "I was alone."

"You're a survivor, Tess."

"Allie used to say something like that."

"She knew you best."

"Maybe." She shrugs. "I couldn't stop thinking about one of Allie's favorite memories. She'd always described it so vividly I felt like I was there, too, even though we weren't friends yet. I can *remember* it, even though I wasn't there. That's how good a storyteller she was. She was camping with her parents somewhere by Steens Mountain, I think, and early in the morning they shook her awake, and they led her out of the tent into the sunrise to see dozens of wild horses grazing at the edge of the meadow. Her dad had whispered in her ear that every horse on the continent was owned by someone except for a few feral herds that still roamed free—no more than a few thousand. These were old breeds brought over from Europe by Spanish conquistadores centuries ago, their manes untrimmed, no shoes or anything. They'd never been touched by a human and never would. Allie always said she envied them."

Tess hesitates.

"When I think about Allie now, I think of those wild horses I've never seen. That's what she always wanted to be." She looks up at the detective. "I like to imagine she got her wish."

Washington nods. *If only.*

But she knows better.

For a long moment, the only noise is the gentle scrape of Tess's finger on the hospital tray table. The same soft motions over and over, like a motor tic.

The detective switches off her voice recorder. "I need to call my boss."

"Wait." Tess snaps back into awareness. "First, can I ask you something?"

"Of course."

"I have to know. It'll bother me if I don't ask." Her finger stops tracing, and she gazes at Washington with hard focus, that ruptured bloodred eye unblinking. "The *asshole* who murdered my best friend. What have you learned about him?"

• • •

The suspect's name is Jacob Herman.

Thirty-six years old. Caucasian. Six feet tall, over two hundred pounds. Callused hands, bristly beard, tanned skin. He's also surprisingly, even unfairly, handsome, like a reincarnated James Dean. His last registered address is a trailer park in Thermopolis, Wyoming, but according to the property manager he hasn't lived there for years. His true residence is unknown, like nearly everything else about him.

Jacob is a walking shadow.

Everything recovered from his heavily modded Jeep Grand Cherokee points to cold-blooded preparation. He'd worn rubber gloves and covered his face with a hard-plated balaclava, likely to avoid shedding skin cells or hairs. He'd brought two rolls of duct tape, two cloth head bags, and a pack of white zip ties. In a leather sheath he carried that steel KA-BAR knife. And, of course, in a crotch holster he carried the .45-caliber Colt 1911 that Tess had witnessed firsthand, its serial numbers diligently filed off. He'd wisely chosen not to bring a phone, likely aware that his carrier's GPS data could be used to place him near the murder.

Other items found inside his vehicle suggest the spartan lifestyle of a man living comfortably off the grid: a light fiberglass kayak on the roof for fishing, a propane camping stove, and a citizens band radio mounted to the dashboard. The floor was littered with yellowed paperbacks—some Nietzsche, some Jack London, and a surprising amount of Tom Clancy. *The Sum of All Fears* was on the console with its spine bent halfway in, right at the chapter where a terrorist's nuclear weapon incinerates the Super Bowl.

Whatever his background, Jacob Herman came to the Devil's Staircase fully equipped to commit a violent crime. And according to Tess, he was already waiting for his victims at the cave entrance with a Green Ridge cover story prepared—before he shot Allie in the head.

This doesn't add up.

Washington misses her old partner. She misses working with a partner, period, and not being relegated to a support role on a four-person team. The lieutenant running the case is educated and pin-sharp, but he's also thirty-five. He wants to be a congressman, not a cop.

"Something is wrong." She paces in the hospital hallway with her phone to her ear. "This is more complicated than we thought."

"How so?"

"What Tess saw . . . it doesn't make sense."

"You think she's mistaken?"

"I think there's something *bigger* happening."

If ideas come too easily, they're not really yours. If answers come too easily, you have to ask why. Occam's razor is not your friend.

Washington thinks back to the first wellness check she'd made during her first year in law enforcement. She'd rung the doorbell at an unassuming house, and an elderly man had answered. Back then he'd reminded her of her own grandfather, although he hadn't been much older than she is now. Apparently his adult children had been concerned about his growing isolation after his wife's death, but the guy had smiled and insisted he was just fine. He showed her the truck he was busy restoring in his garage, an old F-series pickup. The wiring had been chewed up by mice, he'd explained, and the carburetor was gummed up with ancient gas, but he'd been working on it for months as a way to process his grief, and he was close now to taking it on the road. Layla—then only a deputy, so heartbreakingly young—shook the old man's hand and wished him luck.

Twenty-four hours later he was dead.

Never make assumptions. *Ever.*

"For starters, I don't buy this as a random attack," she tells the lieutenant. "A killer doesn't just gear up, rehearse a cover story, and wait inside a cave in the woods for two strangers to walk in. Jacob Herman couldn't have known Allie and Tess were coming that day unless he already knew who they were."

"Focus on your witness," he says.

"We need to look at Allie much more closely. Her past, her associations. And that boyfriend of hers, Ethan—"

"For now," he reminds her, "just focus on your witness."

She can hear the polite denial creeping into his voice.

No disrespect, but . . .

Fucking schoolboy. It may be his case, but he's barely running it, happy to send three worker drones out to gather information and type it up for him so he can review it all at once. It's lazy, compartmentalized work. She knows that the rest of the team sees her as a sad, lost dinosaur, and she was sent to Sacred Heart because Tess's witness statement was expected to tie the whole thing up—not raise new and urgent questions.

God, she misses her partner.

"Hopefully Tess can help me." Washington looks back. "I'll keep you posted."

Returning to Tess's room, she pulls up her chair and restarts her audio recorder. "How famous is Allie Merritt, exactly?"

"Last year she made *Forbes*'s 30 Under 30," Tess says. "And *Keep Calm* gets almost a million unique visitors a month."

"I assume that's good?"

"It's outstanding."

"She started it herself?"

"From the ground up, when she was eighteen." Tess smiles, both proud and wistful. "Ever since she was little, she'd always wanted to be Carmen Sandiego. Her favorite movie was *The Se-*

cret Life of Walter Mitty. While I went to college, she bartended and saved money to pay for these random trips, just wherever she wanted to go—one month it was Peru, the next it was Romania or New Zealand—and then she'd return home and write about the crazy things she did, what she saw, who she met. She traveled cheap and smart. Sometimes just a carry-on, hence the original name. She took red-eyes and puddle jumpers, slept in hostels, used public transportation, walked whenever possible. She loved to walk, miles every day. She even used to hitchhike, which I always told her was a terrible idea. But eventually she didn't need to bartend at all. She changed her name and *Keep Calm* became her day job, as crazy as it sounds."

"What was her name, before she changed it?"

"Alma," Tess says. "She said it sounded too dowdy."

"What was her income?"

"It varied."

"Ballpark?"

"It helps to break it out." Tess counts on her fingers. "On her website, pre-roll and display takes in about four or five thousand a month. Plus two or three more for direct clients we run special placements for, like homepage takeovers. Affiliate links and subscriptions are maybe nine or ten. Sometimes she'll do sponsored content, but she doesn't like to—"

"You're *shitting* me. Allie makes fifteen grand a month?"

"Before expenses and taxes and my part-time pay, yeah." Tess hesitates, suddenly defensive of her best friend. "She works her ass off."

"And you're her manager?"

A modest smile. "More of an assistant."

These are fairy-tale figures. Then again, it's a brave new world out there for content creators. People make a living filming themselves eating cheeseburgers or loudly reacting to movie trailers.

Sometimes Washington wonders if her brain isn't deteriorating quite fast enough.

And at least Allie seemed to deserve her meteoric success. *Keep Calm* and its two subsidiary sites are slick and cleanly designed, her prose snappy and often quite funny. She builds out itineraries by budget tiers, writes packing guides, and lays out her articles intelligently. And she really does seem to be an authority on thrifty travel—using Skyscanner to search for budget airlines, hitting the "shoulder season," safely navigating public transportation—even clever gig-economy stuff Washington never would've thought of, like signing up to pet-sit for local residents in exchange for a place to sleep. Most important, Allie herself is a warm and likable presence in her self-shot videos, grounded and gracious to her hosts and never afraid to try new food. She'd be a fun girl to have a beer with. Her life seemed every bit as charmed as Tess described.

Until Costa Rica, at least. Until *something* happened there.

"So she's successful. She has a public profile with a sizable following. She looks like Taylor Swift. Any of these things could've made her a target."

Tess frowns. "This guy couldn't have known all that."

"Unless he stalked her."

"He got there first."

"*And* he knew you'd both be there."

The survivor hesitates.

"Did Allie have any connection to a guy named Jacob? Did she ever mention dating a guy by that name? Did she ever confide in you that she felt someone might be watching her?"

"Not at all."

"You help with her social media, right? Any creepy messages come in?"

"Mostly fan mail. A few haters."

"Haters?"

"It's the internet. Everyone hates something." Tess shrugs. "Spam accounts trying to sell stuff. Some guy asking if Allie would sell her underwear."

"What did she think of that?"

"She thought it was hilarious. She made nine hundred bucks off him."

Washington says nothing. Raindrops tap the window.

She's always hated the phrase *elephant in the room*, but it's apt here. For the past few minutes she's been trying to coax Tess into mentioning it voluntarily, but she's either avoiding it or unaware of it, and now it's time to change strategies. She sets her notepad in her lap and folds her arms. Once this is said, it can't be unsaid.

The pin can't be put back in the grenade.

She studies the survivor's nonverbal reactions closely. "You were aware of your best friend's recent legal trouble, right?"

Silence.

Tess blinks. "I'm . . . I'm sorry?"

"Allie is currently under federal investigation."

"For what?"

"Wire fraud."

Tess stares numbly, like she can't comprehend the words.

Wire fraud.

Other charges are likely, too. The field office hasn't returned her call, but Washington knows they must be circling something big. No doubt they're scrutinizing Allie's business records and bank accounts, matching up every transaction, looking back years into the past.

Tess looks ill. "That has to be a mistake."

"She would've already been served a target letter. And a boatload of subpoenas." Washington tilts her head skeptically. "She never told you? Even though you were her manager?"

"Assistant."

"If it's true, it means Allie's career, her public profile, everything she built, might have been on the verge of crashing down around her. If charges were filed, she'd be looking down the barrel of multiple felonies."

"Prison?"

"Maybe."

"She already made more money than she could keep track of," Tess says. "She didn't need *more* of it."

Washington says nothing and watches the survivor process her shock. On the monitor, her pulse has spiked again. Understandably.

"I know Allie was your best friend and you loved her." She reaches forward to touch Tess's hand. "But no matter how close you may have been, she still kept secrets from you. And other things happened that day, too, that you couldn't have seen or heard. Have you heard of the Rashomon effect?"

Tess shakes her head.

"It means two people can remember the same event differently. Ultimately, all memories are subjective. You might remember Allie Merritt one way, but the truth, the *real* Allie, might be something else entirely."

The events of the day are an interlocking puzzle. Every person present at the Devil's Staircase saw something wholly unique, and no one—not even Tess herself—witnessed the full picture. What did Allie see? And what did *Jacob* see?

"While I waited in the dark," Tess says, "I heard singing."

Washington blinks. "Singing?"

She nods.

"The killer's voice?"

She nods again.

"Did you recognize the song?"

"No."

"What were the lyrics?"

"It was mostly the same lyric over and over," Tess says. "Maybe that's all there was to the song, or he only knew that part. *The man downstairs, he waits and he waits.*"

The detective looks at her sideways. "An old country song?"

"You know it?"

"It sounds like one I remember."

"And I heard something else from the dark, like . . . grinding machinery." The survivor's voice is faint, shaken. "Almost a screech, like metal on metal. And every few seconds, a click. In a steady rhythm. It started slow but got faster. I didn't know what it was."

Washington does.

And she knows that song intimately, too, in some long-suppressed part of her brain. It's a classic earworm. She was ten years old when it released, and she remembers hearing it on her father's radio almost every night while she did her homework, a scratchy and oddly malicious electric voice from across the kitchen.

The man downstairs, he waits and he waits.
He waits and he waits.
And, baby, he's waiting on you.

PART II

Jacob

15

JACOB HERMAN BRACED HIS SCISSOR JACK UNDER THE BOULDER AND inserted the ratchet handle. Down here, space was tight. Every quarter turn, the handle clicked against rock.

Turn.

Remove.

Reinsert.

At first nothing seemed to happen—and then, just when he was getting frustrated, the suspended boulder shifted with an ancient groan. Loose grit peppered his helmet. With every slow quarter turn, the block was gradually lifting, the twelve-inch gap underneath widening. Soon Jacob would be able to fit his body through.

Behind the obstacle, he heard movement. The trapped woman heard him and knew she was no longer safe. She was retreating, crawling deeper inside the cave.

So Jacob worked fast, flat on his belly. He tried to keep singing as he worked—*The man downstairs, he waits and he waits*—but the cottony tinnitus in his brain kept crowding out the tune. He'd fired his pistol hours ago, but his eardrums still throbbed with pain. Warmth dribbled from his right ear, a clear but yellow-tinged liquid that wasn't quite blood.

Firing his gun underground had been a mistake. A big one.

The whole thing was supposed to be easy. A carefully timed ambush in the tunnel, some scare tactics and zip ties to make her compliant, and a stab-and-twist to the windpipe to bleed her out quick. Five minutes, tops. Then Jacob would've been a ghost, disappearing back down the mountain to burn his clothes and dump his weapons in a lake and hide out in his travel trailer. That should have all happened *hours* ago. Instead, his ostensible victim had escaped the ambush and crammed herself deep underground.

The scissor jack creaked with pressure. He felt the growing tension in every quarter turn. He smelled cracked rock in the air, a smoky gunpowder tang. The entire tunnel felt volatile, a single misjudgment from a fatal collapse. Using an auto jack to lift underground rock debris was probably a Darwin Award in the making, but Jacob didn't have time to play it safe. He had to reach this woman and cut her throat. Fast.

"Don't worry," he huffed. "I won't hurt you."

With a final quarter turn, the jack reached its maximum height. The boulder was suspended roughly eight inches higher. This, he knew, was as good as it would get.

Jacob flattened his body, flinching at the cold water on his exposed belly, and wriggled through the gap like a two-hundred-pound salamander. He had to be careful—*very* careful—not to nudge the scissor jack on his way through. Even twenty inches was a snug fit; the gun in his crotch holster dug painfully into his nuts. He carried his KA-BAR knife in his left fist, the steel blade scraping rock with a rhythmic *click-click*. His headlamp cut into the darkness on the other side, the red glow revealing pale walls and glistening streams of water. And, deeper back . . .

"There you are."

The woman lay prone on her elbows, her eyes reflecting horror. She scooted backward on her stomach, inches from his reach.

"Why are you afraid? I told you, I won't hurt you . . ."

She kept scrambling farther away from him in the confined

space, squirming between loose cobble, fighting to stay ahead of him, ahead of his knife—until something lurched her to a dead stop. Her clothes had snagged.

She was stuck.

Jacob grinned. "Uh-oh."

She thrashed, a surge of trapped-animal terror.

"Caught on something, huh?" He scraped closer. "Let me see."

The woman looked around, her helmet thudding against low limestone. She searched her body and patted herself down with frantic hands, trying to find the snag. Her harness was a tangle of buckles and straps—somewhere, someplace unreachable on herself, a loop must have hooked on a protruding rock. It's the little things that get you killed.

Jacob would insert the knife just under her jawbone. You shouldn't slit a throat from the front like in the movies. The most efficient access point is actually from the side, where there's minimal muscle protecting the carotid artery, jugular veins, and trachea. Sever those and a victim loses consciousness in ten seconds.

Click. Click.

He crawled the final few inches. The woman's face shone brightly in his red headlamp now, her eyes brimming with tears. She shook her head, pleading and helpless. Close enough to touch her now, Jacob could smell the black coffee on her breath. The shampoo in her hair. The onion-sweet odor of her sweat. He'd always loved how girls can stink so delicately.

"It's okay. I'm your friend."

As Jacob said this, he tilted her head to expose her throat.

"I PRETENDED TO BE STUCK," TESS TELLS THE DETECTIVE. "AND THEN, once he was close enough to reach, once he thought he had me—"

Her voice hardens.

"—I plunged Allie's knife into his face."

JACOB SCUTTLED BACKWARD.

Her knife had stabbed his balaclava, the surprise attack barely halted by the reinforced rubber. He'd felt the pressure against his upper lip. He gasped with surprise.

"*Bitch.*"

Now she held the knife out with a trembling hand, the three-inch blade pointed at his face. She caught her breath. No more tears, no more begging. The ruse was over, her intentions clear: *Try that again. I dare you.*

With his free hand, Jacob touched a deep groove in his mask's faceplate. Christ, he'd gotten lucky. She'd missed his right eye by barely an inch. Next time, she wouldn't miss.

She glared at him. *Come closer, asshole.*

He held his own knife, the much larger KA-BAR, low and ready to mirror her stance. Lying on their bellies in this narrow space, he was eye to eye with her.

But Jacob realized with a jolt: he couldn't kill this woman without simultaneously exposing himself to a deadly swipe of her own. To attack here was to go knife to knife, one hand on offense, one on defense. There was no space to stand up or even crouch, no alternate angles to strike from. The single-file tunnel allowed for only frontal attacks.

She jabbed her knife at his face. "Back up."

He grinned, feeling the dented faceplate against his lips. "I like you—"

"Back the *fuck* up."

"You're a tough girl. Maybe even tougher than your friend."

This got a reaction. Rage flashed behind her eyes, personal

and white-hot. Did he hit a nerve? Good. He'd keep pressing, keep her off-balance: "How good a friend was she, anyway? I bet you thought you knew everything about her."

She glared back.

"She had secrets. Things she never told you."

No reaction.

"Who was she really?"

Nothing.

She wasn't allowing him under her skin. She was too smart to lose her composure. And, Jacob was realizing, in this bizarre scenario it didn't matter anyway. The cave imposed its own rules on both sides alike.

We're scorpions in a bottle, you and I.

That was the true dilemma: whoever struck first opened themselves up to a lethal counterattack. It would be near impossible for one scorpion to sting its enemy without receiving a fatal sting in return. Hemmed in by the stifling rock walls, she knew it, too.

Jacob grinned, tasting blood. "She was your best friend. But were you hers?"

"I KEPT CRAWLING BACKWARD," TESS REMEMBERS. "SCOOTING ON MY hands and knees, staying ahead of him. Just out of his reach."

As described by rescuers, the two-to-three-foot crawlspace of the Drainpipe has only a few small pockets with enough space for a crawling human to crouch or turn around. It's more of a waterslide than a cave: cold, cramped, clogged with muddy sediment.

Washington has never particularly cared for waterslides, but with everything she's learned about this section of the cave, it feels like the closest comparison. Years ago she took her kids to a local waterpark, and her oldest teenage son had wanted to ride the highest slide. It had looked like a five-story tangle of blue hamster tubes atop metal legs, precarious and leaking. The Torpedo, it was called. She'd watched him climb the stairs and enter the top, but then he never exited the bottom.

Apparently he'd crossed his arms wrong in there, or he'd tried to sit up or something. Those are details you forget as you get older. What matters is: her son got stuck a third of the way down the stupid slide, stalled in a low dip without enough speed to clear the next rise. Worse, he'd become disoriented inside the three-foot tunnel and hadn't known which direction to crawl. Forward or backward? The curved tube walls were too slippery to climb. He was trapped, panic rising. And what would happen when the next teenager came hurtling down feetfirst like an oblivious human missile? All the while, Washington could only stare helplessly at the blue superstructure, hearing her son struggle and scream inside.

The lifeguards turned off the water and fished him out through a special trapdoor, a process that took fifteen minutes and drew a crowd. Someone made a dumb joke about calling in the Oompa Loompas. Her son was fine—pale with fright, his voice hoarse, but fine—and it still breaks Washington's heart trying to imagine what he'd experienced in there.

And he'd been trapped for only fifteen minutes.

"He knew I was afraid," Tess says.

"But you almost killed him. That's something."

Inside the cave's chokehold, Jacob's gun was temporarily useless to him. Had his victim fled anywhere else, she surely would have taken a bullet to the back. She'd saved her life by venturing deeper underground.

For now.

"The cave felt endless," Tess says. "I wanted to turn around and crawl headfirst, but there wasn't space to turn around. I knew

I couldn't turn my back on him anyway. He kept following me, face-to-face, just waiting for his chance."

Tess, feetfirst.

Jacob, headfirst.

Locked in a crawling, slow-motion standoff inside the waterslide from Hell.

"Did he say anything else?"

"Taunts, mostly."

"Every detail matters, Tess."

"Stuff about Allie. Cruel things. He was trying to get into my head, I think, to make me lash out. He said he'd already dragged Allie's body up to the surface by his Jeep and that he'd done . . . things to it." She blinks away a tear and stares at the floor.

"I'm sorry, Tess."

"He said . . . after he was done with Allie's body, he'd wrap her in chicken wire and dump her in a lake. The same thing he'd do to me."

"Chicken wire?"

She nods. "I don't understand why."

Washington does. Chicken wire will hold a body together underwater as it decays and swells with buoyant gases, preventing any body parts from floating to the surface. There are several deep freshwater lakes within a few miles of the cave, and in such a remote location, they'd be difficult to fully search. A body might never be found. Worse, such specific knowledge suggests Jacob Herman has done this before.

Where did this guy come from?

Where does he live?

She doubts he slept in his Jeep. Even the most nomadic survivalists prefer to camp out somewhere—maybe a yurt in the woods, maybe an RV or camper, maybe a friend's trailer. This guy likely grows his own food, works odd jobs under the table, filters his own water. With little in the way of public records or personal electronics, they might never find Jacob's true base of operations. There's simply too much wilderness out there.

"And I noticed . . . the tunnel seemed to spiral downward." Tess adjusts her pulse oximeter. "It felt like a corkscrew, going deeper and deeper. The whole time, in the pit of my stomach, I knew that every foot I crawled down was a foot farther from the surface."

At this point, Tess and her attacker would have been hundreds of feet from daylight, crawling through an enclosed space with millions of tons of rock and soil packed overhead. And *still* going deeper.

"He told me the farther down I went, the worse it'd get."

This was accurate. With every foot of depth, the danger rises and rescue becomes more difficult. Eventually the chase would lead to a chamber of jagged formations both fragile and dangerously sharp. Rescuers likened the passage, known as Razor Alley, to navigating inside a giant sausage grinder. Deeper still is the Chimney, a deadly forty-foot vertical drop.

Finally, deeper below, is a third and final challenge. This area comprises the lowest, least-understood region of the Devil's Staircase. Much of it remains undiscovered and unmapped. It's where the sprawling rescue effort to reach the trapped woman would be concentrated, where two team members nearly lost their lives. It has a name, too.

Worse Than Death.

In that moment, eye to eye with a murderer, Tess would've had to make a calculation—that for all its unknown dangers, the cave was still less dangerous than the man who'd cornered her inside it. She would crawl *deeper* to keep ahead of him, descending to lower, more punishing circles of Hell. It was her only chance at survival.

Washington remembers the incident commander's unsettling text message, sent during the rescue effort's bleakest hours.

We're losing her.

Things would inevitably get worse before they got better.

"And"—Tess shifts uncomfortably in her bed—"I realized it was worse than I knew."

"How?"

"Even if I took my chances and tried to fight him head-on, even if I somehow avoided his huge knife and stabbed him in the eye or throat and by some miracle killed him, he'd still made sure I'd lose, too. I'd never, ever escape the cave."

"How so?"

"Because," she says, "his body would block the tunnel."

Sealing her inside the crawlspace with two hundred pounds of deadweight.

16

"YOU'RE ONLY MAKING IT WORSE," JACOB WHISPERED TO HER.

He'd expected the cornered woman to try to negotiate for her life, but she hadn't. All the tears and sobbing had been an act to lure him in close, and it had almost worked. She understood the severity of her situation, but she wasn't letting herself fall apart. She kept scooting backward, her kneepads scraping rock and sandy mud. Keeping just beyond his reach.

He lunged for her—she swiped her knife—but he was only feinting.

"Oh." He laughed. "*Almost.*"

He could still find ways to enjoy himself. He'd keep testing her, wear her down, wait for her muscles to tire. All he needed was a split second. Even funneled down a tube together, the faster scorpion can still win, right? It's all about violence of action. Speed, strength, surprise.

Life itself is will to power.

When he was a kid his father used to take him trout fishing out in the Wind River Range. He'd always hated hooking their mouths, no matter how many times his dad assured him that fish can't feel pain. *Their brains are so primitive,* he'd say, *that they don't even realize they're suffocating in the open air.* Jacob pretended to believe him, but he could never ignore how violently they flailed. Nothing fights that hard unless it knows pain and fear.

One evening they returned to the truck and saw a pair of human legs underneath it. A stranger was stealing the vehicle's catalytic converter, and this was the only time he'd ever see his father point a gun at another human. The thief held up his hands and apologized. He was living on the run and starving, he said. Jacob knew his father's temper and dreaded what was coming next, but to his surprise, his old man hadn't seemed upset at all. He listened to the stranger's sob story, and when it was over, he calmly asked the guy to reinstall the catalytic converter's mounting bolts. No harm done. For a few minutes it almost seemed like he might share some fish with him. Then, politely, he asked for the man's wallet.

His keys.

His backpack.

His coat and boots.

Finally, with a rumbling cruelty in his voice, he commanded the thief to strip naked. Boxers, too. It was sundown, early October in the high plains. With the windchill it couldn't have been far above freezing. Even as a kid Jacob had sensed he was witnessing something forbidden and certainly something he should never tell his mother about. But it was also an exhilarating sensation, being *bad* together with his dad. He remembered laughing timidly and asking his father if he could make the guy dance. The thief made a few half-hearted disco moves at gunpoint, his yellow teeth chattering.

Then they left. Riding away with the guy's clothes draped in the truck bed beside an icebox full of trout, Jacob remembered watching the pale figure disappear in the mirrors. He'd looked like a gray alien, chest heaving and barefoot on cold gravel. Jacob and his dad had laughed for miles of dusky highway, their voices joining to form a new melody he'd never heard before, and then miles more of contemplative silence. It felt like an hour passed before his dad finally spoke: *Remember, Jacob. A living being seeks above all else to discharge its own strength.*

Life itself is will to power.

For most of his life he'd believed those were his father's words; it wasn't until later that he learned they were Friedrich Nietzsche's. He'd never seen the man read anything thicker than a *Little Nickel.* As an adult, Jacob read voraciously with a particular interest in the works of Nietzsche, hoping they might offer hints to understanding the enigmatic man now long gone from stomach cancer. Which ones had his father read? What else resonated with him? Or—disappointing but possible—had he only picked up the quote from an action movie?

Now he noticed the cave walls seemed to narrow around him and his victim, the glistening limestone faces constricting closer. The air was cloyingly humid. Even through his balaclava he smelled a sour odor, like wet socks. Wriggling through this sewer-like space took noticeably more effort, and his skin was slick with cold sweat. It was oppressive, staying on your belly for this long under such pressure from all sides. If the woman's harness caught on a rock—for real this time—she'd be in serious trouble.

And *still*, she kept going. Deeper and deeper.

God, he wished he could just shoot her in the forehead. It would be over so fast. But firing a gun inside the Drainpipe would be catastrophic unless Jacob solved two big problems. First, the threat of fragmentary ricochets after the slug exited the back of the woman's head. Second, the cost to his own hearing. He could cover one ear with his hand while he fired the gun, but the damage to his unprotected ear would be ruinous.

It was fine. There were still other ways he could kill her.

"You know I can just guard the cave's entrance, right?" He felt their breaths swirl together in the confined space, nicely intimate. "I can make sure you never leave this place. I've got your phones. I've got most of your supplies and gear. Hell, I can wait all week. You can't. How long do you think you'll last?"

She stared back. "Long enough."

"You know the rule of threes, right?" He counted on neoprene-gloved fingers with his blade. "Generally speaking, you can last three weeks without food. Three days without water. And three minutes without oxygen. Down here, which do you think you'll run out of first?"

She said nothing.

"Ticktock." He tapped his wrist.

She had to know she was cut off and cornered. She could keep retreating to maintain the space between them, sure—but for how long? Eventually she would run into a dead end or a hazard she couldn't navigate. Or the smothering rock walls would open up enough that Jacob could chance one more risky gunshot. To one end or another, her time was running out.

"You could always apologize," Jacob suggested.

"Fuck off."

"I'm serious. You don't know who I am or what I want. Maybe it's money. Maybe it's revenge. Maybe if you apologized to me, really apologized and showed genuine regret for what you did, I'll take pity on you and decide to go home—"

She enunciated: "*Fuck. Off.*"

"How about we make a deal, then?" He pointed at the GoPro mounted on her helmet. "You give me your footage and your knife, and I'll let you live."

"You're lying."

"Cross my heart."

"I know you're lying—"

"Hope to die." He grinned. "Stick a needle in my—"

"Zero chance," she said. She meant it.

This woman had a certain animal cunning that he admired. She knew the survival knife clenched in her sweaty fingers was the only thing keeping her alive.

"I know you don't trust me, but what other options do you have right now?" Jacob patted the low ceiling, the rock bumpy with wartlike growths. "Either you and I negotiate our situation here and figure something out, or we try to fight and slice each other to bloody pieces. In a knife fight, the loser goes to the morgue and the winner goes to the hospital. In all likelihood, neither of us will leave this tunnel."

"Or," she said, "I crawl deeper."

"That's fine, too."

All bad options, dilemmas upon dilemmas. He could see the calculations running behind her eyes as she tried to reason her way out of a no-win situation. "I'm not stupid. I'm keeping my knife." She chewed her lip. "But I might give you the footage."

He grinned. *Here we go.*

"I'll give you the GoPro's memory card under one condition."

"Which is?"

"You leave." She glared back into his red light, unblinking. He could see all of her in sharp detail: the blood vessels in her eyes, the microscopic pores in her skin. "You take the footage and turn your big ass around and crawl back to the surface. You get in your Jeep and disappear. We never see each other again."

"Just like that?"

"Just like that."

"Sounds nice. A happy ending for everyone. But you know, I need guarantees, too." Jacob pointed with his knife. "If I abort my mission and leave you here, I'm just supposed to take it on faith that you won't talk to the cops?"

"You can't," she said. "You have no reason to trust me, either."

At least she was honest.

"What matters is I haven't seen your face yet." She pointed at Jacob's balaclava, at the rubber faceplate scarred by her knife. "I can't describe what you look like. And once I give you the memory card, the police won't have your voice or clothes or any other information that might help them identify you. It won't matter if I spend hours in a little room with some detective, racking my brain and trying to remember every last detail. What matters is I won't have *enough*. And—" Her voice splintered with emotion. "And you already know my best friend won't—can't—tell them anything, either."

Jacob slurped on his lower lip and considered this. *No face, no case,* as they say. He'd already eliminated the first camera. He'd feel better with both removed from the equation.

"That's the offer," she added. "Take it or leave it."

"Fine."

"We have a deal?"

"Deal." He held out a gloved hand.

"I'm not going to *hand* it to you, dipshit." She pointed. "Back up."

Another intelligent move. She knew she'd be vulnerable while she detached the camera from her helmet. Jacob couldn't help it: he was really starting to like this girl.

He held the knife in his fist and used both hands to push his body backward, giving her several feet of new space. He already had a babygirl of his own, but maybe he'd met his match in this woman. Something about the mud and darkness, the threats and bartering, the cold and sweat—it felt natural. The cave was a crucible for predator and prey alike.

Life itself is will to power, my son.

"There," he said. "Feel safe now?"

"I KNEW IT WAS THE SMART CHOICE," TESS SAYS. "BUT . . ."

"What?"

She sighs. "It felt like I was betraying Allie. Cutting a deal with her murderer, giving him exactly what he wanted."

"To save your life."

"Only if he was telling the truth."

It's a difficult decision, and there can be no half measures. If Washington were cornered by an armed killer inside a shoulder-width tunnel, she couldn't be sure what she would do, either.

"I know Allie would've handled it differently." Tess brushes back a strand of hair. "And the whole time, all I could hear was her voice in my head, urging me to stop. Warning me that I was making a mistake by taking the easy option. He was just waiting for his chance to shoot me or stab me. He was a liar. *Never* negotiate with a liar."

"Keeping the footage wouldn't bring her back."

"She would've wanted me to."

"Tess, I think Allie would've wanted you to take any chance to save your life." The detective smiles tightly. "*Any* chance."

Bargaining with Jacob might have been the most logical choice, but it was still risky. The video footage would have been Tess's most powerful leverage. Once Jacob had the memory card, his options would open up. He'd no longer need to recover the evidence from her body, so he'd be free to kill her by more indirect methods. He could stack the Drainpipe's entrance with boulders, for example, sealing the woman inside to die. Thanks to his text message alibis, it would be days before anyone knew to report Allie or Tess missing.

"I knew . . ." She takes a breath. "I knew that even if I hadn't seen his face, he wouldn't leave me alive. Just like how he'd said he just wanted an apology from Allie, if we'd only just zip-tie ourselves. Whatever he said to me was a lie. Giving him the footage wouldn't accomplish a thing. He'd still kill me."

She faced two grim options, then.

Take the killer at his word?

Or double down on a suicidal deadlock?

"So." Washington leans forward. "What did you do?"

"HERE."

Jacob watched her toss it to the gritty mud between them. He picked it up to inspect in his red headlamp—a rectangular memory card no larger than a postage stamp, 128 gigs—and then he snapped it in half.

Hours of footage, instantly gone.

She watched silently.

"You made the right choice." He tucked both halves into his pocket, joining the one he'd pulled from the first camera. He was fairly sure that once a memory card is broken the data is irretrievably gone, but he'd melt the pieces down in his firepit tonight to be sure. No loose ends.

Two cameras, two memory cards. Things were looking up.

"I haven't seen your face," she said. "So hold up your side of the deal and *go*."

At this, Jacob Herman smiled. God, this little dance of theirs was intoxicating. He wished it could last forever, even if he understood why it couldn't.

He pulled off his helmet—"Wait," she said, "what are you doing?"—and the red light changed, casting wild shadows. Then he gripped the edge of his balaclava and peeled it off. Like a reptile sloughing out of its skin, it felt good to remove the sweaty fabric and rubber. His upper lip, starting to swell, felt better already in the cool air.

"Now," he said, grinning, "you've seen my face."

Her heart visibly sank.

"So now I guess I'll have to kill you anyway, huh?"

Her glare turned venomous. *Liar.*

He loved it.

"Sorry, but you knew I was a snake when you picked me

up." Jacob patted the broken memory cards in his pocket. "And honestly, I'm a bit disappointed in you. After everything you saw today, you really thought we could just talk our way out of this and go our separate ways? I'm sorry, but I lied to you. I don't leave jobs half done."

He grinned at her.

"I won't leave this cave until you're dead."

"HE DIDN'T REALIZE I'D LIED TO HIM, TOO," TESS SAYS.

"How?"

"I gave him one of Allie's spare memory cards." A crafty smile flickers across her face. "The real one was still in my GoPro, still recording. I was only testing him."

The clarity in her voice is startling.

"And," she says, "now I had his *face* on video, too."

17

THE DETECTIVE NODS. "CLEVER."

"I promised myself I'd get that footage to the police. Whatever the cost." Tess hesitates, afraid to say the second part.

For Allie.

Washington can't help but be impressed. Tess had tricked the killer into playing his hand, and he was completely unaware of it. She's a skilled liar.

"*Very* clever."

"I tried to think of what Allie would have done," she says, "and do that."

She's tracing triangles on the hospital table again, that same nervous motor tic. If she keeps at it long enough, her finger might wear down to the bone.

"I thought about swallowing the memory card," Tess adds. "So even if he killed me, too, and some coroner had to find the footage in my stomach during my autopsy, the cops would *still* know what happened to us. They'd have his face."

A GoPro's memory card must be at least an inch by an inch, maybe bigger—would it even fit down a human throat? Swallowing an angular plastic chip would be painful. But it might be the only way to preserve objective proof of what happened. A memory card could survive for months or even years inside a corpse's stomach.

Washington winces. "Hell of a plan B."

"I liked plan A better."

"Survive?"

She nods. But then she seems to reconsider.

"It wasn't just about surviving," she admits. "Slowly, I was realizing . . . I didn't just want this man to go to prison, where they'd clothe him and feed him and he could get old and fat reading books. That wasn't enough." She takes a breath. "I wanted to *kill* him."

"I would, too," Washington says.

Tess seems surprised to hear this. Maybe these days it's unprofessional for an officer of the law to acknowledge that some people really do need killing. After an uneasy pause, the survivor asks, "Do you do a lot of homicides?"

"It's almost all I do."

"What's it like?"

"It ages you," Washington says. "I'm actually forty-one."

"No." Tess ignores the joke. She's after something else, something on the edge of her tongue. "I mean . . . what's it like to catch the person responsible for taking a life?"

The detective hesitates, searching for the right words.

Tess waits.

"Most of the time, they catch themselves," Washington says. "They sit down in a little gray room with me for hours, and slowly, with great effort, they dig their own graves. I just hand them the shovel and listen. Everyone wants to tell their story, and every story needs an audience. I give it to them. I smile and empathize and build rapport until they think they can tell me anything. And with every word, every detail, they keep digging themselves deeper and deeper, until they're too far down that hole to climb out. And by the time they realize I wasn't really their friend at all, they've already given me everything I need."

"So bad guys talk themselves into prison."

"I keep them talking."

Tess grins. "Never interrupt your enemy when he's making a mistake."

"Exactly."

Small wins are exhilarating in the moment, but the killer would've still held every advantage over Tess. And he still had that .45-caliber pistol. If she remained so stubbornly difficult to kill, Jacob would eventually weigh the risks and decide he'd rather just be half deaf for the rest of his life. With every passing minute she pushed him inexorably toward that decision. The standoff was temporary.

That gun in Jacob's holster was a ticking time bomb.

"Jesus." Washington rubs her arms, surprisingly cold. "Through all of that, I don't know how you managed to stay calm."

"I was scared shitless."

"I mean, you were composed. You improvised and adapted."

She shrugs. "Fear is power."

"I'm sorry?"

"It's . . . something Allie used to say."

"*Fear is power*?"

"Whenever I was nervous, which was often because I'm a bit of a wreck, she'd always tell me, *Remember all the things your body does when you're afraid*." Tess smiles, channeling her best friend's confident voice. "*Your pupils dilate so you can see better. Your breathing gets more efficient so you can run faster. Even your immune system gets better.* She always told me it's okay to be afraid. Because being afraid doesn't make you weak. It actually makes you stronger."

Nevertheless, the physical and psychological strain of crawling inside the Drainpipe had to be overwhelming. Tess couldn't have been far from an adrenaline crash. Fear may be power, but the body can't stay on high alert forever.

"And the killer?"

"He kept picking at me, trying to get under my skin. He told me it didn't matter how long I stayed alive. He'd outlast me, wait for me to die of suffocation or thirst or hypothermia. He kept singing that stupid song, just the chorus, like it was all he knew."

The man downstairs, he waits and he waits.

"Maybe," Washington says. "But there's an implication there, too. Whether he meant to or not, he was giving you information."

Tess's finger stops tracing.

"Do you understand where I'm going with this?"

"I'd assumed he was bluffing," she says, "trying to scare me."

"And that's still possible."

"But?"

"But I think there's more to it."

A multiday siege on a cave would be a stretch for a lone killer. When, exactly, had Jacob planned to sleep? How would he keep eyes on Tess and ensure she didn't escape through a side passage? How would he guard the entrance to prevent witnesses from stumbling across the scene? The cave was simply too much square footage for one man to control.

"What are you saying?"

"I'm not trying to alarm you," the detective says. "But as hard as you fought that day, I think you only saw part of the picture."

"I don't understand."

"I think there was a second killer involved."

The techs are calling it the *mystery hand*.

A partial glove print—in dried blood, no less—found on the suspect's Jeep. Even in the photographs sent to Washington's phone, it's clearly too small to be Jacob's.

Someone else was present that day, even if this *mystery hand* (she hates calling it that) is the only supporting evidence thus far. This unidentified person might have cleaned the crime scene to hide their own involvement, and they'd almost succeeded—if they hadn't missed the one-inch gap under the Jeep's rear door handle.

"But I never saw a second person," Tess says. "I only saw *him*."

"I think whoever helped him helped from behind the scenes. Out of view."

"Who?"

"I don't know yet. That's the puzzle." Washington smiles gently. "But we'll solve it together, Tess. You and I. Your job is to tell me everything you saw and heard on that day. Every detail you can remember, no matter how small. And while you do your job, I'll do mine. Together we'll attack this thing from two directions: past and present."

Tess says nothing.

This is a major revelation for her, and it'll take time to settle. Washington can see the survivor reframing her thoughts now.

She glances toward the hallway. "That means the second one is still out there."

"Yes."

"Right now."

"You're safe, Tess. That's a promise."

She nods, unconvinced.

"But this is why I need your help." Washington sets her pen down. "I'm starting to suspect that Jacob Herman was only acting under the direction of someone else. Someone master-minded this attack, and Jacob only carried it out. And it's our responsibility now, for Allie. To do right by her, we need to find the true killer."

For Allie.

"Okay." Tess swallows. "Where do we start?"

"Well, it's probably someone who knows you both. Someone

who knew you'd both be at the Devil's Staircase, alone in the woods and far from help."

Tess nods. She's mentally scanning her friends and acquaintances, everyone she's ever wronged in her life. But she's always been a loner. It can't be a long list.

"Maybe someone wanted Allie dead, and you were just there."

"Like who?"

"You're clever. I think you already know."

"Apparently I'm not that clever."

"I think the answer has been right here in front of us the entire time." The detective flips back through her notes. "Let's revisit the start of the day, when Allie first picked you up from your apartment. Remember? There was one person who'd had that mysterious disagreement with her. One person who knew exactly where you and Allie would be that day, and maybe even exactly who was waiting for you at the cave. Maybe he'd stayed home to avoid witnessing the murder firsthand, so he'd appear innocent."

Tess freezes, a dawning realization.

"Not possible," she says. "It couldn't be Ethan."

"Are you sure?"

Tess looks at the detective head-on, a rare moment of eye contact, and something changes in the recycled air. Washington realizes this survivor is even sharper than she'd realized—she's intuitively sensed information is being withheld from her. "What aren't you telling me?"

"I'm sorry, Tess—"

"Just tell me."

"I'm truly sorry you have to find out this way." She feels a weight on her chest as she speaks. "We found Allie's Outback where she'd parked on that dirt road, as you probably figured. And a preliminary search found something interesting: a Bartell's receipt in the cupholder, dated for a week earlier. She'd bought pregnancy tests. Six of them."

Tess blinks.

"Did Allie tell you she might be pregnant?"

She can only shake her head in slow, robotic motions. It's like the floor has dropped out beneath her and opened up a terrible new dimension to her grief. It's quietly shattering.

"Did Allie want kids?"

"She never wanted kids," Tess says. "Ever."

Washington recalls the bumper sticker in the corner of the Outback's back window: *No Baby on Board, Feel Free to Crash into Me.*

"Because her entire career is built around travel, right? Having a baby could change the trajectory of *Keep Calm*, or even force her to abandon her brand completely." She chooses her words carefully. "I think that morning, when your intuition told you something was weighing on Allie's mind, that was it. I think that's what she so desperately wanted to talk to you about but felt like she couldn't."

It all fits together, even if Tess wishes it didn't. Washington can see the pieces assembling themselves behind her eyes, slow acceptance of a new truth. Her best friend had been a few weeks pregnant when they entered the cave together.

Before it all happened.

"Like I said, we'll solve this from the past and the present," Washington says. "You and me, Tess. Between us, we have all the pieces."

"Why Ethan, though?"

"Well, that's the thing." The detective looks her dead in the eye. "Maybe kind, gentle Ethan Ramirez, the nice-guy pediatrician who sends Allie photos of used dental flossers in parking lots, wasn't quite the person she thought he was. Maybe that feeling in your gut was right to dislike him, even if you never knew quite why. You want to know a guy's true colors? Tell him he's going to be a dad. Maybe when Allie told him the big news, he decided he didn't want a baby—or even a pregnant girlfriend."

Silence.

"And maybe he was willing to pay someone to make his problem disappear."

18

THIRTY THOUSAND DOLLARS IS A LOT OF MONEY, BUT WEIGHED against the risks of murdering a woman, it's not a *lot* of money. Sometimes Jacob felt he should've been insulted by the lowball compensation, but in the end he'd still agreed to it.

Time isn't money. Money is time.

Money is gas in the tank and fuel in the stove. Jacob was finished pressing aluminum—he'd long ago sworn he'd never work a regular shift again—but odd jobs are intermittent and his lockbox was thinning out. He knew he was liable to put his 1911 in his mouth when his reserves hit zero, and a fresh infusion of thirty grand kicked that unpleasant can down the street for at least another year. He'd already watched the strongest man he ever knew melt into his own bedsheets like a rotting pumpkin. Jacob understood better than most that all time is borrowed, and once you've made your peace with that, life opens up significantly.

Every day 150,000 people die around the world. That's 6,250 every hour, 104 every minute. Every second, somewhere on this blue marble, two strangers breathe their last and croak. Sometimes he correlated this with the amount of time he spent performing routine tasks. Taking a leak, for example, is roughly thirty seconds from start to finish. That's sixty people dead while Jacob Herman pissed on a tree.

And that's only an average. Consider wars and atrocities, the hundreds of thousands of lives lost in Ukraine and Gaza. Or over a half million dead in the Syrian and Ethiopian civil wars *each*. Industrialized death on a scale hard to fathom. Against such overwhelming numbers, what difference could Jacob possibly make? That's the big secret. In some cave up in the hills of the Pacific Northwest, one more dead woman hardly matters.

Nonetheless, this was turning into the hardest money he'd ever earned. She was *not* giving up. She'd escaped his ambush. She'd dodged his gunfire and turned what should have been an execution into a crawling, close-quarters chase. She'd improvised and used the hostile environment against him to neutralize his advantages—his size, his strength, his weaponry.

But Jacob could improvise, too.

He'd already worked it out in his head. To fire his pistol inside the Drainpipe, he needed to solve two problems. First, how to protect his hearing from the magnified blast. He'd cover his left ear with one hand, and if he braced his head against his right shoulder—while aiming the gun—he could protect his right ear, too. He might come out of this without hearing aids. Second, the risk of a deadly ricochet. After his jacketed round blew through the woman's skull, it was likely to hit rock and come back at him. In this confined space, he imagined bullet fragments zinging around like a bouncy ball thrown inside a phone booth.

But . . . if his aim was precise, and he shot the woman at the correct downward angle, the slug wouldn't exit her head at all. Instead it would tunnel down her neck and, in theory, be absorbed by the rest of her torso.

Yes.

Yes, that just might work.

But he would need to choose his moment carefully. Drawing his gun would be awkward from this position. He'd be vulnerable to her counterattack.

"What's your plan?" he asked her, his vapory breath misting

in the red light. "Just keep crawling deeper and deeper until one of us gets stuck?"

"My money's on your big ass."

"If I get stuck, you'll be sealed in, too."

The woman's foot slipped behind her with a gritty scrape. The tunnel floor was slanting downward, slick with watery clay. This was good.

"Careful," Jacob said with a grin. "Wouldn't want to fall."

The rock faces were smoother down here, cut in uniform ripple patterns like the choppy surface of the ocean. He'd never known stone could look so liquid. Every now and then he'd even glimpse a straight line too perfectly straight to be natural, as if sliced by a laser. It stuck in his mind, refused to fit. This was a new world with new rules.

And it was now impossible to ignore: the tunnel's decline was steepening. As he forced this woman deeper into the earth, her muddy boots were losing traction, and she had to arch her back to keep balanced. Centuries of erosion had wiped away all handholds and footholds.

He could see the calculations running behind her eyes—to retreat any deeper down the slippery tunnel, she would need to use both hands to grip the curved walls. She'd be unable to counterattack with her knife. Not without sacrificing her hold.

One scorpion won't be able to sting. This was about to become untenable for her.

He pressed: "Do you even know what's down there?"

She said nothing.

"You seem like a smart girl." Jacob watched her. "You would've done your homework. You must already know about Razor Alley and the Chimney. And, of course, you know what else is down there, right?"

Still nothing.

"I read that a guy, a gold miner or something, died after being trapped down there for a week. Can you even imagine what that's like? Being alone, no light, unable to move, squashed inside a tiny little tube with solid rock on all sides. It's got to be one of the worst ways to die. Being disemboweled or burned at the stake would hurt like hell, but it'd be over in a few minutes. Imagine this physical sensation spread out over *hours*, or *days*, or *weeks*, crammed so deep and so tight that the only way they can get you out is if they first break your legs with a hammer. That poor bastard probably wished he were dead long before they reached him. And even after he suffocated or his heart failed, they still couldn't hoist his body up to the surface for a Christian burial. They had to cut his arms and legs off and pull him up piece by piece." He whistled. "I mean, holy shit, can you imagine that?"

She didn't blink.

"Down there, the tunnels are barely wide enough for a human to fit. You won't be able to crawl on your hands and knees, like we are now." Jacob scraped the smooth ceiling with his knife. "You'll have to slither on your belly like a salamander. You'll have to take off your helmet and shoes, probably, to even fit. In the narrowest spaces, it's only *ten inches* wide."

He held out a gloved hand, measuring the distance between the walls.

"Even worse, the narrow tunnels change direction, too. Ninety-degree turns. You'll have to twist your entire body to squeeze through. If your legs are too long or your hips can't twist just right, or if you get your body wedged into an angle you can't recover from, you'll get stuck and die just like he did. Way too slowly."

Ten inches. Much tighter than the Drainpipe. Just thinking about it caused the hairs on Jacob's forearms to prickle.

He grinned. "Hence its name."

He didn't need to say it. She already knew.

Worse Than Death.

Gripping her survival knife with pale knuckles, the woman moved again, scooting her body away from him. She was right at the precipice now, an inch from letting go. She kept her eyes locked on him, spotlighted in his red headlamp as she finally spoke.

Her teeth chattered, her voice trembling—"I'm . . ."—but gaining strength:

"I'm going to *make you* chase me through it, asshole."

19

THE DETAILS OF THE RESCUE STILL BOGGLE WASHINGTON'S MIND.

The depth, the danger, the sheer psychological agony of being locked under millions of tons of settling earth. The experience must be worse than any nightmare. Rescuers found the poor woman only because they'd heard her screams echo up through cracks in the porous bedrock, and they were searching the cave deeply enough to hear it only because of a single distress call sent via citizens band radio late last night. Just a few words, really, uttered by a weak and near-unconscious voice. The individual was also apparently inexperienced with radio protocols, having tried several frequencies before finding the emergency channel by luck.

That distress call saved the woman's life. And although it originated from the radio mounted to the dashboard of Jacob Herman's Jeep, the caller wasn't Jacob. In fact, when Tess discovers who it was, she'll be quite surprised. But for now, Washington files that away in her mind and listens to the survivor's testimony. Jumping ahead will only muddy things.

Her story will get there.

"I knew I had to go deeper," Tess says. "Farther down, into a place he couldn't fit."

From there, the Drainpipe slopes downward into a slippery ramp marked with coffee cake layers of shale and mud. Cavers are advised to descend cautiously and use a fixed rope as a backup—but Tess wouldn't have had time to go safely. There was only one option faster than climbing.

Falling.

"I let go," she says, "and I slid down."

"Like a waterslide."

"Basically. But pitch-black." She shuts her eyes, reliving every detail. "My helmet rattled my brain. I crossed my arms and braced my feet against the walls, trying to slow myself."

Sliding feetfirst down the cramped tube would have been a calculated risk. She couldn't have known what she was dropping into below. Every surface inside the cave is as hard as concrete, some of it dappled with unpredictable bumps, some of it sculpted dagger-sharp. If she broke an ankle or knocked herself unconscious, it would all be over. Her only advantage was her mobility, her ability to stay ahead of the killer.

"At the bottom, I landed hard on my tailbone." She pats her forehead. "I think that's when my headlamp broke."

One source of light down. Two remained.

"I couldn't see. I found my flashlight and turned it on, but there was too much mud on the lens to see." She takes a shivering breath. "And he . . . he was catching up. His red light was growing around me."

200 feet, Washington writes.

With her gutsy stunt she'd bought herself thirty seconds, at the cost of her headlamp. Few cavers are determined enough to crawl all the way down the wet, slippery Drainpipe. But those who reach the bottom, it's said, are rewarded with a spectacular sight.

"I wiped mud off my flashlight." Tess's voice wavers. "And what I saw, all around me . . ."

"What?"

"It's hard to describe."

"Allie's surprise?"

Tears glimmer in her eyes. "I think so."

When you go deep enough underground, the laws of physics don't quite work.

Early this morning on a bumpy ATV ride, Washington had listened to a quick primer from a local volunteer on what makes the Devil's Staircase unique. A solution cave's natural formations are all created by the same interplay of gravity and water, he'd explained, and those forces are inherently predictable. Stalactites form where water drips; stalagmites rise from where it lands. Where water pools, rimstone dams form. In almost any cave around the world, a trained eye can easily read the gravitational physics that formed it.

Except here.

In this place, the formations don't grow vertically—they grow *sideways*, almost organically. Like plants or fungus. These gravity-defying sights, still unexplained by modern science, are called *helictites.* The phenomenon is often too deep underground to be formed by wind, the volunteer had explained, and capillary forces aren't strong enough to create structures of such size. Helictites are physically impossible, one of our planet's natural mysteries, and this lower chamber of the Devil's Staircase—a small appendix-shaped room nicknamed Razor Alley—contains one of the largest known concentrations of them in North America.

"It was beautiful," Tess whispers. "Like . . . her last gift to me."

Allie Merritt, who'd cruised the Nile River and sipped cocktails in Lower Manhattan and camped atop Arctic ice floes to watch narwhals, had seen and tasted more of the world than most people do in their lifetimes—and still it seemed to be this underworld that fascinated her the most. The unknown. The dark. The depths.

"For just a few seconds, I . . ." Tess wipes an eye. "I'm sorry."

"It's okay."

"I know it sounds stupid."

Washington scoots closer. "There's nothing stupid about it, Tess."

"I know she's gone. I saw her die. But I swear to God, I felt like Allie was still there with me somehow. Like . . . the last of her was holding on to the world by her fingernails, refusing to move on, refusing to leave my side. Not until I was safe. Not until we killed him."

"Together?"

She swallows and nods.

The sight she witnessed is difficult to imagine. The photos Washington has seen are indeed spectacular, but in a cold and threatening way. She knows one should never confuse beauty with safety. Humans don't belong underground.

"I knew he'd kill me if I tried to fight him head-on." She exhales. "But . . . there was another way I could win."

"How?"

"By being *like* Allie," she says. "By staying ahead of him, by going deeper into the cave, deeper than he could follow me."

Forward momentum at all costs. The Devil's Staircase is a grueling trial, relentless in the ways it attacks your body and mind. Hours later, even expert-level cavers on the rescue team would suffer its psychological effects while fighting to save the trapped woman.

"By outlasting him. By being braver than him."

She takes a breath.

Like Allie would've done.

JACOB HERMAN LANDED HARD ON THE BOTTOM, BRUISING HIS KNEES on rock. He shone his red glow on the walls around him and saw they were wriggling, covered in worms.

His gut dropped.

But his lizard brain was just a fraction of a second ahead of his upper brain. Of course they weren't worms.

They were wormlike formations made of stone, all flash frozen solid. Hundreds of them, maybe thousands. They grew off the walls as thin as angel pasta, wispy and needle-sharp. At his feet, he noticed more strange sprouts emerging from the ground to knee height, crooked *Cordyceps* stalks bending and reaching. He was surrounded by impossible shapes, and the longer he looked, the more of them he saw, like they were multiplying around him.

The odor of wet socks was stronger down here, earthy and pungent.

But Jacob found space to stand up—yes, he could finally stand without scraping his helmet. The cave had expanded to the size of a small bedroom, lowering the chance of a ricochet. His gun was viable again. He knew he needed to end this chase quick, to run the woman down and plant a .45-caliber slug in her brain before she wedged herself someplace he couldn't follow.

Everywhere, more worms blossomed in his red light. More solid tendrils emerged from the walls, some as thick as antlers. Surreal chandeliers hung from above, too, like alien flowers blooming in reverse. He balanced himself against a radiant formation the size of a standing child and it shattered at his touch. Fragments hit the ground like glass shards.

Careful.

A needle of rock had pierced his neoprene glove, impaled right under his thumbnail. With gritted teeth he pulled it out—a bloody toothpick, pale as fishbone.

Very careful.

He knew the woman was close now. But she'd turned off her flashlight, making herself difficult to track. It felt like his opponent had joined forces with this hostile environment somehow, harnessed its power against him—

Movement ahead.

He raised his pistol—his left hand covering his left ear, right shoulder to his right—and jerked the trigger. The blast shook his teeth, a microsecond of nuclear white. Did he hit her? He couldn't tell. His night vision was fried now.

He breathed in the smoky scent of burned gunpowder.

This was hide-and-seek, Marco Polo with a gun. With his red spotlight he pursued the woman through a coral reef of moving shadows, stooping and crawling under jagged shapes. Some snagged his clothes and slowed him down. Some snapped away freely. Tiny forms crunched underfoot like bird skeletons.

Ahead, he glimpsed the woman's helmet.

He fired again.

But she was agile, rolling and crawling and somehow always a half second ahead of him, rock debris peppering her as his bullets tore gouges out of the fragile terrain around her. She navigated this foreign landscape with skill and confidence—but she was running out of space. Jacob knew the Chimney was coming up. He would corner her there at the precipice, shoot her in the head, and finally end this exhausting day. He couldn't imagine any payout being worth all this pain. Not thirty grand, not three hundred.

His ankles bled now. Fingers of rock clawed into his jeans, his socks, his boots. The Colt 1911's single-stack magazine held seven rounds. How many left?

Head shots only, he told himself. He'd have his chance soon.

He passed an aluminum plate bolted into limestone, decades

old and rusted brown. Only the sign's image was visible—the hooded Grim Reaper holding a scythe—and six words.

GO NO FARTHER
You Will Die

"I STOPPED AT THE EDGE," TESS SAYS. "IT WAS A SHEER DROP."

The Chimney.

She was trapped.

"When I looked down, the beam of my flashlight couldn't even reach the bottom. The walls were smooth, like big curtains of wet rock, too slippery to climb down."

"And Jacob?"

"He was close. I heard him crunching through the rock formations, trying to get a clear shot on me. His red light was growing." She shuts her eyes. "I tried to imagine Allie's voice in my head, to remember what she had taught me."

Earlier that day, Tess had rappelled for her first time underground. Now she needed to do it again, alone. And fast.

"I grabbed the last rope from Allie's bag. My hands were shaking so badly, I almost dropped it. I tried to remember—all those hours ago, how did she anchor it? She'd clipped it around a boulder, a BFR the size of a fridge, but all the rock formations around me were too thin, like glass sculptures. Nothing would hold my weight."

From this point downward the Devil's Staircase is off-limits to everyone, regardless of skill level. Green Ridge requires permit holders to sign an affidavit agreeing they will descend no deeper than Razor Alley or face criminal prosecution.

"I found holes drilled into the walls, but all the bolts must have rusted away years ago. The metal had just disintegrated, bled down the walls, become part of the cave." She steadies her voice. "Except for one last anchor bolt."

Corroded by decades of rust.

Bad idea, Washington thinks. The anchor was a time bomb. It might not hold an adult's weight. It could explode off the wall at the worst possible moment, and then she'd plunge into the darkness below.

"Bits of metal flaked off as I clipped my rope to it," Tess says. "I knew it was risky, I knew it would probably fail on me, but I had no choice. I was running out of time."

Next, the hard part.

"I had Allie's rack descender, but I couldn't remember how the brake bars worked. How to thread the rope through, which bars to open and shut. My fingers were numb and stiff and . . ." She hesitates, pulling in a shivery breath.

"What?"

"I heard . . . I heard Allie's voice in my mind." Her eyes glimmer. "I swear, I heard it."

The detective leans closer.

"The same thing she always told me when I was afraid. Ever since her family took me in." She smiles through tears. "*You're a survivor.*"

You're a survivor, Tess.

Years ago it was her mother's bleach. Now, blades and bullets.

Washington imagines this poor woman struggling against unfamiliar gear and a rust-eaten anchor bolt that might fracture at any second. Scooting her legs out over the edge. Her heart in her throat, her palms sweaty inside her gloves, her boots dangling over abyssal black. Maybe she saw her own shadow projected against bright red dripstone, her silhouette in Jacob's sights. Afraid to jump, afraid to stay, paralyzed between two terrors.

But even if Tess overcame her fears and descended the

Chimney's vertical shaft, even if the hundred-year-old anchor bolt held her weight, her death was still certain. Jacob was only seconds behind her, and once he reached the edge he would have a clear shot at her. On the rope, Tess would be exposed and defenseless. In this situation, there were no good choices.

Option one: die where she stood.

Option two: die on the rope.

Tess has been silent for several breaths.

"Did you jump?"

She wipes an eye.

"Tess?"

"I . . ." She steadies her voice. "Allie was the bravest person I've ever met. She was never afraid. All my life, I'd wished to be like her. And I tried to imagine if our places were reversed—if it was Allie there with the rope in her hands, what would she do?"

Tess looks up. The burst vessel colors her left eye vivid red.

At this moment, Washington knows, Jacob would have been just feet behind her, the gun in his hand, brittle formations crunching underfoot as he raced to catch her.

"I realized . . . I had one more choice."

Option three: fight.

20

SOMETHING PUNCHED JACOB IN THE WINDPIPE.

Hard.

Two hundred pounds of inertia carried him and slammed him down on his back. His helmet cracked against rock. He gasped, eyes watering, choking on his own larynx. His thoughts raced—*she tricked me, she set a trap, she used the rope to set a goddamn trap.* The resourceful woman had held her climbing rope up at neck height, five feet off the ground, and let him charge straight into it. He'd clotheslined himself.

Now she tackled him.

But Jacob still had the gun in his hand. He rolled over, twisted the Colt 1911's barrel into her face—but now the rope was tangled under his armpit, and she pinned his wrist like a gooseneck. He couldn't point the gun. His finger jerked the trigger anyway—a tooth-rattling blast into the ceiling—and stalactite chips showered them.

Her other hand, his mind screamed. *Knife.*

Knife-knife-knife—

Coming straight at his face—but he caught her wrist.

His eyelashes fluttered against a pinpoint of steel. The blade had stopped millimeters from the soft jelly of his eyeball. He felt her hot breath on his face. She was already on to her next move, fighting with an untrained but instinctual intelligence, almost feral, repositioning and bracing every pound of her body weight onto that knife. Trying to drive the blade just a little deeper, straight down into his eye socket.

She tried. She used all her muscle, all her leverage.

It wasn't enough.

Jacob was stronger. Fights always end up on the ground, and he was in his element here. He felt her adrenalized strength melt against his.

"Good try," he huffed in her face. "Hell of a good try."

He was back in control and it felt good. He punched the knife out of her hand, sent it skittering into the dark. He elbowed her in the teeth. Then he dug his boots in and rolled his shoulders and threw her off-balance, his own weight catapulting hers. The woman spilled toward the cliff and kept falling, right over the edge—but she caught herself.

Her fingernails slipped on the smooth stone, her legs dangling freely. Gasping, disarmed. She could barely hold on. Her surprise attack had almost worked.

Almost.

But now Jacob was in full command of his body. He coughed, spat, pushed himself upright with the pistol in his fist—still at least a shot or two left—and aimed at her face. Too close to miss now. She was helpless, hanging from the edge.

Her eyes widened with fear.

Jacob covered his ears and pulled the trigger—another concussive blast and searing flash—but the bullet skipped off rock.

She was gone.

"I PUSHED OFF THE EDGE," TESS WHISPERS, "AND DROPPED."

JACOB'S EARS RANG. HE BLINKED AWAY GRIT.

She *let go*?

He almost laughed with disbelief—facing a bullet to the forehead, she'd chosen a blind drop. He sure as hell hadn't expected that. But there was no time to react. Something snarled on the ground beside him like an uncoiling snake, and he realized: as they'd wrestled together, her rope had looped around his chest, around his wrist, around the gun in his hand, and not by accident. *She tangled me in her rope—*

It snapped taut with bone-shattering force.

21

TESS'S BODY WEIGHT, ACCELERATED BY A PLUNGE INTO FREE FALL, would've drawn the rope tight with incredible kinetic force.

Tangled around Jacob's right hand.

Washington nods. "Smart."

"I only dropped a few feet," Tess says, "before the descender locked."

The physics would've been painful for both sides of the equation. To Tess, it must have felt like being hit by a truck in midair: the carabiner yanking her harness to an instant dead stop, the straps digging into her flesh. She would've been whip-lashed, blood in her teeth, sweat in her eyes, dangling over the Chimney's deadly plunge.

"And Jacob?"

"I couldn't see him," she says. "But I heard his voice."

"Saying what?"

"Nothing." A cold smile crosses her face. "Just screaming."

Minute by minute, Washington is seeing a different Tess emerge. The woman who first entered this cave should have been easy prey for an armed killer: a shy introvert abused by her mother and living vicariously through her adventure-seeking best friend. It's difficult to reconcile that version of Tess with this resourceful and capable survivor, underestimated by Jacob, maybe even underestimated by Detective Washington herself. This new Tess was no victim. She could improvise. She could adapt. She could fight with knives and rope and momentum and sheer whatever-it-takes ingenuity. In a real way she was *becoming* Allie Merritt, the woman she'd idolized since her childhood.

And it wasn't just about survival, either. There was a new motivation in play, visceral and hot-blooded and impossible to deny.

Revenge.

"Dangling on that rope, my entire body ached." The coldness grows in Tess's eyes, like ice forming on a pond. "But when I heard him scream up there, tangled in my rope, I knew the bastard who murdered my best friend was hurting *even worse*."

LIVE-WIRE PAIN.

Jacob screamed until his lungs were empty in a raw voice he didn't recognize. He was afraid to look at his right hand. It had all happened in a fraction of a second, but somehow he'd perceived everything in perfect clarity: the braided rope slicing like a noose around his knuckles, ripping the gun away, hooking his fingers, tightening, bending them into a dislocating ninety-degree *snap*—

He tried to lift himself, but the rope now pinned him down, held taut by the woman's hundred-and-some pounds swinging below. A human counterweight. It crushed his ribs like a boa constrictor's grip, and he couldn't breathe.

He didn't know where his pistol had landed, either.

She got me.

Now he understood the woman's true ingenuity—facing a bullet to the head, she'd made a split-second calculation. She knew they were entangled in the same rope, so she'd weaponized her own inertia against him. She'd gotten him, all right.

But . . .

I can still get her, too.

Down the cliff, the woman was suspended over a fatal drop, four stories above a floor of jagged bedrock. As in any survival situation, every choice has a cost. The rope that snared Jacob was *also* the same rope that kept her alive.

With his unhurt hand, he slid his KA-BAR combat knife from its sheath. He rotated the blade in his fingers and began to saw.

"I FELT A VIBRATION DOWN THE ROPE, THROUGH MY HARNESS." THE elation fades from Tess's voice. "I knew he was cutting it."

Of course.

Of course it was too good to be true. This gutsy plan had saved her from a bullet and injured her attacker—but catapulted her straight into another impossible dilemma. Now dangling over a deadly fall, she could only reach out to smooth, slippery dripstone and hold on to it with her fingernails, kick her boots against vertical rock, searching for traction, grasping for any grip to support herself, holding on tightly before—

"I felt the rope go limp," she says, "and drop past me."

No backups, no safeties.

She was now solo climbing.

22

"I HELD ON TO THE WALL," TESS REMEMBERS, "TRYING TO FIND A foothold. A toehold, even."

Hanging by sweaty fingers.

"I was slipping. I could feel my fingernails bending backward. I pressed myself flat, trying to hold on."

But the walls would have been too smooth to grip. The Chimney is almost entirely flowstone, every edge rounded off and frozen into waterfalls of calcium carbonate. In photographs the walls appear unsettlingly biological, all shades of mucus yellow and blood brown like the interior valves of a giant organ. Cave water runs down the sheer walls in glistening sheets, making the surfaces even slipperier.

Hundreds of feet underground.

In total blackness.

"But then . . . my toes found a gap in the rock. Just a thin, little crack, maybe an inch or two wide. I couldn't turn my head to see it, but I could feel it there. I dug my boot into it, twisted sideways, and rested all my weight on that foot."

As narrow as the crevice in the wall was, it was an improvement. She could perch for minutes in this position, instead of mere seconds hanging by her fingertips.

Work the problem, Tess.

"It was too dark to see. My headlamp was broken and my flashlight was gone. All I had left were glowsticks, but I couldn't reach for them. I'd lose my grip. I was afraid to breathe, even. Every time I inhaled, my chest expanded and pushed me away from the wall."

Even if she'd had a light source, climbing the curtains of slick flowstone would have been impossible. The Chimney is akin to an underground elevator shaft. Not even the most experienced caver can ascend it without vertical gear.

Sisu, Washington remembers. The rescue operation's incident commander had said it best. There's no English-language equivalent for such prolonged strength in the face of hardship, and there's no better word.

Sisu.

At this point Tess's muscles would've been strained, rapidly fatiguing. Ice-cold water trickling down the back of her shirt would lower her body temperature and sap her strength. Adrenaline pinned her to this wall, perched like a ballerina with one foot wedged in that tiny crack—but adrenaline isn't limitless. Gravity always wins.

"I needed to press myself as flat to the rock as possible. Every millimeter. So I unclasped my helmet and let it drop."

"With Allie's camera?"

She nods. "I heard it fall for a long time. Then I heard a splash."

"There was water at the bottom?"

She nods again.

Groundwater levels in the cave's lower reaches are known to fluctuate wildly with the seasons and rainfall. As far as Tess would have known, the depth could have been ten feet or ten inches. To let go was to gamble with her life.

And Jacob was on the ledge just above her. With his broken fingers he would've been a furious, wounded animal. Dragging himself to the precipice, his pistol clenched in his good hand, about to aim down at her and fire again—

"I heard him crawling. Toward the edge."

There was no overhang to shield her from a bullet. This poor girl couldn't catch a goddamn break. She couldn't climb up or down—she'd be exposed in the killer's red light, hanging for her life between a bullet and a four-story drop. Below, a life-and-death coin toss.

She knew what she had to do.

Heads: the water is deep enough to break a fall.

Tails: it isn't.

"I thought about Allie," Tess whispers. "I thought about when we were teenagers in that tree behind her house, practicing with her descenders. I could never get the rope stuff right, but she was always so patient with me. Allie loved to be self-reliant, knowing how to tie knots that will literally keep you alive. It's why she practiced with guns. Her dad always taught her to be independent. And she wanted to empower me, too."

Washington nods gently.

"It was like . . . we were those kids again. And I was squeezing my harness and remembering to breathe and trying not to puke, and she was urging me to be brave and jump. And she's looking at me with those green eyes—her eyes have always been so emerald green, tropical, like a chameleon—and she's telling me I'm a survivor, that I survived my mother and I can survive this, too. To trust her and jump."

Her voice breaks.

"And I . . . kept telling her I couldn't. That I wasn't like her, that I'll never be brave like her. And I know it wasn't real, and I was really clinging to a wall with her killer above me. But all I could see was teenage Allie in that tree."

Washington imagines a gasping, furious Jacob reaching the ledge. His gun in his fist. Aiming down at her.

Squeezing the trigger . . .

"And you let go?"

"No." Through tears, Tess smiles. "Allie *pushed* me, one last time."

JACOB AIMED HIS RED LIGHT DOWN ON HER—BUT A HEARTBEAT TOO late. The woman dropped off the sheer wall, into blackness.

A second passed.

Longer.

Then he heard a reverberating splash far below. The echo rang off the cave walls like a grenade. He heard water droplets land, ripples lapping against rock.

Goddamn it.

Staring down into the darkness made him dizzy with vertigo. He scooted back from the ledge and sprawled onto his back, cradling his hand. He dreaded seeing the damage. Peeling the neoprene glove off his broken fingers would be excruciating.

This whole thing was supposed to be simple. It should have been over in five minutes, an easy execution—zip ties to bind her wrists, a KA-BAR to cut her throat, and a gun for backup. And now five *hours* later, here was Jacob Herman with leaking eardrums and mangled fingers, God only knows how many floors underground, with his prey far below and out of reach.

Still, he knew, the situation had a reassuring upside. He couldn't reach her down there at the bottom of the Chimney, true. But with her rope cut, she had no way to climb the smooth curtains of vertical flowstone.

She was confined down there.

"Nice stunt," Jacob shouted, hearing a distorted echo swirl below. "I'm impressed. I really thought your friend was the brave one. Joke's on me, right?"

No answer.

But he knew she was somewhere down there treading water. Rubbing her eyes, shivering in the pool's piercing coldness. Trying to plan her next move.

"You're cut off from the world." He forced a wincing grin. "You know that, right? And I won't leave this cave. I'll camp out here for as long as it takes, until you freeze or suffocate or starve. I'm patient. I can wait days. Weeks, even. No one is coming to save you."

He caught his breath.

"*The man downstairs, he waits and he waits . . .*"

His voice was hoarse and off-key. His hearing was spongy, fresh fluid pooling inside his ear. He cradled his smashed hand and almost laughed at the wild hilarity of their chase, the bullets and broken bones and close calls. He'd found his match in her, all right. But her victories were only temporary.

"*And, baby, he's waiting on you.*"

23

DETECTIVE WASHINGTON IS LOSING HER LIEUTENANT'S PATIENCE. IT'S late in the day, the unknowns are accumulating, and this phone call is going significantly worse.

"It's all in Tess's statement." She flattens to a wall as nurses wheel a bed past. "Just listen to what she's saying and you'll see it, too. Have we questioned Allie's boyfriend yet?"

"It'll take time."

"Whatever Ethan's story is, we'll need to compare it with Tess's statement. Lay out his version and hers, side by side—"

"No disrespect, Layla, but I'll handle the big picture."

No disrespect. Again.

"Focus on your witness," he repeats. "Finish up with Tess."

"I'll do that."

After she hangs up, Washington curses under her breath. A nurse glances her way but pretends not to hear.

She may have been railroaded into a support role, but she still knows where this investigation is headed. With most of the cave's physical evidence contaminated by the rescue operation, the investigation will all come down to statements. Conflicting accounts, different perceptions of one objective truth. And the human mind is the ultimate unreliable narrator.

On the way back to Tess's room, words echo in her mind.

Apple. Chair. Umbrella.

From her cognitive exam, repeated once at the start of the

appointment and then again at the end. A simple memory test. And of course they had to be basic words, written on a whiteboard in primary colors like a kindergartener's homework.

Apple. Chair. Umbrella.

Washington wasn't too proud to take a cognitive screening. She wasn't bothered by the inconvenience of splitting up a busy workday on short notice. She didn't even mind that now, five days later, those three childish words are still engraved in her mind like a chorus to a maddening song she can't forget: *Apple. Chair. Umbrella.*

What bothers her is that at the start of the test she'd been given five words to remember, and she'd retained only three.

As she returns to Tess's room and restarts her digital recorder, Washington is starting to feel like she's grasping in the dark: "Did Jacob say anything else? While you were trapped down there, treading water—did he say anything else that suggested why he was really there, or who he was working for?"

"I don't think so."

"Try to remember everything, Tess."

God, she wishes she could enter this survivor's mind and know what happened for certain. Play back, pause, rewind, like Allie's all-important GoPro camera. Study every detail embedded in her memory. All the grit and tactile sensation.

Free-falling dozens of feet into subterranean water would have been an out-of-body shock, and Tess has the bruises on her thighs and forearms to prove it. So much sliding, jumping, dropping, spiraling to new depths. So much *letting go*. How many stories underground was she now? Twenty? With this final calculated risk, she'd left the killer injured and stymied, her own certain death leveraged into a stalemate.

But there's another layer here.

Washington knows it. And it's time to take a calculated risk of her own.

"Something is bugging me," the detective admits. "It's been under my skin ever since the killer cornered you and Allie in the tunnel. And I'm sorry, Tess, but . . . I'm going to have to ask you something uncomfortable."

Tess nods, uncertain.

"Let's take it back to the moment you saw Allie die. I need you to concentrate and search your memory. The shock and emotion of the moment might have tricked you, made you misremember, so try to focus on specific senses. Only things you saw and heard. When this stranger put a gun to Allie's head and pulled the trigger, did you instinctively look away?"

This is a jarring question, and Tess has to think. Then, reluctantly, she nods once.

"Did you see her blood?"

"No."

"Did you see the hole in her head?"

"*No,*" Tess says. "Why are you asking me this?"

"Because my team has searched every inch of the Upper Vault, where you saw the murder happen. And . . . well, Allie's body isn't there."

The temperature of the room seems to change.

Tess blinks. "No blood?"

"Nothing."

"Have you searched the lakes?"

This being the next logical step. While Tess was cornered underground, the killer would have had several hours during which his movements were unaccounted for—plenty of time to make Allie's body disappear. Down the valley are Blue Lake and Lake Jackson, twin glacier basins dozens of square miles across and more than seven hundred feet deep. It will take months or even years for divers to scour both lakebeds, and if Allie's remains are down there wrapped in chicken wire, as Jacob claimed, there's a high chance they'll never be found at all.

This explanation is entirely possible.

Plausible, even.

But Washington already knows: Allie Merritt isn't at the bottom of some lake.

"Why?" Tess looks at the detective head-on, her voice wavering with a sudden dread. "What *other* possibility is there?"

JACOB LEANED AWAY FROM THE PRECIPICE, CRADLING HIS BROKEN fingers, and glanced back to his girlfriend. She'd finally caught up, wiping mud from her kneepads.

"Well?" she asked, frowning. "Is she dead yet?"

24

THREE WEEKS EARLIER, UNDER THE STARLIGHT BY JACOB'S TRAVEL trailer, she'd first proposed her idea to him: "I want you to murder my best friend."

He'd coughed up a mouthful of smoke. "That's dark, Babygirl."

"Don't call me that."

"Sure thing, Babygirl."

"It'll be simple. I'll take her someplace isolated, so it'll just be me and her." Her voice had been so confident, so precise. "And she'll have no idea you'll be waiting for us."

"Dramatic."

"Put down the joint. I need you sharp while we talk about this."

Ever since he'd watched that shivering naked man disappear in the red glow of his father's taillights, Jacob had wondered what it might be like to take a human life. Years ago he'd made a pact with his best friend to crash their senior prom with a pair of twelve-gauge Mossberg Cruisers, but they'd both gotten cold feet at the last minute. The class of 2006 had no idea how famous they'd almost become as they sipped their sparkling cider. That's how it goes, though. You only hear about the planes that crash.

"But you'd be the one who saw her last," Jacob told her. "Your best friend dies while she's out with you, and you instantly look guilty."

"That's why we'll stage it. It'll look like she and I were both attacked."

"A cover."

"Exactly. I'll tell the police we were ambushed at gunpoint by some anonymous scary killer played by you, to rob us or rape us or whatever, and while my best friend was murdered, I barely survived."

He felt himself nodding in agreement before he'd even agreed. This was her subtle charisma, like stepping into a river's current. It was easy to get caught up in the things she said. And sure enough, if you've decided you must murder your best friend, this had to be the cleanest and most elegant way to do it. Enter Jacob Herman to anonymously do the ugly work while leaving her, the sole survivor, with enough injuries to look innocent.

"It'll only work if I'm hurt badly enough," she said. "So you can't just give me a few cosmetic cuts and bruises. It'll have to be convincing. Real."

"I can shoot you up close and make sure the bullet grazes you."

"That's a *horrible* idea."

"Here's how it'll happen." Jacob aligned his index finger on the side of her face. "Scary killer executes you, but the bullet only grazes your cheekbone. He thinks you're dead, so he moves on and kills your best friend, too, and takes your purses and wallets and leaves. You crawl to safety. No detective will question your story. No woman on earth would be crazy enough to take a bullet burn to the face."

"Including me."

"Just let it marinate."

It was fun to sit here with her and float hypotheticals, if only because what-ifs won't send you to prison. He was well aware of the risks.

"You'll wear gloves and boots," she said, "and a ski mask to cover your face and hair, so you don't leave anything for forensics to pick up. Nothing. Zero. Not a single skin flake or fiber. Whatever you wear, you'll burn. Do you understand? The cops will study the scene afterward, every centimeter of it. So there can be nothing connecting the murder to you, and *nothing* suggesting I had any knowledge of what was about to happen to her."

"I fully understand," Jacob said. "I've read a lot of detective novels."

"Not funny."

"I think I'm delightful."

"Not when you're stoned." She was thinking aloud, her mind buzzing with an altogether different high. "And to be safe, you and I don't know each other. None of my clothes can be in your trailer. None of my fingerprints. No texts, no emails, nothing that leaves an electronic trail. Police can look all that up, and as far as they'll know, you and I have never met, Jacob. I can't have them wondering who my secret boyfriend is."

"Can we still meet up?"

"Discreetly."

"Can we still bone?"

"Please stop making jokes."

"Remember, I haven't agreed to kill your friend yet."

She looked at him with clear eyes. "You will."

Somehow this felt like an insult to Jacob, a class thing, and he no longer felt much like joking. It was the quiet certainty in her voice. She knew damn well the power she held over him, how much money it was, how anyone would want it. Jacob had seen a man stripped and humiliated over a truck's catalytic converter.

On a clear night out in the Gypsum River valley, far from the power lines and radio towers, the sky is an ocean of stars. This place felt like an old world, still wild and full of secrets. His father had always told him they had Comanche blood.

The trailer hadn't changed since Jacob was a kid—he just towed it with his Jeep now instead of his dad's old truck. He used to spend entire summers in these forests with his dad, moving from plains to riverbank just like their ancestors. Salmon in July, whitetail in August. He'd learned how to tell time with shadows and the sun, which plants were edible, and the irreplaceable flavor of meat cooked over pinewood. One autumn Jacob remembered returning home to find his mother gone, her closet emptied. She'd left a window open somewhere and the entire house had been cold.

He eased back into his camping chair. "We're like Bonnie and Clyde."

"We're nothing like Bonnie and Clyde."

"I think we are."

"I swear to God, Jacob, when you say things like that, it makes me nervous about doing this with you."

He laughed. He loved to pick at her.

"We've already crossed a line," she added. "Even us talking about it, right now, makes it premeditation. That bumps it up to first degree."

He'd always believed you could look back on your life and identify the little hinges everything turned on. This conversation under the galaxies on the sandy bank of the Gypsum River was one of them. At the time he hadn't fully understood why they were targeting her best friend, and he honestly didn't care. There'd be time for questions later. It felt like the start of a science fiction book he'd read as a child, something wild, dark, exciting.

And dangerous.

Jacob wasn't that pizza-faced kid with a duffel bag full of Walmart buckshot anymore. Suicide by cop sounds romantic only when your teenage brain hasn't finished developing. "This friend of yours. You're sure she won't suspect a thing?"

"She trusts me."

"Will she try to fight me?"

"She's a hundred pounds."

"I'm just covering my bases," he said. "She lives in the city, right? So how will you get her to willingly go somewhere isolated enough for this? It can't just be some campground or bike trail. It has to be somewhere truly remote, where there's no way she can call for help. Lots of places sound remote in theory, but there's always a chance some random dipshit will hear a scream or a gunshot. Babygirl, if I'm going to do this for you, I need a controlled location that *guarantees* the three of us are alone, with one way in and one way out."

For a moment, she said nothing.

Then she plucked the joint from his fingers and took a long drag. She exhaled hot smoke into his face, and it curled over her lips like canine fangs.

"Jacob," she said, grinning. "Have you ever gone caving?"

"THE TALENTED ALLIE MERRITT," WASHINGTON SAYS. "WHAT CAN YOU tell me about her?"

Tess hesitates.

"Come on. Don't feel like you have to flatter her. You've known her since junior high. You lived with her family. You have to know where the bodies are buried. Who is Allie, really? Has she ever lied? Has she ever cheated on a test? Anything she's ever said to you that secretly disturbed you, maybe sent a chill down your spine?"

Tess doesn't blink. "Nothing."

"Any secret boyfriends Ethan doesn't know about?"

"She'd never."

"Any history of violence?"

"None." But then she reconsiders, a subtle doubt.

There it is.

"Except back in junior high," she remembers. "Allie split a guy's lip, but he deserved it."

"He bullied her?"

"He bullied me."

"So Allie can fight."

"Anyone can," Tess says, "if they're pushed hard enough."

And, of course, Allie isn't just anyone. She's worldly, intelligent, an enviably successful travel influencer, and apparently a crack shot with a handgun. She's also the target of an ongoing federal investigation—at this very moment, every transaction her personal business has made over the past five years is under a microscope.

Almost 50 percent of digital advertising is estimated to be wasted. Metrics are weightless and theoretical. Impressions can be faked. Tracking pixels can be spoofed. If you traffic the ad space or boost the social media deliverables yourself, as Allie does for her wide network of partners, it might be tantalizingly easy to take a client's payment while only telling them you're running their pre-roll or cobranded post. She'd reinvented herself from Alma to Allie, shedding her identity with apparent ease—to Jacob, was she *Babygirl*? What has she really been doing with *Keep Calm*, behind all the sponsored tropical trips?

"What about her moral character?"

"She's always been nice to me."

"Not what I asked."

"She was basically perfect."

"I'm sure her breath still stank in the morning." And, of course, no one should ever confuse being *nice* with being a *good person*.

A stillness falls over the room.

Washington's eldest son is forty now, but back when he was

in elementary school he'd had two teddy bear hamsters, littermates named after his favorite Nickelodeon cartoon. One night he came running into her bedroom, sobbing and red-faced with blood on his hands. He'd been crying too hard to speak. Without warning, Stimpy had chewed the flesh off Ren's skull.

Her husband hadn't known what to say. Honestly, neither did she. *They're animals,* she'd tried to rationalize. *Sometimes animals are just unpredictable.* She'd later learn online that hamsters can happily cohabitate for years before suddenly resorting to violence and even cannibalism. And, as she hadn't had the heart to tell her son, humans are just as capable of sudden, seemingly unmotivated, and self-defeating evil.

Tess shakes her head. "Allie's dead. I saw it happen."

"Memory can be unreliable, Tess."

The survivor shifts forward in her bed, her too-starchy sheets crinkling, her muscles tensing almost imperceptibly. Her gaze meets the detective's. "I know where you're going with this."

"Do you?"

"And I'm telling you, you've taken a wrong turn. Whatever the feds think they saw is a mistake. I lived with Allie and her family for years. I know her, maybe better than anyone. She wasn't a criminal. She wasn't leading some secret life under Ethan's nose. She was a genuinely good person." Tess is searching her memory for examples. "When . . . when we were younger we used to play this drinking game with her cousins called Changeling—"

Washington jots this down. "*Changeling?*"

"It's like a monster in disguise. And whoever is randomly selected to be the changeling has to play it cool and shift the blame onto someone else. And Allie always lost. Always. She was a terrible liar, and I could always read her like an X-ray. That's her flaw: she was too honest."

"Were you jealous of her?"

This catches Tess off guard. "Sometimes, sure."

"Her success?"

"Just . . . her."

"Her life?"

"The person she was. Completely fearless." Tess smiles wistfully. "I mean, she'd already died once before—what did she even have left to be afraid of? Nothing seemed to stop her. I used to think she was like a shark, like she'd die if she stopped moving. She could walk into a bar anywhere in the world without knowing a word of the local language and make friends. She could load her carry-on with two changes of clothes, her passport, and her toiletry bag and just *go*. The people she met, the places she wrote about—her life seemed too amazing to be real, like she was the main character in a movie." Tess shrugs, almost embarrassed. "I think that's why I finally broke down and agreed to go caving with her."

Washington narrows her eyes. "She asked you?"

"And I said yes because I wanted to break out of my comfort zone, to try something a little dangerous, to feel like Allie, maybe, for a few hours."

"That reminds me." The detective lifts a page. "When entering a cave, how many people do you need, at minimum, to make it a safe group?"

"I don't know."

"Guess."

"Two?"

"Three," Washington answers. "No fewer. So if someone falls off a rope or gets pinned by a big rock, one person can go to the surface and call for help while the other can stay with the injured person. Four people is better, but three is the absolute minimum. That's quoted directly from the National Speleological Society's website."

"I didn't know that."

"You wouldn't. But *Allie* would have."

Silence.

"And she took you, an amateur, alone into your first cave. She knew there'd be ropework involved, confined spaces, dangerous falls, and she still declined to bring a third person along for safety. Why would she do that?"

Tess sighs. She wants to argue, but she has no answer.

Allie is charming and charismatic, but those who suffer from antisocial personality disorder often are. They can learn to navigate social interactions like any other complex system, memorizing the accepted dance moves and drawing upon their often high intelligence to mimic and persuade. It's been said that one in every hundred individuals is a sociopath. And, despite decades of negative stereotyping, most sociopaths and psychopaths aren't even criminals at all. Many are aided by their natural antisocial traits to become high achievers in sales, the legal profession, and executive business management.

But . . . why would a woman who's visited six continents and works her own self-designed dream job wake up one morning and decide to murder her best friend? In Washington's experience, the people who possess the most tend to also be the most afraid of losing it. Tess worked part-time as Allie's assistant—could she have witnessed something damning in the books somewhere? Maybe Allie paid Jacob to murder Tess as a cover-up. And then there's Allie's mysterious recent behavior to consider—chief of all her trip to Costa Rica, cut conspicuously short.

"What happened to her in Costa Rica?"

"She wouldn't tell me."

"You never pressed?"

"I respected her privacy," Tess says. "She always respected mine."

Stymied silence.

But the pieces are all there, Washington knows.

The survivor looks uneasy, her face going pale. It's understandably sickening to consider your best friend might have tried to have you murdered—and if so, she's now lost Allie in two distinct ways. The shock and grief must be unfathomable. Washington leans forward to squeeze Tess's wrist. Her flesh is soft, her lacerations still scabbing.

We'll solve this, you and I.

Together.

Tess bites her lip. "I saw her die."

"Maybe you saw what she wanted you to see."

"I *know* her."

"My old partner used to say that no one ever really knows anyone," Washington says. "It sounds nihilistic, but it's true. It's a reality of being human. You just have to accept it and think of people in layers, like a Russian nesting doll. We all have exterior versions of ourselves, polite and polished and professional. The whole world knows that layer of Allie, the smiling, globe-trotting influencer. And there are interior layers, the parts of ourselves we only show our closest friends and family, and then even deeper, the secret person nested inside. The true self. Who we are in the dark, when no one's looking and the lights are out."

Tess nods.

"So, who was Allie in the dark?"

25

JACOB WOULD NEVER ADMIT IT, BUT HE'D ALWAYS BEEN A LITTLE afraid of her. It was in her eyes, maybe. The muscles in her face smiled and smirked, but those eyes never lost their clarity or focus, searching, scanning, judging.

I'm a bad person, she'd sometimes lament. *I think something is wrong with me. Like I'm broken, missing a part everyone has.*

It was true that his girlfriend could be a bit of a basket case, moody and obsessive, deeply lonely inside her own mind. Most guys would find this exhausting, but most people are boring. Jacob loved her for her hidden complexities, and when she suffered from these spells of melancholy, he'd always reassure her with the same monologue: that *everyone* is a bad person. Everyone. It's the way of things. The natural order is built on survival, self-interest, discharging strength. This wasn't quite Nietzsche but more of a Jacob Herman original—he'd always invite her to think of the most altruistic people in the world: the charity workers, preachers, teachers, and volunteers. They're generous, yes, but only because doing the right thing makes them feel good. They're still satisfying a need like anyone else. Selfless people are selfish, too. They just get off differently.

I'm a bad person, she'd repeat.

Maybe. He'd kiss the top of her head. *But you're* my *bad person.*

Earlier today he'd been thinking about this conversation while he spent almost an hour following the two women into the cave.

He'd listened to them prod and encourage each other, the rattling of their gear and shared water bottles, their laughter ringing off wet limestone. It had all sounded so authentic. He could never occupy two headspaces like that, smiling and bonding with your best friend while secretly luring her to the site of her planned death.

And now that plan had badly deteriorated.

"This is bad." Jacob winced as he peeled off his glove. "She's too far down."

"So follow her," she said.

"My hand is wrecked."

"She's half your size."

"She's tough."

"You have a gun."

"I can't rope down there *and* hold a gun with one hand." He pointed over the edge. "I'll be vulnerable. If she jumps me again, she'll win."

Those clear eyes glared, focused enough to melt steel. Babygirl was used to getting her way, like she had all her privileged life—but she was also cunning enough to know when to pivot. She never committed to losing battles.

"So we change the plan, then." She stood up and paced around the jagged, plantlike rock structures. "We just camp out here, in the cave. We wait for her to die down there. She has, what, three days until she dehydrates?"

"There's water down there."

"Can she drink it?"

"The microbes might give her the shits, but it'll keep her alive."

"We'll seal her down there, then." She pointed at the ramped slope leading back up the Drainpipe, the peanut-butter-colored rock glistening wetly in her headlamp. "We'll stack every boulder we can find and block it. She'll starve to death."

"That'll take weeks."

"I know."

"We *don't have* weeks. We have two, three days at most." Jacob wished he hadn't already smashed the two phones—they were committed to their alibis now. "And even if we had more time, this is a popular cave. We can't just leave her. More groups will come by. They'll see a big stack of rocks and wonder what happened."

She'd gone blank. Out of ideas.

The true danger was now sinking in. What would happen when the next group of cavers arrived here with their ropes and jingling gear, trogged up and ready to explore the Devil's Staircase? How long could his Green Ridge cover story hold these new witnesses back without raising suspicion? The trapped woman's screams might echo up the tunnel. It would take only a single 911 call.

Cave water dripped somewhere, a slow metronome. *Tick. Tick.*

Something about this place made Jacob viscerally uncomfortable. More tendrils seemed to gradually sprout at their feet as they spoke. The walls and ceilings were covered with wriggling creatures all frozen into stone, blazing red in his headlamp like a life-sized Hieronymus Bosch painting. He wanted to leave. Badly.

"She's your friend, Babygirl."

"Stop calling me that."

"I'm just saying, maybe you should be the one to—"

"I can't touch her." She jabbed a gloved finger into his chest, her voice a breathy hiss. "Everything here has to show she was murdered by someone else, someone bigger and stronger than me. I can't have any trace of it on my body. No gunshot residue, no suspicious bruises. None of her blood. Every inch of what happens here needs to be airtight."

He knew they were a hell of a long way from *airtight*. At this point, was it even possible to cover their tracks? He'd scattered

Razor Alley with brass casings and bullet fragments and even some of his blood. The unplanned chase could have already left behind something damning, something that put Jacob Herman squarely in the sights of investigators.

"You know her inside and out, right?" He nodded toward the edge, keeping his voice down. "Why don't you just try and talk her into coming back up? Drop a rope down, feed her some horseshit about how you miraculously survived the bad guy's attack and how you're pretty sure he's given up and gone home. Then you'll guide her up the rope to us, and I'll be waiting right here." With his good hand, he made a stabbing motion.

"Won't work. She's too smart."

"Or you could make a deal with her."

"We're past that."

Both sides of this standoff were working against the clock—so whose time would run out first? Arguably, the desperate woman cornered at the bottom of the underground pit might even be in the better position. It made him sick.

The droplets kept counting. *Tick. Tick.*

"Whatever." She pouted. "I'm sick of waiting up here. This has gone on for hours already. I'm sorry you're hurt, Jacob. I'm sorry she kicked your ass, but you need to put on your big-boy pants and go down there and shoot her in the head."

She didn't know yet.

And he didn't want to say it. But he couldn't hide it any longer.

She sensed his discomfort. "What?"

He'd been avoiding this conversation. Saying it aloud would make it real, a solid and objective problem. For the past twenty minutes he'd searched every inch of Razor Alley with his headlamp and flashlight. Behind every radiant growth of alien rock, inside every crevice, under every shadow with rising dread. He couldn't find it.

"I dropped my gun," he said.

"You *what*?"

"When her rope broke my fingers, it ripped the gun out of my hand. I know it landed somewhere. But it's . . . it's not up here."

Her mouth opened. "Where is it, then?"

Jacob pointed over the edge, into the darkness below. "With her."

The more Jacob thought about it, the worse their situation was. It felt like an impossible riddle: *How do you kill a woman who's wedged herself hundreds of feet down a tiny crawlspace?*

He sighed.

And she stole your gun?

With that gutsy rope stunt, she'd managed to both injure Jacob and disarm him. He had to assume the firearm was in her hands now. Confronting her directly was out of the question. Forget scorpions in a bottle—she'd outwitted him and turned this into a true stalemate. She couldn't climb the slippery walls of the Chimney to escape, and Jacob didn't dare go down to face her.

Both sides were now paralyzed, unable to make a move.

"Whatever happens, we can't leave this cave until she's dead," Jacob said. "If she survives to talk to the police, you and I go to prison."

"That won't happen."

"So how do we fix this?"

"I'm thinking."

"How do we kill someone we can't even reach?"

"I'm *thinking*," she said. "Let me think."

She was always thinking. That was her problem. Even the day they'd met, when Jacob first spied her across the tiny margarita bar by the airport, she'd been absorbed in her laptop and oblivious to the world. Of course he'd noticed her legs first. He'd glimpsed palm trees on her computer screen and wondered what she did for work—it looked like something called *Keep Calm*, involving vacations or travel? It seemed glamorous. He'd wanted to talk to her, but he hadn't known how. She wasn't just out of his league; they weren't even playing the same sport. What could he possibly offer her? And apparently he wasn't the only one who'd noticed those legs—some drunk guy in motorcycle leathers took the liberty of sitting by her. She kept politely declining his advances. He kept pressing. At one point he waved his hand in front of her laptop screen, trying to get her attention. Finally she'd paid her tab and left her beer half full.

Motorcycle Guy slurped the rest of it and followed her into the parking lot. She speed-walked. Then she ran. By her car, he grabbed her wrist.

She screamed.

The man's exact intentions remain unknown to this day, because Jacob Herman had silently followed and delivered a single, precise haymaker to the back of his skull. It's actually possible to punch someone in the head so hard that an eyeball pops out. This is a fact supported by science and confirmed by his own firsthand (*pun intended*) experience. The physics of it are sickening and so much worse than he'd intended. Motorcycle Guy was instantly incapacitated, crying and cupping his hands to his face with one soggy red eyeball bulging from its socket.

Every great love story begins somewhere, right? Jacob wasn't stupid. He knew he wasn't a catch in the conventional sense. But he was a type of man from a bygone era, rare now—a man who could get things done, a man who could hunt food and make fire with only sticks. Enlightened liberals liked to pretend men like Jacob weren't needed any longer, right up until the electricity went out and the supply chains failed. He understood his value.

Even now, who *really* needed who?

"You're in over your head, Babygirl." It felt good to unload a few things. "You always were from the very start, because you can't stand to get your hands dirty. You need someone else to do the real work for you. You don't want to see it happen or even listen to it. You just hang back in the shadows and hide."

She stared at the ground, still lost in thought. Ignoring him.

"Go on. Say something."

Nothing.

Jacob winced as he wrapped his fingers with medical tape. This was, romantically enough, the second time he'd broken his hand for her. His ring finger was merely dislocated—he'd already managed to reset it with a rubbery, eye-watering pop—but his pinkie finger was clearly fractured. The rope had hooked under his fingers when it tore the gun away, peeling them ninety degrees backward. His entire hand thrummed with radiating pain, almost electric, like his bones were vibrating on a strange frequency.

Christ, he didn't want to be down here, squatting in a gloomy, damp place that looked like the inside of Cthulhu's asshole and bickering with his girlfriend. He didn't even care about the thirty grand anymore. Money is only time, after all, and time was running out.

"Will you please say—"

Something, he was saying, when she leaned in to kiss him, the unexpected stir of her tongue on his lips. It startled him, like touching a snake. She'd always thrived on surprise.

"Jacob," she said, "I know how we'll kill her."

26

"COULD YOU HEAR ANY VOICES ABOVE YOU?" WASHINGTON ASKS. "Arguments? Planning their next attack?"

Tess shakes her head.

"Any clues at all?"

"Nothing."

I'm reaching, the detective knows. The bottom of the pit was forty feet down, and the killers would've known to hush their voices.

Tess had managed to defeat Jacob in a hand-to-hand fight, but now she faced new and urgent problems. The first was hypothermia: immersed in cold water, a human can suffer heart and respiratory failure within an hour. She needed to keep her body out of the pool or she wouldn't survive long enough to face the next threat.

Washington recalls the incident commander's grim text, now hours ago.

We're losing her.

One relentless challenge after another.

The bottom of the Chimney breaks out into a few tertiary chambers with just enough space to slither between hundred-ton boulders or even stand uncomfortably to let her soaked clothes dry. Maybe she'd eaten a granola bar for some quick energy. With every passing minute, the killer—or *killers*, plural—plotted their next move.

Escape was impossible. Tess was twenty stories underground with a broken headlamp. She'd lost her knife and flashlight. The only light source remaining was her pack of emergency glowsticks. In the chemical green light, her exploration of the lower chambers would have been methodical and dangerous.

"Then," Tess says, "I found his gun."

Washington perks up.

Jacob's Colt semiautomatic was sturdy and powerful—the 1911 is arguably one of the finest handguns ever designed—but the single-stack magazine held only seven rounds. How many had he fired at her already?

"I hadn't touched a gun in years," Tess says. "Not since Allie's dad took us to the shooting range when we were teenagers."

"How many rounds were left?"

"I . . . found the button to eject the clip."

"And?"

She shakes her head.

It feels almost cruel. After hours of fighting for her life, the embattled survivor had finally managed to turn the tables, broken the killer's hand, and taken control of his gun—only to find it empty and useless. And even if it had been loaded, a gun would've realistically been little help in her situation. To shoot your enemy, you must first *see* them. Tess was sealed deep underground at the bottom of an unscalable pit. Jacob would have known to keep his distance from the edge and not expose himself.

She was sealed off with an empty gun. All she could do was wait.

Washington realizes Tess has fallen silent, disconnected. Something seems to be weighing on her. "Are you all right?"

"I'm fine."

"It's okay if you need a sec."

"I just . . ." The survivor chews her scabbed lip, and Washington senses their earlier conversation isn't quite finished. "Have you ever killed anyone?"

The question is startling in its bluntness.

She considers her answer before she speaks. "Not in the way you mean."

"How so?"

"It means I've never shot anyone before. But I've made mistakes that have arguably contributed to people's deaths. And more times than I can remember, I've sat in a room with someone and pretended to be their best friend while helping them end their own lives in every way that matters."

"Is it satisfying?"

"It used to be."

"And now?"

Washington exhales and massages her sore knuckles. "When my phone rings, it's because someone's daughter has been found half buried in the woods or someone's elderly parents were shot to death in their bed. And the best-case scenario, the happiest news I might hope to tell a grieving family, is that we think we've caught the bad guy. That's it. That's the most I can offer them. When someone loses their life, I come in to balance the equation by ruining the life of whoever took it, and then I move on. Punishing someone . . . well, you quickly learn it isn't the same thing as saving someone."

"Maybe you are, though," Tess says. "Maybe by catching someone who's likely to re-offend, you're really saving the *next* person."

Washington smiles. But platitudes don't help, and Tess can see it.

"Why do you still do it, then?"

It's a good question. Her husband, long retired from his university job, has asked her this. So have her four adult children. When her grandkids are old enough, they'll ask, too. Why get up at five or earlier every morning on arthritic knees and wear a gun? Why continue to work in a high-pressure, emotionally corrosive profession even as she feels herself slowing down?

Apple. Chair. Umbrella.

She knows her cognitive fitness test is a time bomb. Whatever the results were, they'll find their way to her lieutenant's desk, and she'll soon be having long-avoided conversations about lightened duties and end dates. In another year, the department's mandatory retirement age will forcibly expel her anyway. What can she possibly do?

Somewhere down the hall, a patient coughs. An ugly, wet hacking.

"The situation looked hopeless," Tess says. "But I realized . . . it wasn't."

"Why not?"

"I remembered something from Allie's little story that morning. A small detail at the time, but now critically important. A hundred years ago when they were rescuing the trapped prospector, she described how they'd crawled down to help him from both sides. One team rappelled down the Chimney. The other went another way."

"Meaning?"

Tess smiles. "There's *another* way."

Yes.

"From where I was stuck, there still had to be a second route to the surface, to daylight. It's the only way Allie's story made spatial sense."

Washington nods.

Tess's instincts were, once again, dead-on. The eventual rescue effort would follow similar routes through the intricate labyrinth. Even without a map, she could surely find her way back to the Upper Vault and, eventually, the surface. It was simply a process of following the moving air and eliminating dead ends.

But first, she would need to traverse an infamous passage.

"And"—her voice hardens—"Worse Than Death would take me there."

The rest of it lingers in the air, unspoken.

If I could survive it.

Washington knows the dynamics of the standoff were about to change. "While you formed this new plan, the other team was making moves, too."

The other team. Like it was a football game.

"We know Jacob spent some time up there in Razor Alley splinting his fingers, treating his wounds, taking stock of his supplies. And then he seemed to get a new idea—or someone gave it to him. He did something unexpected."

Tess blinks. "What?"

"He went back up to the surface, got in his Jeep, and drove away."

Leaving Tess alone inside the cave was a massive risk—unless, of course, Jacob had left his accomplice behind to guard the entrance.

"Where did he go?"

"A nearby town called Flour Gold."

Flour Gold has a population of fewer than a thousand. Being the closest settlement to the cave and having both a fire station and enough flat ground to land a helicopter, it would eventually serve as an unofficial base camp for the rescue effort. Motel 6 would become a communications center. The Sasquatch Diner would generously deliver Styrofoam containers full of hash browns and eggs. Residents would donate their four-wheel drives and help ferry supplies and personnel to the cave. For hours today an entire town held its breath, everyone equally invested in the rescue of this poor, embattled woman deep underground. But that operation wouldn't begin for at least six more hours.

Tess appears unsettled. "Are you sure he drove into town?"

"We have him on security camera. Twice."

"That's strange."

"Why?"

"Letting himself get caught on video just seems . . ." She shrugs. "Sloppy, I guess."

"Everyone gets videotaped every day." Washington hates to give Jacob Herman credit, but there was a clear logic at work. "He would've been just one guy in a thousand filling his tank on some gas station camera. It would only matter if we already knew who we were looking for. In other words, Tess, if you *survived* to tell your story."

"So he stopped for gas."

"Yes."

Tess tilts her head. "And . . . his second appearance?"

"Admittedly, this one is different."

"How?"

At the end of the town's main drag stands Flour Gold Hardware, a water-damaged building with a gravel parking lot and a QAnon sign in the window. After questioning the manager this morning—a bit of a moron, to be polite—Washington had pulled footage from the store's single interior camera. It confirmed Jacob Herman entered the store just after four p.m., noticeably hiding his splinted fingers in his pocket. Even in grainy playback he'd looked like hell, sweaty and wincing. He'd avoided both clerks and walked straight to the lawn and garden section in the back. He'd known exactly what he was there for.

A weird shopping list, the manager had said. *I mean, really weird.* And it would seem to be, unless you knew what came next.

"With cash, he bought a wrench and two rolls of heat-resistant tape," Washington says. "And every garden hose they had in stock."

27

I KNOW HOW WE'LL KILL HER.

Her voice echoed in Jacob's mind as he drove back. Usually while off-roading he liked to sing along to oldies channels or chat up truckers on his CB, but this time he drove in anxious silence. He chewed aspirin while the Jeep's shocks rolled and bounced. Every motion vibrated the broken bones in his hand.

It'll work, she'd assured him. *It's certain to work.*

For all the things that had gone catastrophically wrong today, at least the cave was suitably isolated. The nearest dirt road was a fifty-minute hike, and the nearest paved highway was considerably farther. Even with his four-wheeling beast of a Jeep, his little shopping trip into Flour Gold had eaten up almost two hours. His face and license plate had been captured on at least two cameras back there, too. He didn't like it, but he'd had no choice. Like any survival situation, every action was now a trade-off. Lighting a fire costs matches and fuel. Boiling potable water costs time. Building shelter costs calories. You make your decisions and commit to them. Let fear paralyze you, and you're already bug food.

When he returned to the Devil's Staircase, the sun was low in the sky. This time he didn't bother hiding his Jeep in the brush by the streambed. He gunned the engine and drove right up the hillside. One more good rock climb.

At the cave's entrance he saw Babygirl seated on a mossy boulder with her legs crossed in a meditative pose, looking a bit too relaxed for guard duty. Jacob set the brake and stepped out. "There's no chance she can climb out, right?"

"Zero."

"You're sure?"

"It's almost fifty feet straight up. The walls are slick as ice. *Yes*, Jacob, I'm sure."

"And Worse Than Death?"

"Not an option for her." She didn't elaborate further, like it was a secret. "Trust me."

Jacob wasn't so sure. He'd already gotten his fingers bent backward today by a skinny little thing he'd thought he could handle. He wouldn't make the mistake of underestimating their target—never again—and he wouldn't trust she was dead until he saw a body.

He opened his Jeep's back door and showed his haul. The hoses looked like neatly coiled snakes: three hundred-footers, two fifty-footers, and three twenty-five-footers. Mismatching brands, some green, some brown and black. He hoped they would be enough.

She chewed her lip. "How many feet, total?"

"Four hundred and seventy-five."

She flattened her paper map against the door and traced with a gloved finger. She was checking the distances, adding up surveyed measurements. "That should reach down to the Drainpipe, at least. Maybe farther."

"Far enough?"

She refolded the map. "It'll have to be."

First, Jacob would remove his Jeep's catalytic converter and affix a hose directly to the exhaust manifold. Then they would uncoil the eight hoses as far into the Devil's Staircase as their lengths would allow, joining each one end to end with airtight seals of heat-resistant tape. He'd check every foot for kinks or leaks. Lastly, he'd return to the surface and start the vehicle's engine, flooding the enclosed space with suffocating exhaust.

The air would turn to poison.

Same basic concept as a gopher bomb. As a kid, Jacob remembered helping his dad asphyxiate pests with a hose fitted to his truck's tailpipe (*Easier than the .22,* he'd say with a wink). This cave was much larger than any rodent warren, of course, but Jacob could run his engine for hours. He had a jerrican in the back, and he could make multiple trips to Flour Gold to refuel. He could take all night, or longer.

It'd been a hell of a day, no question. Their victim had escaped her preplanned death, fighting back with rope and momentum and startling grit. It didn't matter that Jacob was near certain he'd already fired his Colt 1911 to empty—they had to assume she had a loaded gun with at least one round remaining. She'd dug herself into the earth like a tick, deeper than Jacob could follow her. She'd made herself untouchable, or so it seemed.

No one is untouchable, Babygirl had whispered in his ear. *We can't follow her down there, but we don't have to. We'll suffocate her instead. We'll kill her from up here without touching her, without even leaving a mark on her body.*

All from the turn of a key.

I told you. It'll work.

She really did scare him sometimes. He never would have imagined a gopher bomb on such a scale, but she was a creature of terrifying ingenuity. She could think laterally around any problem. Jacob knew every inch of her body, but he couldn't begin to comprehend the things that happened inside her head. She was a master of the oblique solution, the kill without contact.

He was starting to feel better.

"Okay," he said. "Let's gas the bitch."

TESS WAS RUNNING OUT OF TIME, WASHINGTON KNOWS.

Her only route to the surface led through an infamously narrow passage called Worse Than Death. But that wasn't her only problem.

"I kept looking." Tess studies the hospital room's pastel walls. "Everywhere was a dead end. Every side tunnel led nowhere. I found a smaller chamber that turned into a low crawl, but a few feet in, it shrank too tight to fit and I had to backtrack. I kept feeling with my hands in the dark, checking every inch with my glowstick. But there was no breeze. Nowhere to go."

With her index finger, she traces a nervous triangle on the tray.

Slowly accelerating.

"I know . . . I *knew* I had to be missing something. I was positive the way into Worse Than Death was down there with me somewhere, but I couldn't find it. No cracks to squeeze through on my knees, no crevices or secret gaps. Just cold, wet rock. Everywhere."

Up on the surface, the killers were racing to implement their deadly plan. Funneling the internal combustion engine's exhaust down into the cave would rapidly choke out the available oxygen—but the true danger Tess faced wasn't asphyxiation.

It was the carbon monoxide.

With every breath the odorless, tasteless "suicide gas" would accumulate in her bloodstream, bonding and adhering to her cell walls. If red blood cells are essentially buses transporting oxygen throughout the body, carbon monoxide is an imposter quietly sneaking aboard to steal seats, and every seat taken is one fewer for life-sustaining oxygen. You may feel like you're breathing normally, but you're actually suffocating inside your own body. Modern automobiles are built with emission control devices to convert carbon monoxide into less toxic components, but Jacob had been aware of this and knew to remove his Jeep's catalytic converter. In such a tightly confined space as the Chimney, the invisible gas would reach lethal levels within minutes. In high enough concentrations, just a few breaths can be fatal.

Washington knows this firsthand.

The day after her very first wellness check on that kind elderly man who showed her his beautifully restored classic F-series, young Deputy Washington was dispatched to conduct another wellness check. It was to the same address, presumably called by the same concerned family member. She remembers climbing those concrete steps under the same blue sky and ringing the same doorbell—but this time, no one answered. The interior lights were off, and the windows were opaque with a sooty haze. She broke a window. The acrid air inside made her gag. Every room was smoky and dim, but she found the old man's naked body on his living room floor, his arms folded over his chest like a mummy, his hairless head reclined on two pillows. In his garage he'd chosen to leave his classic truck idling overnight with every window and door shut.

She remembers hearing her own dizzied voice echo back at her on the radio, coughing as the sirens wailed closer. *I dragged him outside. No pulse. I don't . . . I don't understand.*

The corpse's skin had been colored with what the paramedics called *blood livores*. To her inexperienced eyes it had looked like a full-body sunburn, covering every inch from his sunken chest to his ankles. Cherry-red livores are a common postmortem indicator of carbon monoxide poisoning, but somehow this was worse than any photograph she'd seen before or since. The man's flesh was colored so vibrantly he'd looked like a cartoon character, painted as Technicolor red as the old truck that killed him, silly in a nightmarish way. And in the shock of the moment, of realizing she'd spoken to this man hours before he killed himself and missed every sign, Deputy Washington hadn't even realized how much carbon monoxide she'd inhaled herself, until she collapsed on the lawn beside his body. The paramedics had to take her, too.

From sixty seconds inside that house.

Just a few breaths.

"There was nowhere to go," Tess remembers. "It was like I was buried alive and Worse Than Death didn't exist at all. I was starting to panic. I lost control and screamed at the walls around me. And I threw my glowstick."

Her voice lowers to a whisper.

"It landed in the water and started to sink."

Silence.

"And . . . it confirmed my hunch. Because the green light kept sinking, sinking, until it was almost completely gone under the dark water. But it stopped at the bottom, at the deepest part of the pool, and it illuminated a tiny black hole in the bedrock. Maybe a foot and a half wide, at most. Barely the size of an air vent."

Washington feels a growing coldness inside her chest.

"It was right there all along." Tess exhales. "When I'd first landed down there, I had no idea I was treading water a few feet above it."

Worse Than Death was *underwater*.

The maze of ten-inch squeezes and bone-dislocating bends is already infamous—but with recent rain and snowmelt coming off the mountains, the entire lower crawlspace was also submerged in frigid water. Impossible to survive.

"I was trapped."

28

"WHAT IF THE HOSES MELT?"

"They won't," Jacob told her as he worked.

Removing the Jeep's catalytic converter had taken longer than he'd expected. The bolts were all caked with crud, and his right hand was splinted into a clumsy lobster claw. But he managed. He remembered that thief who'd tried to remove this very same part from his dad's truck over twenty years ago. Was the guy still alive? Probably not, but Jacob hoped so as he wrapped loops of adhesive tape around the exhaust manifold to join the first hose. Every seal would need to be airtight and resist several hundred degrees of sustained heat.

He stood up and pointed at the stack of hoses. "Help me carry those."

"I can't touch anything."

"You have gloves."

"Rubber leaves prints, too. And they can be matched." She looked at him, her eyebrows raised like he was five years old. "You're the bad guy, remember?"

Jesus Christ, Babygirl.

For all her ingenuity, she was still hopelessly deluded. Even after everything that had gone wrong today, she still believed it was somehow possible to walk into a police station and spin her best friend's death as a random attack. How, exactly, would she explain a daylong standoff, several hundred feet of garden hose, and a murder by carbon monoxide poisoning? She was a hell of a gifted liar, maybe the best he'd ever seen, but this was simply impossible.

"Fine." He was too exhausted to argue, and he'd learned when to simply let her be. Without her help, he'd just make multiple trips.

Maybe people like her could will the universe into rearranging itself if they wanted it badly enough. She'd certainly succeeded at turning *Keep Calm* into her own secret digital piggy bank. But Jacob worked with his hands. He traded in real things, sweat and blisters and sleeping hard. He *used* his body. Sometimes he found her unsexy, even pathetic in a childlike way, her too-small features and her soft hands and her stolen, pampered life. She'd seen enough of the world to have her opinions, too, especially about poor people. She'd go on unprompted tangents about how wealthy places were unquestionably better: better houses, better bars and food, better people. She'd list off all the things she'd hated about her childhood, the bargain-bin DVD stands and potholed parking lots and wilted grocery produce. She loathed how stupid poor people were, how proud they were of their own stupidity, how they'd vote for any politician who spoke their stupid, simple language. Get her going and she'd never stop.

Jacob looped the first hoses under his arm and unspooled them foot by foot into the darkness. He retraced the cave's familiar tunnels and took shortcuts wherever possible—the Upper Vault, the fixed rope at the Great Wall, the smothering hands-and-knees crawl of the Drainpipe—and stopped to join each threaded aluminum socket with more generous loops of tape. He laid the hoses carefully, ensuring they wouldn't rub against any sharp rocks.

After an hour of sweaty work in the red glow of his headlamp, he was midway down the Drainpipe and attaching his last remaining hose. This daisy chain of death ended just a few feet short of the Chimney's edge, just forty feet above the captive woman.

"Perfect." He couldn't have done it better if he'd measured it.

This was far from the clean little murder he'd been promised weeks ago under a starry sky, but there was a blunt-force certainty to this new plan that Jacob liked. This tough, resourceful woman had escaped their ambush, dodged his bullets, and turned the cave's hostile geography against him. But she still needed to breathe like any other creature.

Everything left here would be forensic evidence. He needed to find his first aid kit and recover his pack. As he crouched under tendrils of wormy rock to gather his things, he couldn't resist shouting into the darkness: "*Plot twist*, bitch. My Jeep is parked up top with a full tank and five hundred feet of brand-new garden hose. All I have to do is turn a key."

God, it felt good to hold the power again.

"But you never know, right?" He held back a guttural laugh. "Maybe, if you apologize, I'll still change my mind."

"SO," WASHINGTON SUMMARIZES, "YOU WERE CORNERED AT THE BOTtom of a deep vertical pit, twenty stories underground."

"Yes."

"You were injured and hypothermic."

"Yes."

"He was about to flood the cave with carbon monoxide."

"Yes."

"And all you had left was"—she lifts a page on her notepad—"three glowsticks, a water bottle, a granola bar, and an empty gun."

Tess hesitates. "Not exactly."

"What do you mean?"

"There's . . . something I didn't mention."

Washington leans in, now curious.

"I realized I'd forgotten something," Tess says. "Guns were always Allie's thing, not mine. It'd been years since her dad took us to the range together, and I'd forgotten almost everything. But one little detail had stuck in my mind." She smiles, a dawning realization. "When I'd picked up his gun, I'd checked the clip for bullets and found it empty."

But . . .

There are many public misconceptions around firearms—like Tess's common error in calling a magazine a *clip*—and Washington knows a semiautomatic's operation by muscle memory. Some safety fundamentals are drilled in so deeply that they can never leave your brain, no matter how many years it's been. A magazine can be empty, the magazine itself can even be removed, but the weapon is still live—because if there's one final cartridge left, it simply *won't be in the magazine anymore*.

The detective grins. "You didn't clear the chamber, did you?"

29

"I AIMED STRAIGHT UP." TESS DEMONSTRATES BY LEANING BACK IN her hospital bed, both bandaged hands clasped. "I waited for him to expose himself over the edge."

It was far from a sure thing.

She had one bullet. She couldn't afford to miss. And she'd already admitted that she hadn't fired a gun since she was a teenager, long enough to forget the very fundamentals of how a semiautomatic firearm operates.

The pit was over forty feet deep. Hitting a man-sized target at such a distance was reasonable enough for an amateur—back in her deputy days, Washington used to drill grapefruit-sized groups into the x-ring at nearly twice that distance, before her vision went to hell—but other factors would have made the shot exponentially more challenging. The angle was steep. The lighting was poor. The gunshot would be eardrum rupturing.

It would be a difficult shot. But not impossible.

"I scooped up mud and stuffed it in my ears to plug them. I tried to remember the basics Allie's dad taught us all those years ago. Focusing on the front sight. Squeezing the trigger gently, letting the shot surprise you so you won't flinch. I waited."

Washington holds her breath.

"But"—Tess deflates—"it didn't matter."

"Why not?"

"He never showed himself. He didn't peek over the edge once."

Of course. Jacob wasn't stupid.

He'd known not to expose even an inch of himself. He'd already won. He was only finishing his cleanup; he was minutes from ending her life, and this miraculous final bullet in the weapon's chamber was just another false hope.

"I tried to trick him into showing himself," Tess says. "But it didn't work."

"IF YOU TURN THAT KEY," JACOB HEARD HER SHOUT, "YOU'LL BE MAKing a mistake."

"Oh, yeah?"

"A big one."

He wouldn't fall for it. He knew the trapped woman was changing tactics now, trying to bait him. He imagined her down there with his own gun in her muddy hands, her finger curled around the trigger, aiming her Hail Mary shot. Could an amateur really hit him at forty feet? Hell, anyone can get lucky.

He forced a laugh. "You must think I'm stupid."

"I do."

"I missed our talks."

"I didn't."

"Why not shoot yourself instead? Save me the gas money." He scooped up loose ointments and wipe packets and stuffed them back inside the first aid kit. He squashed it with his knee so the zipper closed. "I'll admit, you've got me thinking maybe I picked the wrong horse. You're a hell of a fighter. You don't give up. You would've made a nice babygirl, I think. I shouldn't say this in case she's listening, but maybe even an upgrade from the current model."

"Hard pass."

"I bet I could make your toes curl."

"I'd rather die."

"That's the plan."

"You're making a mistake, Jacob."

The woman's tone was strangely confident. Derisive even, like she knew something he didn't. And hearing his name echo up from the blackness gave his stomach a sickly swirl. But he ignored the feeling. It was time to wrap this up.

He slung his pack over his shoulder. He'd made the arduous crawl to the surface several times today, but this would thankfully be the last. "I promise it won't hurt," he shouted down to her. "I know you won't see it this way, but carbon monoxide is a gift in disguise, practically euthanasia. My old man would've loved to go like this. Just nestle yourself into a cozy spot down there, breathe it in, let yourself fall asleep, and you won't even—"

"Remember when I gave you my memory card?"

He froze.

An icy pit opened up in his stomach.

"That was just a spare." The woman's voice hardened. "I still have the footage. I've had it this entire time. I even have your *face* on video."

The pit grew.

"And if you start that engine, I'll die with my footage. The cave will be full of exhaust, too dangerous to enter for days or weeks or maybe even longer. You don't have the equipment to reach my body all the way down here—but I'm guessing search crews will, won't they? It's simple: if you kill me, you'll perfectly preserve my video for the cops."

His knees turned to slush. He had to sit down.

“Go ahead.” The voice below shivered with laughter. “Turn the key.”

She outsmarted us.

Again.

“I hope you got a good deal on all those garden hoses, *asshole*.”

30

JACOB HAD NEVER SEEN HIS GIRLFRIEND SIT SO STILL BEFORE. SHE'D entered a state of intense concentration, no calories wasted, her body's every nonessential function suspended. Every resource diverted to that million-dollar brain.

Finally, she spoke. "The camera is waterproof, right?"

"Probably."

"What about the memory card?"

"Those can last for years. Even underwater."

She said nothing.

Their biggest threat today was never the survivor herself—it was the camera mounted to her helmet. Jacob imagined the inevitable search parties converging on this cave, rescuers finding the low tunnels choked with toxic gas. They'd send in specialists kitted out with rebreathers and oxygen tanks, and ultimately they'd find the woman's body with her GoPro in her stiff hands or a swallowed memory card in her stomach. On it, a perfect record of the day's events. And a last laugh frozen on her purple lips.

The sun was low now, blazing like an orange fire behind the trees. Babygirl squinted directly into it, refusing to look at him. "You said you tricked her into giving it up. Hours ago."

"It was blank."

"You didn't watch it?"

"I didn't know she had more than one."

"Verify everything, Jacob."

Verify everything. Her stupid childish mantra.

"We can't leave without her camera." Her voice was low, perfectly controlled. "If that footage stays with her body, we're both going to prison."

"I'm aware of that."

"I am *not* going to prison, Jacob. Try talking to her again."

"She'll never give us the camera."

"Then threaten her."

"With what?" He hurled his first aid kit at the ground. "She knows that footage is the only thing keeping her alive. Whether she lives or dies, she still wins."

She wins. God, he hated saying it.

This bitch was supposed to be unprepared and oblivious, walked into an ambush by her trusted best friend. Instead the situation had devolved into a total soup sandwich. And Jacob knew he needed to be honest with himself—he wasn't even here for the thirty grand. He was here because he'd relished being needed, and a small, naive part of him had imagined this would consecrate their relationship. He never should have gotten involved.

Now Babygirl stood by his Jeep and hesitated, working her jaw soundlessly. She was building herself up to say something truly serious, something she dreaded.

"I love you."

"I love you, too."

That wasn't it. Jacob waited, watching her as she controlled her breaths and formed the words: "We'll go down and *fight* her, then. Both of us."

He was admittedly impressed she'd found the balls to propose this. But it wouldn't work, either. "There's nothing to tie a rope to in Razor Alley," he said. "There's only one anchor bolt left and it's rusted to hell. It could break at any second. Anyone who follows her is likely to get stuck down there with her."

"We have to risk it."

"And she still has my gun."

"You said you shot six times, right? That means she only has one bullet left." She lowered her voice. "There's two of us."

He felt a cold breeze on his skin. This was getting truly dangerous.

"She's smart. If she misses, it's over. So she won't take her only shot unless she absolutely has to. She knows the gun can threaten both of us but only kill one of us. We can use that against her." Her eyes burned with focus, and for the first time today, Jacob felt less like her hired badass and more like a chess piece between two skilled opponents. "If you pretend to surrender, I'll sneak up behind her and—"

Jacob held up a hand, silencing her.

He'd always had what his father called *hunter's eyes*, a subconscious attention to shapes that don't belong. He could pick out motion at a hundred yards, and sure enough, across the streambed and shadowed in a grove of darkening evergreens, he just barely recognized the subtle outline of a human figure.

His blood turned to ice water.

"Someone else is here."

I'M MISSING SOMETHING, WASHINGTON KNOWS. *STILL.*

She's reconstructed the violent stalemate—two killers above, a desperate survivor below—but too many variables remain, too many unknowns. Her brain feels overmatched, her cells cluttered with stray thoughts, a city on garbage strike.

As if sensing the unease, Tess frowns. "Something has been bothering me."

Washington glances at her. "What?"

"I've been thinking about Allie. Her actions . . . they don't make sense."

"How so?"

"If she . . ." Tess hesitates, still struggling with the idea. "If she *really* brought me to that cave so her secret boyfriend could murder me, why'd she give me a camera to wear?"

A good point, the detective knows. Bringing helmet-mounted cameras along while you commit murder is a spectacularly bad idea and out of character for such a clever woman.

"Maybe Allie was considering appearances," Washington suggests. "She always brought her GoPros caving, right? So it would have been suspicious if the one day you were murdered by a random psycho was also the day she didn't bring them."

"And why did I only ever see Jacob? Why didn't I see or hear Allie once?"

"Because she hung back. She let Jacob do all the work and ordered him around from the shadows. She didn't want to be seen by you."

"Why?"

"You were her best friend, Tess." Washington rubs her arthritic knuckles. "She grew up with you. When your mom abused you and tortured you with bleach, she empowered you to tell the truth. When you were bullied at school, she stuck up for you. Her family took you in. You're like sisters, almost. And now for some still unknown reason, she'd just arranged your murder. When that plan went to hell and you refused to go quietly, did you really expect her to look you in the eye?"

"That just seems . . ."

"Cold?"

"Cowardly," Tess says. "She wasn't a coward."

Maybe.

Allie Merritt remains a troubling mystery. She's not dead—at least, not yet—and her true role in the day's events is still uncertain.

"The question we need to answer is this." Washington leans forward, keeping her voice gentle and professional. "What motive would Allie have to kill you?"

This visibly hurts Tess. "I have no idea."

"Have you ever had any disagreements?"

"Nothing major."

"Was she ever jealous of you?"

"If anything," Tess admits, "I was jealous of her."

"Maybe you were, but it's all in the open now. We know Allie's life wasn't as glamorous as she made it look on *Keep Calm*. We know she's under federal investigation for wire fraud. What other secrets has she kept from you?"

She says nothing.

"And you were a potential witness, Tess. You didn't realize it, but you were right there at the scene of the crime. You had access to Allie's emails, her bank accounts, her lines of credit, her correspondence with her networks of sponsors. Maybe you were about to discover a discrepancy. Maybe you even already saw it, and you just hadn't connected the dots yet. And Allie needed you gone, before you realized what you'd seen."

"Stolen money?"

"Or something worse."

"How much worse?"

"You tell me."

Tess shakes her head. She looks nauseated.

There's an old Balkan proverb quoted on Allie's website. It must have resonated with the enigmatic woman because it's displayed prominently under the title header: *It is permitted you in time of grave danger to walk with the devil until you have crossed the bridge.*

A streetwise travel motto? Or something more sinister?

For a decade, the world has been Allie Merritt's playground. Airports. Train stations. Resorts. Hostels. Every place has an underbelly. What kinds of people has she crossed paths with? What criminal activities might a solo traveler have gotten herself unwittingly entangled in? The drug trade? Human trafficking? Who might Allie owe? What secrets might an intelligent and successful young woman be willing to kill to conceal?

And somehow, Washington senses Costa Rica is the key. The timing of Allie's conspicuously aborted trip is too close to be a coincidence. Something happened to her there, just a few weeks ago. Something that altered the course of her life. "That night she called you crying from Costa Rica, where in the country was she?"

"The Northern Zone, I think."

"Is that a rainforest?"

"Yes."

"Remote?"

"Very." Tess hesitates. "Why? Do you think it's connected?"

Washington gives no indication.

I'm missing something, she knows. *All of the pieces are there inside your head. I just haven't connected them yet.*

"We'll solve this, Tess. Both of us. Keep remembering."

The survivor glances toward the doorway, as if expecting someone else to enter the hospital room. "Don't detectives usually work with partners?"

"Mine retired last month."

"I'm sorry."

"It's all right." Washington smiles gently. "I have you."

31

JACOB STOOD BESIDE HIS JEEP AND CALLED OUT A GREETING, TRYING to hide the pain in his voice. The stranger answered immediately: "I need help."

Cold sweat prickled on Jacob's back.

"I'm looking for some people." The figure crossed the creek, his hiking boots splashing through shallow water. He was young, dark-haired. Glasses. Hispanic-looking. "My . . . my girlfriend, Allie, and her friend Tess."

It's you, Jacob realized with a shiver. He'd seen the guy only in photos.

Ethan.

What the hell was he doing here? He'd been assured that Ethan would be at home, many miles away. Why was he here, and why *now*?

Jacob stood still. "I haven't seen anyone."

Shit, shit, shit.

And this oblivious boyfriend kept advancing up the rocky slope, just twenty paces away now. Jacob's stomach coiled, and he concealed his splinted hand behind his waist. If this guy came any closer, he'd see something impossible to explain—

"Wait. Stop."

Ethan slowed but didn't halt.

"The entire cave system is closed. There's . . ." Jacob grasped for his rehearsed story, prepared for a situation like this one. It felt like years ago. "We're quarantining an outbreak of white-nose syndrome."

This stopped him.

"I'm with Green Ridge." Jacob smiled effortfully. "They sent me here to put up signs."

Not his best performance, but Ethan seemed to accept it. He'd halted ten paces away, just under the crest of the hill. One step closer and he would've seen the rubber hose affixed to the Jeep's undercarriage and leading into the cave. The only thing blocking his view was a rise of land.

With his heart in his throat, Jacob glanced back to wide-eyed Babygirl, crouched behind the Jeep's tailgate, holding her breath.

If Ethan saw *her*, he'd recognize her immediately.

Instinctively Jacob touched his carry holster, but of course, no gun. He still had his knife, though. If he moved fast he could close the distance and plunge the steel blade into the boyfriend's chest. But he'd get only one chance. Ethan seemed soft—he'd likely never been in a fight before—but he was also lean and fit. Jacob remembered being told once that the guy ran half-marathons. If Ethan sensed an attack coming, if he escaped the area, it would all be over. Worse, he surely had a phone. He could call 911 at any second.

"The people I'm looking for would've come here sometime this morning," Ethan said. "I'm worried something happened to them."

Jacob nodded, pretending to listen. Ethan Ramirez was a doctor, right? Something specialized. Assuming he lived in the city, this meant the poor guy had driven an hour into the mountains, then hiked another hour on foot—just to check on helpless little Allie. That was marriage material, all right. Too bad for him.

You poor, clueless bastard.

You have no idea.

"I've been out here all day." Jacob palmed sweat from his forehead, careful to keep his splinted right hand behind his hip. "Maybe your friends changed their plans and—"

"No." Ethan shook his head. "They're here."

"How are you sure?"

"I found her car."

Jacob's heart sank. He knew they should've moved the damn car. He'd even suggested twice to Babygirl that she hike down there and hide it. This time the silence was longer.

Five seconds.

Ten.

Somewhere in the world, he knew, twenty people just died.

A tumor of dread was slowly expanding inside his chest. The situation was one mistake away from exploding into violence. Out of the guy's view, Jacob slid his unhurt hand behind his waist to lift the leather flap, resting his thumb on his Marine Corps knife.

Ethan subtly tensed. He'd sensed the hidden motion. He definitely suspected something now.

Jacob had a question of his own: "Have you reported them missing?"

"I called it in. But they're not overdue yet."

"Then what's the problem?"

"It's complicated." Ethan stood still on the uneven ground, his eyes difficult to read, his hands at his sides. "Allie texted me a few hours ago. She told me everything was fine, that she and Tess were going to camp down at Blue Lake for the next two nights."

Jacob nodded, trying to hide his impatience. He knew this already. He'd watched Babygirl send that very text hours ago, before they'd smashed both phones with a rock. To his eye, her message had looked like a faithful girlfriend assuring her boyfriend of a perfectly plausible change of plans. What mistake could she have possibly made?

He took a step forward—and Ethan took a matching step back. Loose rocks skittered underfoot. The sloped ground was unsteady.

Ethan's eyes stayed locked on Jacob, as if staring down a rabid animal. "Allie made an . . . appointment on Monday."

"An appointment?"

"It was important. It's strange that she'd forget it."

Goddamn it, Babygirl.

Of course she'd forget some small detail on the calendar. Of course she'd be too clever for her own good. Throughout their relationship she'd loved to flesh out her lies with details. Pointless details, sometimes. It was irresistible to her, maybe even pathological. But every detail is a bear trap planted somewhere in the future.

Ethan took another step back, keeping his balance. Trying to politely disengage now. "Sorry to bother you. I'll keep looking on the trail."

"Maybe she rescheduled."

He nodded once. "Maybe."

Yes, the boyfriend was definitely suspicious. He'd sensed the strain in Jacob's posture, the tension in his voice. He'd already guessed that Jacob was guarding something out here, that he knew exactly what happened to Allie and Tess. Ethan was only playing along, and as soon as he reached a safe distance, he'd call 911. That was the smartest way to play the volatile situation he'd stumbled into.

Ethan kept backing away. He knew better than to turn his back. Eye to eye on the unstable footing.

Jacob matched his steps, turning his boots sideways on the crumbling earth. But the boyfriend was too careful to allow him within reach. He couldn't quite close the distance. Predator and prey danced a halting, uncertain dance.

If he bolts, it's over. The guy was a runner.

I'll never, ever catch him—

Then Jacob heard a rustle of motion behind him. He looked uphill to see Babygirl—the quiet, clear-eyed woman Ethan only *thought* he knew, the root of today's mess—step out from behind the Jeep and into view.

"Ethan," she said. "I'm sorry."

The boyfriend froze.

Distracted for just a half second.

It was all Jacob needed. He bolted forward, closed the distance, and plunged his steel KA-BAR into Ethan's stomach.

Jacob twisted the knife—he felt the guy's slippery guts squirm around inside—and then Ethan fell free with a choked gasp and toppled down the hill, rolling, landing in the creek with a splash. This was now a double homicide.

The blood was oily red on Jacob's knife, like new transmission fluid. Maybe it was the dreamlike cocktail of adrenaline, but he realized a part of himself was disappointed. He'd actually been *rooting* for the boyfriend, somehow, secretly hoping the poor, decent guy would escape anyway—just like he'd always still felt bad for his father's hooked fish—and Ethan had gotten so heartbreakingly close.

Two people die every second, he reminded himself. Will the world bat an eye, then, if for just this one second he bumped it up to three?

Ethan splashed and writhed in the creek as Jacob approached, clutching his newly opened stomach with both hands as if trying to hold his organs in. The shallow water clouded red around him, long tendrils following the current. A knife in the gut was a nasty way to go. At least Jacob could grant him the mercy of a quick death.

"Wait." Babygirl slid down the hill after him. "Give me the zip ties."

"Why?"

"Just do it."

He passed the bundle to her. She pushed past him and pinned the boyfriend with a knee into his back. Ethan turned his head sideways to breathe, coughing on dirty creek water as she clasped his wrists together. His glasses fell off.

She pulled the bindings tight around his wrists with a plastic snarl.

"It doesn't matter," Jacob said as he watched. "Whatever we do here, we're both going to prison anyway. Your friend down there has already won, because she'll never give us the camera—"

"You're wrong."

"How do you figure?"

Her lip twitched; she was trying to smile. Her muscle movements were jerky, unnatural, like a corpse jolted with voltage. He knew it was all posturing and she was scared shitless just like he was. She knew damn well what was at stake. But her voice was disturbingly confident: "She'll give us the camera."

"How?"

"We'll make her."

She rolled the boyfriend over with her hiking boot. He sprawled painfully onto his back, his chest heaving with wheezing breaths, his jacket soaked with blood where Jacob's knife had opened his guts up. His eyes focused on her. Disbelief, then sadness. His lips moved: "*You*—"

She looked away, suddenly nauseated.

She belonged to Jacob, of course, but part of her still cared for Ethan, and this gave Jacob a morbid satisfaction. All her life she'd skirted accountability, micromanaged how people saw her, kept her little hands clean—but today that was no longer possible. Separate halves of her life, matter and antimatter, had just made violent contact. There would be no more secrets.

She picked up Ethan's glasses and steadied herself.

Inhaled.

Exhaled.

"Now," she told Jacob, pressing the glasses into his hand, "we have a hostage."

32

"SOMETHING SPLASHED IN THE POOL BEHIND ME," TESS SAYS.

"What?"

"A pair of glasses."

"You recognized them?"

She nods once. "They . . . looked like Ethan's."

Proof of life, Washington thinks, *or something close to it.* The foreboding opener to any hostage negotiation.

"Jacob . . . he'd dropped them down to me." Tess shifts uncomfortably, like something is pressing down on her chest. "I couldn't see him up at the top. But he told me Allie's boyfriend was here now, that Ethan was tied up on the surface and he'd been stabbed. Bleeding badly."

"Why did he come there?"

"I have no idea."

"What else did Jacob say?"

"He demanded I give up the footage," Tess says. "He told me he was going to start counting down from three, and if I didn't throw the camera up to him before he reached zero . . ."

Her eyes brim with tears.

". . . he'd go back up to the surface and kill Ethan."

JACOB SHOUTED: "THREE."

His own voice swirled back up at him from the darkness. The

woman below didn't answer, and he didn't dare peer over the edge. Not even for a second. Not now, while he was so close to winning.

He waited.

"Two."

Still, only dead quiet below. The steady *tick-tick* of dripping water.

"I'm not an evil person. But I *can* be. And you're giving me no choice."

He thought of the restraints cutting into the flesh of Ethan's wrists and ankles, the cloth bag Babygirl had zip-tied around his throat because she couldn't bear to see his horrified face. He'd looked like one of those poor bastards from Abu Ghraib.

"Honestly, Ethan seems like a nice guy. A doctor, a concerned boyfriend, a guy who sends pictures of used dental flossers. He's an innocent victim here. He doesn't deserve this. And I hope you have a strong stomach, because his glasses were just the beginning."

He scraped his knife along limestone, a rusty chalkboard screech.

"Next, I'll start dropping his fingers down to you. Then maybe his ears. His tongue. His eyelids. *No me gusta!* I'll cut pieces off of Ethan Ramirez and deliver them to you one handful at a time, while you hide down there like a coward. Tell me, please, how much of this poor guy's suffering is your life worth?"

He caught his breath. Spittle hung from his lip.

"*One.* What's your choice?"

"I KNEW HE WAS LYING TO ME," TESS WHISPERS. "HE WAS DESPERATE and running out of time. Whatever I did, he'd kill Ethan anyway."

But a flicker of doubt invades her voice. *Right?*

Washington affirms with a sensitive nod.

"If I threw the camera up to him, he would just murder his hostage." She steadies her breaths, a painful dialogue with herself. "Then he would start the engine and kill me, too. He only needed the camera. I knew his tricks by then. He was a liar."

Washington knows the type. She's interrogated men like Jacob Herman before. They're not particularly clever or persuasive, but they'll say whatever combination of words it takes to achieve the results they want. Such people can't be negotiated with. Any promise Jacob made was weightless, worse than nothing.

The instant Ethan's life was no longer useful to the killers, he would die. The instant Tess no longer held the incriminating video footage, she was dead, too. In such a soul-wrenching dilemma, there are no good choices.

Option one: give the killers the camera, sentencing both Ethan and herself to death.

Option two: refuse, and let Ethan die.

For a long breath, Tess is silent.

"If it were you," she finally says, "would you have given him the camera?"

"It doesn't matter. I wasn't there."

"I know . . ." Tess hesitates. "I think I know what Allie would've done."

"What?"

"She would've known the right choice—the only right choice, and what Ethan would have wanted for her—was to keep the camera."

This would have forced Jacob to make good on his threats. Ethan's final moments alive would have been nothing short of hell on earth. But the only other option guaranteed death for them both. This is not a choice Washington considers lightly, but setting aside emotion, the answer is clear: keeping the footage would have been the only way to keep at least one innocent person alive. Whatever the cost.

Hopefully Ethan saw it that way, too.

"Allie would've put the memory card on her tongue and swallowed it, so that no matter what happened to her, the autopsy would tell the truth." Tess pauses. "But . . ."

"What?"

She blinks. A tear darts down her cheek.

"What is it, Tess?"

"Imagining Allie's ghost, always asking myself what she would do . . . it was a distraction." She takes a breath, finding the words. "One way or another, I've asked myself that question for half my life. And maybe you're right, and I never knew the real Allie Merritt at all. And this fictional version of her that I'd built up in my head was something I needed to overcome, like a tumor I needed to cut out."

She's reached a new clarity.

"I've always lived in her shadow. I was so jealous of her, and in my jealousy I'd convinced myself that she was somehow greater than human, and I was less than her. Not as brave, not as smart. Just a supporting character in her story. And I told myself that to get through this moment, I wouldn't try to be her. I was done trying to be Allie."

Her voice hardens.

"I'd be *me*."

AFTER A LONG PAUSE JACOB HEARD THE WOMAN'S VOICE ECHO FROM below, faint and beaten. "Okay. I'm . . . I'm throwing the camera up to you."

He exhaled. *Thank God*.

"Just please . . . please don't kill Ethan—"

"I won't," he lied.

"Give me your word."

"Cross my heart, hope to die, stick a needle in my eye." Jacob was speaking on autopilot, digging his boots in and hooking his elbow around a protrusion of stone. He'd need to be careful not to lose his footing.

"Ready?" she called.

"Ready."

Sure enough, a tiny shape hurtled straight up from below. The plastic gadget clacked against rock, bounced off the stalactite ceiling, and before it could drop back down—*Yes!*—Jacob leaned out to swipe it from midair with his good hand. The woman's GoPro was finally, *finally*, a solid object between his fingers.

"TO CATCH THE CAMERA," TESS SAYS, "HE HAD TO LEAN OUT OVER THE edge for just a second. I saw his headlamp, that floating ball of red. I was ready."

Her voice lowers.

"I aimed. And fired."

33

JACOB HERMAN'S CAUSE OF DEATH WAS DETERMINED TO BE A SINGLE .45-caliber bullet to the throat, nicking his carotid artery. This fatal shot was fired from some forty feet below.

"I thought I'd missed at first," Tess says. "I wasn't sure I got him."

"You got him, all right."

It wasn't a direct hit—the jacketed round had only grazed the killer's neck and exited below his jaw. But it had still dealt its intended damage. The bleeding would have been relentless, impossible to stop without immediate medical attention.

The autopsy is still in progress, but the medical examiner estimates Jacob died within thirty minutes of taking that glancing hit. Before succumbing to blood loss, he'd managed to stagger back up to the surface with the GoPro in his hands. At last he'd recovered the damning footage, at the cost of his own life. Jacob's blood trail would lead to just outside the cave entrance, where his body was found slumped in his Jeep's driver's seat.

Good riddance.

Not every death is a tragedy. It's not an investigator's job to make personal judgments, but Washington can't deny the visceral satisfaction in seeing Jacob slain by his own gun.

"That was a hell of a shot, Tess."

She nods.

"The distance. The angle. The low light." To say nothing of the speed and coordination required, all from an out-of-practice shooter. With that daring Hail Mary of a shot, Jacob Herman was eliminated from the world.

"It doesn't matter." Tess sighs. "Ethan bled to death anyway."

"You did everything you could for him."

"It wasn't enough."

"I think you're a hero."

She winces at the word. "All I did was survive."

"Tess, survival is victory. Maybe you think you don't deserve it, or maybe you're beating yourself up for fighting back because that's how the world tells women to feel when they take charge of their fates. You aren't disposable. You don't owe anyone anything. No one else was looking out for you that day. Your last best hope was *you*." She glances at the waxy chemical scars on Tess's exposed shoulder. "Fourteen years ago, you survived your mother. And maybe that's what made you strong enough to survive this, too."

Another contemplative nod.

"Jacob was a monster. And you stopped him."

"I wish I could've saved Ethan, too."

"I know," Washington says. "But maybe you saved the *next* person."

"You're right. That doesn't help."

The detective manages a gallows laugh.

For a long moment, no one speaks. Somewhere down the hall, a monitor beeps and a nurse's rubber clogs urgently squeak on tile.

"Okay, Tess. I'll say this once, because I think you've earned it." Washington sets down her notepad and exhales. "You know the curse of being good at something? You're asked to keep doing it. Homicides are my thing. No thefts, no narcotics, nothing else. If someone isn't dead, my phone doesn't ring. My partner and I would rotate to Multnomah, Clackamas, Jackson, anywhere someone was having the worst day of their life. And a few years ago I was talking to a man who'd lost his teenage daughter on her walk home from school. Just a half mile between her bus stop and her house, a ten-minute walk up a gravel road, and someone found her body on a mattress by the river with her hands cut off and cigarettes put out in her eyes. And I was sitting there in a dining room, speaking to a grieving father who was still processing the fact that he would never see his daughter, Isla, go to college or build a career or get married, and while we were talking his phone vibrated with a text message. It was just someone from the funeral home confirming they'd received the girl's body for burial preparations, but the way they'd worded it—*We have Isla here*—I saw it in his eyes, this awful lurch of hope. You feel before you think. It's how our brains work. A part of him thought, for a split second, that this whole nightmare was just an awful mistake and Isla was somehow alive. And that stupid text message, the emotional whiplash of it . . . God, I just wished I could fix it, so badly."

She swallows something heavy.

"So I can't stop. I feel like I'm not done yet, even though I know my body is. It's like a score I have to settle with the universe, maybe. Just once I want to sit down with a victim's parent or wife or child and look them in the eyes and tell them, *I have something incredible to show you. Your lost person is alive and okay, and it's not a misunderstood text message. You'll see them again and touch them again.* I want to bring someone back."

She smiles, her vision glassy.

"That's why I haven't retired yet, I guess. I'm holding out for something impossible."

"And then?"

"Then"—Washington shrugs—"I'll stop working for free."

• • •

As Tess finishes her statement—the harrowing details of her survival in the depths, her dizzy and half-remembered conversations with paramedics, her journey to this very hospital bed—Washington finds her thoughts drifting to Allie instead. She senses yesterday's violent standoff at the Devil's Staircase isn't over. It's only entered its next phase.

The survivor gathers her thoughts. "That's . . . everything, I think."

"I appreciate it, Tess. Truly."

Every word spoken in this ninety-six-minute interview has been recorded, and the detective's carpal muscles ache from six pages of handwritten notes. Her mind is buzzing. It'll take hours to sort and fully digest, to compare with the rest of the team's questioning, to match up with the bullet fragments and spent brass and blood droplets found inside and outside the cave. And of course, to track Allie's true path through the day.

Near Jacob Herman's body, a GoPro camera was found discarded on the ground with its MicroSD memory card removed. The all-important footage was missing. Presumably, Jacob had destroyed the chip like the others—or *someone* took it.

The day is a bloody puzzle, and it's still missing a critical piece.

"We'll find Allie," Washington says. "I promise."

Tess nods, unconvinced.

She's survived hell already. Her body is a patchwork of freshly scabbed cuts and purple bruises, an eardrum ruptured, a wrist and an ankle sprained. Still, hospital staff are optimistic. She's proven she's tougher than she looks—*Tiny but tenacious,* one nurse had remarked—and they plan to discharge her tonight.

"I'll be in touch if I need anything clarified." Washington closes her padfolio and stands up on sore knees. "What's next for you?"

"Sleep. For a month."

"You earned it." She squeezes her wrist. "And thank you again, Tess. For everything."

The survivor smiles.

"If you remember anything else, you can reach me at any time." She lays a business card flat on the plastic tray. "Call my cell. Not the office."

"Thanks."

"If you feel unsafe, call me immediately." She rests a palm on her holstered weapon. "I don't care if it's just a bad feeling or an eerie noise outside your apartment. Trust your gut, Tess. Your intuition is what kept you alive in the Devil's Staircase. If you get the slightest suspicion your life might be in danger, the sheriff's office has resources to protect you."

A nurse enters and steps between them to recheck Tess's vitals. The clock is running out, Washington knows, and it's time to wrap this up. The survivor's discharge paperwork will be signed soon.

Still, she lingers in the doorway for a moment longer. "You're like me, you know."

"I doubt that," Tess says as the nurse wraps a blood pressure cuff around her arm.

"I mean it."

"How so?"

"We're both underestimated," Washington says. "And maybe you've gone your whole life believing it's a weakness, but it's not. It's a strength, Tess. It's how we win, even when the odds are against us. We adapt, we pivot, we surprise. And ultimately, we trick our enemy into defeating himself."

Her phone vibrates in her pocket. A call incoming.

"Or," she adds, "*herself*."

• • •

Speaking of being underestimated?

The most crucial insight into Allie Merritt wouldn't come from Tess at all but from Ethan—the poor, uninvolved boyfriend who drove all the way out to the Devil's Staircase on a bad feeling and paid for it with a knife to the gut. The phone call was from a man Washington had been trying to contact for hours, an emergency surgeon up at Providence Portland who also knew his coworker Ethan socially, and with a shaky voice he relayed the disturbing things Ethan had told him. The details are shocking but not exactly surprising.

This statement confirms suspicions she's had from the very start.

It all *finally* fits together now.

She dials her lieutenant's number, but her thumb hovers over the call button. She rereads her notes and chugs the rest of her coffee, even the gritty black sludge at the bottom. She knows exactly what she has to do. Like the heroine cornered at the bottom of the Chimney, the killer's stolen pistol gripped in her knuckles. Sights aligned, a single .45-caliber cartridge seated in the chamber, waiting for the killer to expose himself for just a moment.

I can do this.

The badass woman in the cave had managed to hit her target, if only barely.

So can I.

Washington takes a breath and presses the call button. She imagines Jacob Herman, dealt a fatal bullet, clutching his throat and staggering up to the surface with time most definitely *not* on his side. He'd had less than a half hour to live.

But a lot can occur in thirty minutes.

When the lieutenant answers, she speaks first: "I know what happened."

34

BY THE TIME JACOB STAGGERED BACK UP TO THE SURFACE, NIGHT HAD fallen. He'd bitten off his glove and clamped it to the side of his throat, feeling his heartbeat through his fingers. He wouldn't dare lift his hand. He'd already lost an alarming amount of blood.

She got me. She really did it.

Unbelievable.

Catching the camera was a calculated risk, yes, but an acceptable one. He'd exposed himself for only a second. How the hell did she make that shot? Throwing the GoPro with one hand, taking a two-handed grip and forming a sight picture, squeezing the trigger—did she practice every month at the gun range, too? It was almost hilarious. What miserable luck.

He staggered to his Jeep and nearly tripped over the garden hose. He found Babygirl down by the creek's edge, kneeling over Ethan's body. The boyfriend lay motionless on bloodstained rocks, his belly open and his wrists bound, a bag crudely zip-tied over his head.

"Ethan's dead," she called up to him without looking. "No pulse."

Jacob didn't give a shit.

She gasped audibly when she saw the bloodstain on his jacket. He turned away from her, gripping his throat like he could somehow hide it, assuring her he was fine in a croaking voice he didn't recognize.

"Jacob—"

"Give me a sec." He needed to sit down.

"Jacob, what happened?"

He half sat, half fell on his ass, but managed to keep pressure on his throat. He dreaded what would happen if he removed his hand. He unzipped his first aid kit—upside down by mistake—and sutures and antiseptic wipes dumped onto the dirt. *Goddamn it.* He unrolled the last bit of gauze, just a few inches left, and pressed it to his neck.

When she reached him she hugged him. He couldn't remember the last time they'd hugged, and it made his insides melt, a feeling he couldn't articulate. The GoPro was an uncomfortable lump in his pocket. He tossed it to the ground.

She saw it and froze. "You got it."

"It doesn't matter."

"We have the footage now—"

"It won't help us." It hurt to speak, and explaining would take too many words. As he tilted his head back and wrapped duct tape around his throat, he realized the treetops were swirling counterclockwise around the dusky sky. He was sober, but he had the goddamn spins. And the gauze was already saturated like a clammy warm towel. The bleeding wouldn't stop.

She wasn't listening anyway. "We can still salvage this, if we're fast."

"Wait."

"I'll start the engine." She hurried toward his Jeep. "We'll run it down to a quarter tank. That'll guarantee she dies down there, while leaving you enough gas to—"

"*Stop.*"

She whirled to face him, her eyes diamond hard.

"It's over." He adjusted his grip and felt a new surge of warmth leak down the front of his shirt. "I need to get to a hospital."

To this, she said nothing.

But he swore he could see something break inside her. Her eyes widened, just a microscopic change, and he recognized shock. Then panic, then anger, and then a bone-deep hatred. Or maybe it was all in his head. She'd always been a human inkblot test.

"We're done here. Forget killing your friend. Forget all of this." Jacob struggled to stand up and felt a tingling sensation in his toes. Disturbingly, his injuries barely seemed to hurt anymore. His brain was full of cotton.

Her birdlike eyes flicked between him and his Jeep, processing their dilemma. To save Jacob's life, they needed the vehicle. To suffocate the woman in the cave, they needed the vehicle. Doing both was no longer an option.

She stepped closer. "Do you understand what that means?"

"Yes."

"If we go to the hospital with a bullet hole in your neck, the cops will question us. And then it's all ruined. Everything. The whole plan. And we both go to prison."

"I'm aware of that."

"I am *not* going to prison, Jacob."

"Then stay here."

"That wasn't the plan."

Well, your best friend just slam-dunked your plan into the trash, Jacob tried to say, but his tongue felt oddly sluggish. His voice came out like a wheeze.

From out here in the mountains the nearest hospital was almost an hour away. Not good. He wasn't sure if he could stay conscious for the drive. He'd already lost quarts of blood through his fingers and it was still coming, a slow but steady leak, no matter how much duct tape and gauze he wrapped around it. Again he tried to stand, but his legs were jelly. It felt like he weighed a thousand pounds. The short walk to his Jeep looked like a mile.

He suspected he was dying but tried not to think about it.

Instead he pictured Motorcycle Guy's prolapsed eyeball. Life rarely cooperates with your fantasies, but that moment outside the margarita bar was like something from one of his dad's action movies. The timing, the surprise, the perfect haymaker. The terror and relief in Babygirl's eyes as she saw him for the first time, the stranger who'd saved her.

"There's a better way," she said now. Her voice was almost too faint to hear.

"What?"

"I have a solution."

"To what?"

She smiled bleakly. "Everything."

"Yeah?" He matched it with a dizzy grin of his own. "It must be a doozy."

She touched his cheek with her hand, her glove's studded fingers sliding through the hairs of his beard, and for a moment he thought she might kiss him. Then her smile melted away and her eyes dimmed with sadness.

"It is," she said.

She ripped the bandage off his throat. An arterial surge exploded out of him, hitting the ground with a splash. He clawed at his neck, too late to stop it, and liquid warmth spurted between his fingers. "Babygirl—"

"For the last fucking time," Tess said, "stop *calling* me that."

"SHE LIED TO ME." DETECTIVE LAYLA WASHINGTON GRIPS HER PHONE. "Her entire story. Every word, every minute, she looked me in the eye and lied. The second killer that day wasn't Ethan, and it wasn't Allie."

On the line, the lieutenant says nothing. A staticky pause.

"It's Tess."

35

"TESS ARRANGED HER BEST FRIEND'S MURDER."

It was *always* her.

"We've had it backward. It was Allie who escaped the ambush with her helmet camera. Allie who broke Jacob's fingers with rope." Washington catches her breath. "And *Allie* who finally shot the bastard in the throat."

Silence.

"And with Jacob bleeding to death, Tess knew she was in deep trouble. She couldn't hide what happened to her hired killer, but she's smart. To conceal her involvement, she came up with a new story. A version of the day where she's the hero."

Finally, the lieutenant speaks. "Clever."

"Not just clever. Ingenious."

Their perfect murder might have fallen apart, their designated victim might have fought back and kicked the designated killer's ass—but cunning Tess DeWater still found a way to land on her feet. She'd surveyed the crime scene, adjusted the evidence, and created a new cover story that explained everything. She'd understood a constant as old as human history, from shipwreck to massacre alike: the sole survivor gets to tell the truth.

The dead can't speak.

Washington has her digital recorder in her pocket. She's captured ninety-six minutes of Tess's lies, every detail chosen for maximum effect. The survivor's performance from her hospital bed was flawless—her tears, her regrets, her survivor's guilt, the expertly calibrated waver in her voice. The unmistakable raw talent of a pathological liar.

"Tess had to make sure we never found Allie's body. So in her story, her best friend took a bullet to the head. Then she made sure to suggest to me, *several times*, that the killer dumped Allie's body in some lake with chicken wire. It was all a misdirect, so we'd send our divers out there for months and search the wrong places, so we'd never find Allie's remains at all."

"And we'd have to accept Tess's story."

"Exactly."

Throughout the survivor's statement, an attentive listener might've detected subtle contrivances in Tess's storytelling—nothing impossible or unlikely enough to challenge, but merely convenient. When Tess fought back in the tunnel, why did she conveniently have Allie's knife and rope? When she tricked the killer, why did she conveniently have Allie's baggie of spare memory cards? And when she ultimately shot him, how did she, an out-of-practice amateur, conveniently land that difficult shot?

It was really *Allie* all along. Fighting for her life.

"Holy shit," the lieutenant says.

Washington feels her skin tingle with adrenaline. She's always had a knack for remembering faces, but Tess has become a worrying hole in her memory, like trying to remember a dream. Dark hair? Pale skin? Small features? Her classmates used to call her Wednesday Addams—but Christina Ricci or Jenna Ortega? Tess is an optical illusion, solid enough to touch when seen from one angle, intangible from another.

"I don't see a motive," the lieutenant says. "Why murder her best friend?"

"I don't know yet."

Tess had admitted herself that she was jealous of Allie's wealth, her prestige, and her jet-setting life with Ethan—honestly, who wouldn't be?—but Washington senses the women's friendship has other, hidden depths. She thinks of Stimpy chewing Ren's head to a skeletal nub, the shock and grief in her son's sobs and the hamster blood on his trembling hands, the sudden pivot to violence after years of peaceful cohabitation.

No one ever really knows anyone, her partner used to say.

"Whatever her reasons," she says, "Tess masterminded the attack."

"If you're right."

"I am."

"Or she's just Jacob's puppet—"

"Do *not* make the mistake of underestimating this woman. Everyone who's underestimated Tess has paid for it. I've spent an hour and a half in a room with her. I've looked her in the eye. She's one of the best liars I've ever seen."

Over the past ninety-six minutes she'd watched Tess tell her thrilling final-girl tale from a hospital bed. Washington herself had played the role of audience, gasping and cheering the self-described heroine at all the correct moments—building trust, feeding the survivor's vanity, letting her get comfortable and believe she was in the clear while Detective Washington quietly assembled the true picture in her mind.

Never interrupt your enemy while they're making a mistake.

And now, finally, it's time to go on offense.

Her walkie-talkie crackles. "Baker-twelve, we're at the hospital. South lot."

"Hang on." Washington holds her phone to the side of her face, her walkie to the other. "Baker-twelve, stand by in the parking lot. They're going to discharge Tess any minute. I'll send her down the south elevator to you."

"Baker-twelve copies."

From the fourth-floor window by the nurses' station, she watches the roof of a marked vehicle glide under sodium vapor lights to park at the roundabout. Light bar dark, engine silent. A sleek predator in wait, occupied by Deputies Harris and Dunn.

She waves to them. "Baker-twelve, be ready."

Then, speed-walking down the hallway, Washington switches back to her phone. "I'll take Tess myself. I've got a marked unit outside to transport her to—"

"No. Not yet." The lieutenant's voice is solid brick.

"What?"

"Layla, *wait*."

She halts. From here, Tess's room is five down.

"Call off the deputies," he says. "You're moving too fast. We need to work as a unit. First, let's all sit down tonight and listen to your audio. You locked Tess into her story, and now we need a strategy to break it. I fully agree with you—Tess was involved and we can prove she lied—but right now, she thinks you swallowed it whole. Her guard is down. If you rush us to the next step, we lose that advantage. And . . ." His voice tightens with strained etiquette, a politician boxed into an uncomfortable corner. He's reluctant to say it, but he has to: "And no disrespect intended, Layla, but you're not at your best anymore."

There it is.

Oh, fuck you.

"Time is running out." She swallows a ball of white-hot anger and glances back to Tess's room. "Any second now, they'll sign her discharge papers—"

"Then let her go home. We'll prep tonight and break her story tomorrow."

"It has to be now."

"When we make arrests," he says, "it'll be my call."

"This is a mistake."

"I'll own it."

"*No disrespect intended*, but you don't understand this woman," Washington says. "If we don't take Tess into custody now, if we let her out of our sight, she'll disappear."

JACOB FELL TO HIS KNEES. BLOOD SURGED THROUGH HIS FINGERS TO the slowing beats of his heart, spattering heavily on the rocky soil. He couldn't stop it, any of it.

He stared up at her dizzily.

Who are you?

Who are you, really?

Babygirl—or Tess, or whatever she really was—watched him fade with wordless disinterest. She'd gone blank, now a silhouette in his red light. She stepped back so his blood wouldn't touch her clothes. The air smelled like copper.

She was a creature, all right, and this mystery had enchanted him at first. She was a small-boned thing when he saved her life at that margarita bar, petite like a doll—*Babygirl*, he'd designated her—and maybe that was his first mistake. He remembered the moment his fingers first touched the scaly flesh on her back, like she was a shape-shifting alien caught mid-transformation. *I'll tell you later,* she'd whispered in his ear.

And she did, eventually, tell him the story of how she single-handedly destroyed her mother's life. How fourteen-year-old Tess stood in her shower with grim determination and poured bottles of bleach down her own shoulders and back, twice a week, for almost an entire summer. Just to get out of her mother's tiny house with a leaky roof and bad water pressure, to get away from the woman's rules and chores, to be adopted by a new family, *Allie's* family, with two parents and fresher groceries and faster wi-fi. She was a hermit crab, he'd reckoned, and she would always want a bigger shell.

Even if adolescent Tess's teary-eyed claims of abuse were just inconsistent enough that the charges were ultimately dropped—maybe her gruesome details didn't quite add up, or maybe there were some flaws in her performance—her poor mother lost custody of her only child. Then she lost her job and was shunned by friends and family. Eventually she killed herself, Tess confided in him once, although she never explained how.

She'd outgrown her mother.

She'd outgrown her best friend.

Of course Jacob would be her next meal.

Now Tess paced with catlike footsteps, quietly surveying the crime scene she'd helped create today. She hopped from rock to rock, her boots never touching soil or mud. Minimizing her footprints, Jacob observed thickly. Cute.

"It doesn't matter," he gurgled. "You're going to prison anyway."

"This is your fault." Tess's voice circled him, flat and hateful. "You never took this seriously. You parked your Jeep right where she'd notice it. You waited at the entrance in plain view. You called me *Babygirl* right in front of her."

All fair points. But none of it mattered now.

"The cops won't believe you." He forced a smile with unfeeling lips. "Whatever story you come up with won't last five minutes in an interrogation room."

She kept pacing, in deep focus.

"They'll *eat you alive*."

She ignored him.

"You'll crack under pressure. You'll slip up and make a mistake, just like last time. You'll be that scared little teenager all over again, trying to send your mom to prison—"

"You're wrong." Tess crouched to meet his blurring gaze.

"This time, it'll be my word against three bodies. The truth is whatever I say it is."

She smiled.

"And when I'm done, I'll walk right out the door."

DETECTIVE WASHINGTON ENTERS THE DOORWAY WITH HER PHONE clasped to her ear. She sidesteps a nurse and finds the recovery room empty. The amenities are being rotated, surfaces sanitized, bedsheets stripped out. Tess DeWater is gone.

"Where is she?"

The nurse erases a whiteboard. "She's been discharged."

36

JACOB NEVER LEARNED EXACTLY *WHY* TESS DECIDED TO DO IT.

He liked to think discretion and deniability made him a more appealing confidant—and this deed would surely lock them together for life, more ironclad than any marriage vows—but in truth he'd asked her several times after their fateful conversation by the Gypsum River and received only vague nonanswers. As far as he could tell, it wasn't about revenge or score settling. She'd always been jealous of Allie, of course, but jealousy wasn't enough of a motive, either. Why pay someone to murder your best friend?

Tess never said.

She'd plotted out the date, the location, and the inevitable aftermath (*verify everything,* she'd repeated like a mantra). She'd rehearsed the story she'd tell police. She'd even warned him that Allie might bring her GoPro, but a helmet camera wouldn't be a problem as long as the "unknown killer" remembered to steal it on the way out. Everything else was logistics.

Where to do it? The bottom of the Upper Vault.

How to do it? Knife to her carotid.

How to safely get close enough? Coerce her into zip-tying her wrists.

The nylon zip ties had been Tess's idea, too—once both women were bound and helpless, Jacob would be able to cut Allie's throat without risking a counterattack. Tess, meanwhile, would heroically "escape" into daylight, flee the cave on foot, and tell her harrowing tale of surviving an unidentified, untraceable killer. Her plan was simple and near flawless.

The only blind spot?

The target herself.

Allie was no victim. She never would have zip-tied herself, whatever he'd threatened. She'd known, perhaps from her years of street-smart travel, that women who surrender to their abductors are often never seen again. *Of course* she'd try to bargain with her PIN. *Of course* she'd conceal a knife behind her back. They'd underestimated Allie Merritt, and the planned ambush had stalled.

Leaving Tess standing paralyzed, with no choice but to break character: "Jacob, just *shoot her in the head*."

He'd drawn his gun—but Allie was fast. She was already in motion when he fired, ducking under two earsplitting gunshots, fleeing the only direction available, *down*, headfirst into the narrow Drainpipe. With her helmet camera still recording.

"Follow her." Tess had shoved him. "Finish it."

And God, how he'd tried.

Over nine hours, he'd tried his very hardest.

Now he felt Tess's boot dig into his kidney, doubling him over on the ground. He was too weak to catch himself. He felt her fingers claw through his pockets until she found what she'd been looking for.

His keys.

Sprawled sideways, he watched Tess stand up with his key chain held in her sleeve—still careful to avoid transferring her own fingerprints—and march toward his Jeep. Of course, she had one last thing to do.

It'll be my word against three bodies, she'd said.

And she was right.

Three bodies, indeed. Jacob knew he was bleeding out (*one*), Ethan was dead (*two*), and once his Jeep finished the job and suffocated Allie (*three*), not a soul would be left alive to dispute Tess's story. No living witnesses would remain at all. Just like she'd originally planned, and despite everything that went wrong today, Tess had still found a way to appear innocent. What an incredible magic trick it was. As the sole survivor of the bloodbath at the Devil's Staircase, the truth would be hers to tell.

Except, he knew, for one minor wrinkle. One little detail she hadn't considered.

And it was *delicious*.

He watched Tess open the Jeep's driver's-side door with her sleeve, leaning inside and clicking the key into the ignition—and he couldn't hold it back any longer.

He started to laugh.

She froze. "What?"

He couldn't speak. His throat rattled with deep belly laughs.

"What is it?" Tess held the key mid-twist.

Jacob tried again—but Christ, he just couldn't stop laughing. Maybe it was the delirium of blood loss, but this was the funniest, most karmically beautiful thing he'd ever seen in his entire life. His lips were numb, his tongue a dead slug in his mouth. He'd die with this shit-eating grin on his face. He gasped: "She . . ."

"What, Jacob?"

With splinted fingers he pointed at the ground, at the GoPro. He strained to enunciate his words, pushing air through his teeth: "*Verify everything*, remember?"

Tess didn't understand at first.

Then her eyes widened.

She moved fast, too fast for Jacob's glazing eyes to track. She left the driver's-side door swinging ajar. She grabbed the GoPro from the ground and turned it over, prying the camera's side port open with her thumb—and with a gasp of horror, finding it empty. The memory card was missing.

Allie had kept it.

"You're right, Babygirl." Jacob lay back and let his eyes slide shut. "It'll be your word against three bodies."

He choked on a final, clotted laugh.

"*And* her video."

PART III

Allie

37

TWENTY STORIES UNDERGROUND, ALLIE MERRITT PLACED THE MEMory card on her tongue.

She tilted her head back.

Swallowed.

The hard-edged little plastic square cut her throat on its way down, pricking her eyes with tears. She coughed. Gagged. It almost came back up, like regurgitating a razor blade. But she clenched her muscles and held it down until the sensation faded.

It was done.

Allie's life had changed in Costa Rica.

Symptoms first appeared on days one and two, in the dry lowland forests of Guanacaste. Traveler's stomach, she'd told herself, or maybe too many sugary drinks while writing by the pool. By day three she was hiking deep in the dense rainforests of the Northern Zone and the heat and humidity were nauseating. She barely saw the capuchin monkeys her guide pointed out, or the poisonous blue jeans frogs, or the rare sloth. She'd hardly taken any photos, no notes, no sketches, no local profiles. She'd been too sick, unable to focus.

Don't throw up.

Eventually the trail opened up to a hundred-foot suspension bridge. She gripped the bungee-cord railings with sweaty fingers, the footbridge sagging and swaying with every step. The treetops were far below her hiking boots, like walking on a slippery chain-link fence. She counted down the hours until she'd be back at her hostel.

Don't you dare throw up.

On her way back, the crowded public bus lurched up the mountain pass, and Allie's seat belt had been too tight, her insides now cramped and watery. The single-lane road was all switchbacks, washed out with streams of red volcanic clay. The bus heaved with every turn, and rainwater blurred the windows, and other passengers' elbows kept bumping her side. She gripped her seat and tried to focus on the murmuring Spanish voices around her.

I will not throw up on a crowded bus.

But there was no lavatory. Asking the driver to stop wasn't an option; the bus was currently finessing its way up the cliff like a ten-ton mountain goat.

She couldn't fight it. Her mouth was salivating. She kept swallowing spit.

I will not.

I will not.

I will not.

Days later, after she'd cut the trip short and returned home exhausted and sick with aching breasts, it was still too early to take a pregnancy test, but she'd told Ethan anyway when he picked her up from the airport. He'd processed the news in silence—and then with a growing boyish excitement she'd never seen before. By the time he dropped her off at her apartment, the sky was graying with dawn and she only wanted to sleep, and he'd kissed her forehead and told her it was the best news of his life. This shattered something inside Allie. Of course Ethan would be enthusiastic about having a kid. It wasn't his body or career.

Allie's career was every airport, rail station, and bus stop in the world. She'd built her identity around traveling hundreds of miles a day, fast and thrifty and light. She imagined navigating customs with a stroller and a diaper bag, washing formula bottles under rural water spigots, installing a twenty-pound car seat in every bus and taxi—and she had to stop, because the anxiety became a physical weight atop her chest. How would she adjust to this? What would happen to *Keep Calm*? Allie's life, her identity, everything she'd worked so hard to build over the past decade, was all about to be obliterated by the time bomb growing inside her.

She'd been too embarrassed to tell anyone else, even Tess. She'd researched her condition in private like it was a shameful disease (and, she'd reasoned, isn't pregnancy just the ultimate sexually transmitted disease?). At some point, she saw an online chart breaking out fetal sizes by week—week six was a lentil, week seven was a blueberry, week eight was a raspberry—and the lovey language and saccharine colors made her want to puke all over again. She hadn't been afraid of the fer-de-lance bite that killed her or the deepest, blackest caves her grotto could find, but miles into the Northern Zone of Costa Rica, she'd finally found her personal worst-case scenario, a thing that truly scared her.

Back on that crowded public bus, she did throw up—but quietly, into her satchel.

Only one passenger noticed.

"You didn't have to do that," he'd said in Spanish as she zipped her bag up, the fabric full and warm. But Allie Merritt had always prided herself on solving her own problems. Even then, she already knew she wanted to terminate her pregnancy.

Now, shivering and alone inside an ancient chamber hundreds of feet underground with mud-slick hair, bruised elbows, and a

MicroSD card in her stomach, it occurred to Allie that it was a Saturday, which meant she was now exactly five weeks along.

Five weeks.

According to that stupid pink chart? The size of a sesame seed.

Well, this isn't an ideal situation for either of us. But if we're stuck here together, we might as well introduce ourselves.

Nice to meet you, sesame seed.

I'm Allie.

38

"WE'RE IN UNCHARTED TERRITORY NOW."

Detective Layla Washington sits in that same stiff hospital chair. Now the curtains are open, the monitoring machines are off, and Tess's bed is empty. The Starbucks cup sits on the tray table, untouched and long cold.

She hears the lieutenant sigh over the phone, a staticky crackle.

Whatever happened next at the Devil's Staircase is known only by Tess and Allie. The truth is often a secret shared by killer and victim. But Washington has a theory.

"I think Allie kept the memory card," she says.

"Clever."

"This would have put Tess in one hell of a dilemma. She'd taken care of Jacob and Ethan already, and she had Allie trapped at the bottom. She was *so close* to winning, but she couldn't take that final step. If she started the engine, she'd seal the memory card down there with Allie's body for us to find. This left her with one choice."

She hears a smile in the lieutenant's voice as it comes together. "To rope down into the Chimney herself."

"Yes."

"And fight Allie."

She nods. "Hand to hand."

No more hiding behind Jacob. No more lies.

Tess DeWater is an intelligent and cold-blooded creature.

She would have reasoned that Allie's last bullet was spent and the gun was no longer a threat. She would have armed herself with whatever weapons she had available. Jacob's steel KA-BAR knife? Most logically. And her map. Plus her headlamp, her flashlight, and any borrowed climbing gear she had left.

She'd been forced into the very situation she'd fought so hard to avoid: a direct confrontation. She might have planned to watch from the sidelines and let her accomplice do the throat cutting, but Jacob Herman never stood a chance against gritty, determined Allie. Maybe this final battle was always inevitable. It certainly feels like it's all coming full circle, back to the clear red morning Tess had first described hours ago.

Two best friends visited a cave.

One returned.

And now, we know who the real heroine is.

"Whoever won the fight," Washington says, "would tell us the story."

"And Allie lost."

She looks to the empty bed and says nothing.

39

I CAN DO THIS, ALLIE TOLD HERSELF. *I'VE LASTED THIS LONG.*

I can survive this, too.

Forty feet up, she saw light.

Faint at first, but it slowly grew into a blue-white glare. Shadows swirled across stalactites as the light source crept closer to the Chimney's edge, just out of view. Then soft noises echoed from above: a pack unzipping, rope uncoiling, the click of descender bars. Allie listened to the rustle of gear and waited for her former best friend to say something before she began her descent, to justify her actions or even apologize, and it took a few heart-sinking moments to accept that Tess had nothing to say to her at all.

This fight would be different—and so much harder—than the clownish and sadistic man she'd shot in the throat. While her enemy prepared above, Allie would prepare below.

I can do this.

First, she needed a weapon. The male killer's .45 was slide-locked empty. Her survival knife was long gone. She searched loose cobble to find a rock the size of a baseball—light enough to swing, heavy enough to crack bone. It would have to do.

I can do this.

She kicked off her boots, waterlogged and heavy. She would move faster on bare feet. She peeled off her harness and slathered her arms with handfuls of cold mud. It would camouflage her, make her slippery in a hand-to-hand grapple.

I can do this.

Surprise was her best advantage. She tossed her glowstick into the pool—it would only give away her position—and concealed herself behind an overhang of dripstone. She nestled into its contours comfortably, until blackness shrouded her.

The glowstick projected watery ripples across the chamber, a dizzying aurora of green light. She steadied her breaths and closed her eyes, letting them adjust to the dark. She listened to Tess rappel from the ledge above using the same single-rope technique they'd practiced as teenagers and swallowed a solid mass of emotions—shock and betrayal and heartbreak and rage—all at once. She didn't know what to feel first, so she strangely felt nothing at all.

Those familiar sounds crept closer: the soft jingle of a carabiner, rope feeding through stainless steel bars, wet boots wall-walking down rock.

And halfway down: a jarring metallic gunshot.

Allie heard a heavy splash and the slap of limp rope. She already knew Tess's fall was nonfatal, broken by the pool, but all the same, she felt a jolt of adrenaline: the last anchor bolt up in Razor Alley had finally broken. Its corroded, century-old hook had shattered under the strain like she'd known it would, and whatever happened next, Tess and Allie were now trapped inside the lower chamber together.

Both were fully committed.

All right, sesame seed.

I have a few things I need to get off my chest.

First, you, my little friend, must be the unluckiest clump of cells in the entire universe. And I'm not just referring to our current situation.

You had the extreme misfortune of coalescing into existence inside me, Alma Lynne Merritt. Me, of nearly two billion fertile women on Earth. Whatever maternal instinct is, I don't have it. I'm not nurturing. I'm not patient. I have zero interest in wiping crap out of an infant's butt crack or building a toddler bed or waking up early in the morning to pack a school lunch. I've never, ever wanted to make a family, and to be brutally honest, I've wanted to punch most of the children I've met. Let's face it, little guy or gal, you and I were never going to work.

Second, I just want to make this perfectly clear, so you don't get your hopes up. Whatever happens in the next few minutes, if I survive this fight, if I somehow make it to the surface—I'm still killing you on Monday.

I already made the appointment.

Sorry, sesame seed.

Nothing personal.

Allie flattened her body against cold rock.

Her enemy's LED flashlight scanned the walls of runny dripstone, much closer and brighter now, but it still couldn't see everything. It would need to search every blind corner and check every shadowed space. And in one of them, a crouched and mud-slathered Allie waited with a rock clenched in her fist, ready to swing.

As the light crept closer, she felt a tickle atop her bare shoulder: finely haired legs creeping one step at a time.

They climbed her throat.

Her chin.

Brushing the spider away would risk making a sound, so Allie relaxed her muscles and let it crawl up her cheek, tickling her eyelashes, and then onto the wall behind her. This was *her* world, not Tess's. Since she was nine years old, she'd spent cumulative weeks of her life underground, and she was such a natural part of this landscape that its blind denizens didn't even notice her. The cave spider didn't even realize it was walking over a human face.

A dead man's voice echoed in her mind, a droning loop.

The man downstairs, he waits and he waits.

This time, the lyrics emboldened her. Allie had the element of surprise now, and she only needed to wait for her moment to strike.

As the LED light crept closer, it illuminated the glistening floor, almost touching Allie's bare toes. She tucked them in and pressed herself lower, her body aching and tense. Rock textures lit up around her—mineral grays, egg-yolk yellows, rust reds, glistening streams of calcium carbonate poured like molten slag. Eye-wateringly bright now, the light infiltrated every crack and crevice, and Allie's hiding place shrank to a sliver of darkness.

No noises now. She held her breath.

The light stopped a few feet away, hovering just barely out of view. She knew Tess was standing just around the formation's edge, almost close enough to touch. She could hear the woman's breaths, the flex of her harness, the water dripping off her drenched clothes. One more step and they'd be eye to eye—and Allie would swing her rock.

It was almost over.

Almost.

With her lungs in her throat, Allie waited for that final step.

Instead, the LED light snapped away. The woman's footsteps retreated. The light source raced back to the base of the Chimney, leaving Allie alone in the dark. She struggled to process this. Something had just suddenly changed, but *what*?

Then under her own heartbeat she heard it, too. A faraway echo off wet limestone, so faint and muffled that she'd mistaken it for another layer of the cave's ambience. It could have been there unnoticed for minutes, a low and throaty rumble, like a predator's growl.

Every cave has a Minotaur, Ethan used to joke, but she knew this was something worse.

40

"BACK ON THE SURFACE," WASHINGTON SAYS, "JACOB HAD ONE LAST surprise."

Even in death.

"He crawled a bloody trail to his Jeep, dragged himself up into the driver's seat, and, with his last few seconds of consciousness, turned the key."

With a dead man slumped at the wheel, the Jeep would idle uninterrupted for hours. Piped through several hundred feet of rubber hose, the internal combustion engine would flood the confined space with carbon monoxide. The air inside would become poisonous to breathe within minutes, a death sentence to Tess and Allie alike.

"He got his revenge on them both."

41

ALLIE COULD ALREADY TASTE IT.

The fumes tickled her throat, sooty and nauseatingly dense. Like inhaling campfire smoke. She could feel the weight of it descending the Chimney, a blanket of smoggy air. How long, already, had the engine been running unnoticed?

She watched Tess scramble along the chamber's edge, clawing her fingernails on smooth flowstone, searching for handholds, footholds, anything to climb.

It wouldn't work.

Allie stepped out of the shadows, still gripping her rock. "Are we still fighting?"

Tess ignored her.

"Are we fighting or not?"

"It doesn't matter." Tess hurried from wall to wall, her voice choked with desperation. "We're both fucking *dead*."

Allie knew the four-story shaft was impossible to climb. She'd already tried it for hours today, searching methodically with her fingertips for any thin gap. She'd even tried creative solutions, like tying her remaining rope to her water bottle to fashion a crude grappling hook, but there was nothing up there to latch on to. Nothing worked.

Escaping the Chimney was impossible without a fixed rope. And that last surviving steel bolt, corroded by decades of moisture, had been the only anchor point.

Now destroyed, too.

"There's no way up." Tess coughed, wincing at the acrid stench. "And we're . . . we're running out of air—"

Allie focused on controlling her own breaths. She inhaled through her nose, counted to four, and let it out through her mouth. "Slow your breathing, so you use less of it."

"It doesn't matter."

"And sit down."

"We're dead anyway."

"And limit your talking. That uses air, too—"

"What does it matter?" Tess shrieked, her voice raw.

Allie ignored her and sat down. She knew the vertical chamber was an hourglass filling with poison and every physical exertion now had a cost. Every second, the air grew worse. With every breath, more carbon monoxide accumulated in their bloodstreams. She pulled her lighter from her pocket and flicked it—just a weak orange flame the size of her thumbnail.

Her heart sank. Oxygen was already low.

"We're . . . we can't stop it." Tess kept trying to scurry up the slick walls like a pathetic trapped animal, her boots slipping, tears in her eyes. "It doesn't matter what we do. There's no way to shut off the Jeep from down here. It'll keep running all night, for hours and hours, until the entire tank is—"

"Tess, will you *shut the fuck up*, please?"

She froze, as if struck.

Allie flicked her lighter shut and stood up. She approached the pool's edge and stared into the dark water, at her green glowstick glimmering at the bottom like a bioluminescent cave worm. It illuminated that black underwater opening, no bigger than an air duct. She took another measured breath.

"You're wrong," she said. "There's one way out."

• • •

Allie had never entered Worse Than Death before.

She always stopped her summer expedition groups at Razor Alley. The team was usually made up of amateurs, and after an oppressive hands-and-knees crawl down the Drainpipe, everyone was muddy, sweaty, and ready to see the sky again. The Grim Reaper sign did its job in deterring most sensible cavers, but there was always one or two who couldn't resist the call of the depths. Allie had always been curious herself, maybe more than anyone, but the entire group's safety was her responsibility.

She knew all the horror stories. She'd read all about the ill-fated prospector and the ensuing rescue attempt, and even the gory, but disputed, particulars of how they recovered his body. She'd memorized every detail of the man's famously horrifying death, true and mythic. She knew it was illegal to enter Worse Than Death under even ideal conditions, and right now she didn't have her pack, her gear, or even her map.

Also, conditions were far from ideal.

It was *underwater*.

"Tess." She looked back. "You had a map. Where is it?"

But Tess wasn't listening. She kept pacing in a tranced panic, her boots sloshing through the pool's shallows, gulping more precious air. Caught in her own cruel trap. Her boyfriend's ugly steel knife was in her hand, and when Allie approached, she slashed at her.

"I don't give a shit about fighting right now." Allie kept her distance, the rock in her hand. "Do you have a map or not?"

"I have it."

"Show me."

Holding the knife blade-out, Tess dug into her pocket and

unfolded something. The map wasn't even laminated. Just flimsy paper, already soaked.

"How long does it say Worse Than Death is?" Allie pointed. "How many feet?"

"It doesn't say."

"Look at the scale, dipshit."

"It's . . ." Tess's voice broke apart. "*Two hundred feet.* Without air."

Through a winding, hostile crawlspace.

In some places, ten inches wide.

Underwater.

It wrenched Allie's stomach, the enormity of it. Claustrophobia and drowning: two primal fears combined. Only professional cave divers would attempt such a plunge, and air tanks and flippers would never fit in such a confined tunnel anyway. Such a distance would take several minutes to swim through, at minimum, and she didn't have the training to hold her breath for that long. To try it would be certain death.

Her eyes and throat burned with irritation now. A headache pierced her thoughts like two hot knives behind her eye sockets. Soon, she knew, would come dizziness, fatigue, and confusion as her body started to shut down.

Then unconsciousness.

Convulsions.

Respiratory arrest.

Death.

"Fuck it." Allie paced on shaky knees. "There have to be elevated spaces down there, cavities in the ceiling where pockets of air might be trapped. Even if it's just a small bubble. Anything to get to the next breath and keep going—"

"You're *insane*."

"When water rises, air has to go somewhere."

"If you're wrong, you'll die."

"I'll die if I stay here, too." Allie gazed down into the black water, inhaling slowly with her diaphragm. Practicing efficient breaths, trying to prepare herself. This would defy every self-preservation instinct in her body, her lungs, her brain. It would be so much easier to sit and wait here with her former best friend, inhale more invisible poison, and let herself fall asleep. Like euthanasia, the male killer had said.

Not happening, she told herself.

If I have to die today, it won't be in my sleep.

"It's worse than that." Tess coughed. "You know it's not just one tunnel down there, right? There are offshoots and dead ends, like a flooded maze. It's not even fully mapped—"

Yes, yes, and *yes*. Allie knew all of this already. Worse Than Death was an underground cardiovascular system branching into tangles of smaller veins and arteries. Hitting a dead end inside a tight squeeze is already dangerous—without space to turn around, a crawling human must instead wriggle in reverse and backtrack. This can take several minutes. Underwater, while holding your breath, you don't have several minutes. Underwater, one wrong turn is fatal.

"I can't die here with you," Allie said. "I won't."

"It's suicide."

"Stay. Follow. I don't care what you do." She waded up to her knees in icy water and felt a sickening dizziness fall over her, like an instant inner ear infection. Another bad sign. She snapped her last glowstick, a fresh burst of green. Without her headlamp, without her flashlight, it would be her only source of light underwater.

"I've done squeezes before," she coached herself. "I can do this, too."

"You're really serious?"

"I have to try."

This is my world, she thought. *This is what I do.*

"It looks like the tunnel goes straight for . . . about ten feet." Tess studied the map with her flashlight. "Then it turns and splits. I can't tell, but I think the left side widens."

That widened space, Allie knew, would be her best chance at finding a pocket of breathable air. If one even existed. This would be a gamble with suicide, an underwater game of Russian roulette, and she couldn't even be sure Tess was telling the truth. Unknowns upon unknowns.

She flicked her lighter again—this time, just a spark.

No flame at all.

It was getting difficult to breathe. Every gulp of air felt strangely solid in Allie's chest, like inhaling cotton candy. Her thoughts were starting to swim with hypoxia. "So I'll go left. Give me the map so I can see the rest of the—"

"I'll tell you if we make it that far." Tess stood up. "I'm following you."

"Give me the fucking map."

"I'm keeping it." Tess tucked the wet paper into her back pocket, her boyfriend's knife in her other hand. "For insurance."

Allie felt a spreading coldness in her stomach. Her best friend had always been quietly savvy with calculations. Even here, even now.

She considered fighting anyway in the dwindling air—hurling her rock at Tess's face, feinting left, hitting right, trying to rip the fragile paper away without damaging it—but her enemy still had that vicious combat knife. Even if Allie won the fight, she'd likely take a stab wound, and then she'd never make the long swim. Fighting over the map was suicide, a waste of air, energy, and time.

Whether she liked it or not, they had a fragile alliance.

Until we don't.

Allie told herself she'd solve one problem at a time. That's all anyone can do. When plans went awry in unfamiliar places, she often remembered something her grandfather used to say: *It is permitted you in time of grave danger to walk with the devil until you have crossed the bridge.*

But this would be one hell of a narrow bridge.

"Fine. Try to keep up." Allie waded up to her chest in chilled water, her bare feet touching jagged hidden rocks. Worse Than Death was a keyhole in solid stone, like a vent at the bottom of a swimming pool. Her rock would only slow her down, so she dropped it. In the tight tunnels there would be no space for shoes or a helmet or any gear at all except her water bottle, which she clipped to her wrist. It was empty, drank hours ago, but that was the point—the bottle itself was an emergency air reserve. One last breath on backup.

Treading water, she inhaled before the plunge.

"Allie, *wait*."

She looked back.

"For whatever it's worth"—Tess's eyes glimmered—"I'm . . . sorry."

The woman's form seemed to shift in the watery green light. Her face kept changing with the rippling reflections, her features swirling in inhuman ways, and Allie thought about those late-night games of Changeling at her cousin's house, the room's shared gasp of disbelief that the secret monster could be shy, innocent little Tess time and time again. A changeling is a tragic creature, an imposter planted by the devil in the place of a stolen child. They're masters of mimicry, dirt and dead wood enchanted to look and sound human but lacking a soul, and sometimes changelings even unwittingly trick themselves. Sometimes, as grown adults, they don't even remember what they are. Allie couldn't tell if she hated Tess or pitied her.

She breathed deeply and submerged her face.

I can do this.

I can do this.

I can do this.

Please, God, help me do this.

Up close, the hole was even smaller than it had looked from the surface. The murky water was full of particles, like swimming inside a snow globe.

Her lungs burned already.

Allie gripped the narrow opening with her fingertips, bit the glowstick with her front teeth, and wriggled inside. No time to hesitate. The physical sensation of enclosure was immediate; knives of rock scraped her body on all sides, but she ignored her fear and struggled through. She'd survived squeezes before, some almost as bad as this. The only difference was the water. She estimated the tunnel was eighteen inches wide, and it would only get tighter.

She needed to breathe. Soon.

Caterpillar-crawling underwater, progress was painfully slow. Was she already too far down to swim back up? She reminded herself that it didn't matter—she'd only run feetfirst into Tess and drown anyway. Her only chance was moving forward. At all costs. She felt the jagged walls change shape around her—yes, this was the turn Tess had described. She had to rotate onto her back and squeeze, fighting her gag reflex as cold water trickled down her nose.

Next, the crawlspace split into two paths—a right and a left—but she already knew the way. *Left.* She twisted her body to fit with the green glowstick in her teeth, through swirling particles of ancient sediment—her lungs were aching now, ballooning against her ribs—but a jolt of panic stopped her cold. Her stomach dropped.

Despite all her efforts, she hadn't seen the map.

Only Tess had.

I can't trust her directions.

Tess had every reason to lie to her, to send her down an unmapped dead end to drown. To die somewhere her body would never be found.

Did she lie to me?

There was no time to swim back. Allie's lungs were about to explode. Either way, right or left, led to a 50 percent chance of drowning. Life and death would come down to this, a blind underwater coin toss. She thought of the way Ethan had flipped that coin on their first date, their penny date, the expectant laughter between them as it twirled and caught a spark of sunlight. At one intersection he'd fumbled the toss and it fell down to the pedals as he drove, so Allie unbuckled her seat belt to retrieve it—*Tails,* she'd called triumphantly—and it would be the first time she'd touched Ethan's leg, their bodies still then unexplored. "Little Talks" by Of Monsters and Men on the speakers. The cinnamon-cookie scent of his cologne that she'd teased him for. God, she wished to be in that moment and not this one.

Left?

Or right?

Allie had to make a choice. Her time was up. And if she chose wrong, she knew, it could be Tess telling this story to the police instead.

Left, Tess had said.

So Allie went opposite and swam *right.*

• • •

I'm going to let you in on a secret, sesame seed.

Death is no big deal.

Really.

I mean it. I know this because I've literally done it before. I lost consciousness in the back of some nice Mexican dude's pickup with a swelling hand and woke up in a hospital bed without even realizing my heart had stopped. No angels or demons or Heaven or Hell. Cardiac death was just a glorified nap. It felt like nothing at all. That's the big secret of all mankind, the thing everyone seems afraid to admit: to the beholder, death is no worse than falling asleep.

Heck, technically we've all been dead before, haven't we? For billions of years across the span of time, while Earth was a half-formed ball of magma, during the Crusades, during the Roaring Twenties, you and I were both as dead as doornails and it didn't hurt us one bit. Only life hurts. But oblivion? It's painless.

That's a promise, straight from your mama.

Whatever happens to us next, there is nothing to be afraid of.

42

SHE FOUND AIR.

With her fingertips, Allie felt a narrow cavity in the limestone overhead—barely enough space to inhale. It tasted musty, sour, like bathroom drain mold. She didn't care. It was the best damn air she'd ever breathed in her life.

The low ceiling scraped her forehead and glistened with rows of symmetrical ridges, eerily organic-looking, like a rib cage. She couldn't turn her body around. She could barely move her legs and arms. Traversing the shoulder-width tube felt like belly-crawling down the long stomach of a python, neck-deep in stomach acid. Cold water lapped at the curved ceiling, just a few inches of breathable air.

This was beyond claustrophobic. Whatever this was, words hadn't been invented for it. If she survived this she'd never even begin to describe this enveloping full-body horror, the weight and pressure and strangling visceral *closeness* on all sides—

A gurgle of displaced water rose behind her. A gasping voice inhaled.

Tess.

Allie twisted her neck to look back. "You lied."

The woman wasn't listening. Too much wild-eyed adrenaline. She coughed on dirty water, her hair plastered to her face in black tendrils.

"You lied to me," Allie repeated. "It was *right*, not left."

"I . . . read the map wrong."

"You went right."

"I was following you."

Lies, lies, lies. All of it. Everything Tess said was too dangerous to trust. Allie knew she'd been a single wrong choice from a nightmarish death, from frigid water racing down her throat to fill her lungs as her fingernails clawed against rock.

For decades, no human had dared to explore Worse Than Death. The survey maps were all incomplete—hundreds of feet underground, below the Drainpipe and Razor Alley and the Chimney and everything else, a human body lost in an unmapped dead end would likely never be found, let alone recovered. A complete search of such a cramped and intricate tunnel system was impossible, and Tess surely knew it.

She needs me to die down here.

Her spine chilled.

Someplace they'll never find my body.

She needed that map, somehow, but it was physically impossible to fight here. The single-file tunnel wouldn't allow it. And even though Tess had the knife, she couldn't attack from behind, either—if she slashed the arteries in Allie's ankles, her body would block the passage and trap her, too. Guaranteed death.

Tess coughed. "I still smell exhaust."

"It's following us." Allie spat water. "Through cracks in the rock."

Time was running out.

Ahead, the crawlspace submerged again into dark water. Another blind plunge. Another life-and-death gamble that there was another pocket of air deeper inside, that it could be swim-crawled to fast enough. All of it, all over again. Allie's heart sank.

"Pass me the map"—she reached back—"so I know what's next."

"I'll describe it to you."

"Fuck you. Give me the map."

"It . . . splits into three tunnels," Tess described. "A left, a right, and a middle. We have to go down the middle—"

"You're lying again."

"Trust me."

"I don't."

Wedged on her back in the flooded tunnel, Allie felt crushed from all sides. Relentless pressure. Carbon monoxide penetrating the porous bedrock behind them, their shared air dwindling, their body temperatures dropping. Tess's knife carried inches behind her unprotected feet. So many deaths in pursuit. She took a shivering breath.

I can do this.

"Trust me," Tess repeated. "What choice do you have?"

Okay, sesame seed.

Maybe I was a little harsh.

About aborting you on Monday, I mean. If I was, well, I'm sorry. I know you're just a clump of cells, but I shouldn't be glib about it. Humor has always been my way of avoiding things I'd rather not deal with. I'll even admit that you and I have a few things in common, although you probably look like a tadpole right now.

We both have a heartbeat (according to that stupid chart).

We both require oxygen.

We're also both—let's not sugarcoat it—in extreme fucking danger.

We're hundreds of feet underground and wedged inside a flooded trench the diameter of an air duct, and the only thing more dangerous than this cave is the woman we're trapped with. We're crossing a narrow bridge with the devil, all right, and it'll only get narrower. She holds the map. She can't fight us physically, so she's fighting psychologically, using the cave against us. But your mama won't go quietly.

I'll find a way to beat her.

I swear.

If it's any consolation, sesame seed, I promise: no one kills you but me.

As she swam through the murky water, Allie's glowstick revealed artifacts littering the cramped tunnel. She had to push them aside.

Rust-eaten tools and chisels.

Pulleys.

Decayed ropes.

Like wreckage on the ocean floor, this was the epicenter of an unsuccessful rescue operation more than a century ago. This was where it happened. Every item was left exactly where it had been discarded, the men who carried them all long forgotten.

Her chest ached with building pressure. She'd been submerged for too long already and she was in danger of losing consciousness—but finally, the crawlspace widened a few inches into the three-way split Tess had described, and this time she couldn't afford to second-guess herself. There were three routes. Two led to death. She had a one-in-three chance.

The middle, Tess had said. But she was lying.

Left or right, then?

Fifty-fifty. Better odds, but still not good. Stars pierced her vision like fireworks now. She couldn't hold her breath for any longer. She needed to make another blind choice, another all-or-nothing coin toss. In her hypoxic thoughts she saw that penny twirling, slapping down on Ethan's forearm as it led them closer and closer to their first date at the cemetery, the *cemetery* of all places. Heads or tails?

Left or right?

Left or right?

Left or—

Allie ignored both and swam straight down the middle. Left and right were both wrong. She knew Tess's tricks, the subtle ways she played the room, how when the changeling suspected the group's suspicions were turning against her, she didn't get flustered or try to argue. She smoothly changed her tactics.

Reverse psychology.

This time, Allie guessed Tess had told the truth—the middle—and staked two lives on it.

43

ALLIE HAD A PLAN.

Twice now, she'd survived by intuition and luck. She wouldn't survive a third dive. "No more mind games, Tess." She spat out her glowstick and stopped in the neck-high water, letting her body block the narrow trench. "I'm not moving until you give me the map."

Behind her, only the lap of water.

She waited for Tess to respond, breathing through her teeth while they both lay wedged single file on their stomachs. Their bodies crushed flat in the cold water. No space to turn around. She imagined millions of tons of earth suspended overhead, like they were belly-crawling between the jaws of an industrial press. At any second, the slab of moon-gray rock could shift a few inches and *crushed like a bug* wouldn't even begin to describe the totality of it. One tremor and they'd both cease to exist.

Still, Tess said nothing.

Allie raised her voice and repeated, "Give me the map, or we both die—"

"It doesn't matter."

"Why?"

"The paper's soaked." Tess's voice quivered with fear. "It's mush. I can't read it."

Allie's heart dropped. She hadn't considered this.

Please, God, no.

"Pass it to me anyway," she said.

"I can't reach your hand."

"Then hold it up." She craned her neck under the low ceiling—to look back in the cramped space, she had to submerge most of her face. Icy water rushed up her nose.

Sure enough, the waterlogged map really was disintegrating. Tess had preserved only a corner of wet paper and pressed her flashlight behind it like a slide projector. The maze of tunnels was blurred with running ink.

Allie squinted. "I think I see—"

The last of it melted away. Tess cried out and tried to scoop mushy pieces from the water, but they were unrecognizable.

The map was gone.

"It's okay." Allie spat water. "I saw enough."

"What did you see?"

"There's one more dive, maybe twenty feet ahead." Allie shut her eyes and concentrated. "We'll go down. Then left. Then up, and we're out." Then on to the Upper Vault, and up a few hundred feet more of crawls and scrambles.

Tess repeated: "Down, left, up—"

Then, finally . . .

The surface. Open air. The sky.

"And then?"

"Then," Allie said quietly, "I guess we'll have our fight."

"I won't fight you."

"You're lying again."

"If we make it out of this, I swear to God, I'm done." Tess's shivery voice rattled in the confined air. "I'll give you the knife. We'll tell the police everything, together."

More lies, Allie knew. *More manipulation.*

She felt a strange disappointment in her former best friend. Being lied to now, still, after everything, hurt in a soul-deep way.

It was all gaslighting. Every word was designed to trick her into lowering her guard. Then once they reached the surface, the truce would end and Tess would surprise attack with her boyfriend's knife. It could even come now, at any second, if Tess decided the tunnel's dimensions allowed it. Whenever the attack came, Allie knew she'd be at a disadvantage and unarmed. Against a knife, without the element of surprise, she wouldn't stand a chance. In all outcomes, Allie's death was near certain.

But she had a plan for that, too.

First, she'd need to walk with the devil a little longer.

The tunnel constricted around them as they crawled deeper, all rock surfaces tightening closer. Eighteen inches of width shrank to a snug fifteen, and Allie had to contract her shoulders to fit. Her knees and elbows scraped on all sides. She felt the weight press down against her, like something heavy was sitting on top of her. Then even tighter, *tighter*, until there wasn't enough space to crawl with her limbs and she had to wriggle her entire body like a giant inchworm instead. The ceiling forced her mouth underwater, and she gagged. To cram herself through the narrowing space ahead, she had to dig out mud and gravel in shaky handfuls.

Some cavers call it the *rapture*. To Allie, it had always felt like a sort of sleep paralysis: a locked-in sensation so intense and unrelenting that your entire body wants to turn itself violently inside out. She heard rapid breaths behind her—Tess was hyperventilating.

"Stay calm."

"I can't . . . I can't *breathe*—"

"You're wasting our air." Allie braced an elbow and rotated her body to fit. "Roll over. Press your mouth to the ceiling. We'll scoot on our backs."

The cracked gray ceiling lowered to ten inches now, flattening

Allie's nose. Her eyelids fluttered against it. Water lapped at the edges of her mouth, and she had to purse her lips against cold rock to inhale—*ceiling sucking*, it was called. She could feel the pressure on her chest, forcing her to take shallow breaths. Squeezes trigger a claustrophobic *get me out of here* terror, but she understood the true danger was just ahead and out of view. It's actually the turns, the unexpected changes in direction, that get cavers stuck.

"Okay." She felt with an outstretched hand. "I feel a sharp turn ahead."

"How sharp?"

"Ninety degrees, at least."

She couldn't even say the worst part yet. This was the deadliest variation dreaded by the most experienced tunnel crawlers: an S-bend. Two ninety-degree turns placed closely together, bending in opposite directions to form a deadly natural chokepoint. The human body can hinge in only a few places—waist, elbows, knees—and survival can come down to the length of your shins. She thought about the prospector, wedged so tightly in this place that the only way out was to have his legs broken with hammers. To be sawed apart and excavated limb by limb—

A boulder shifted overhead with a sudden tectonic creak. The ceiling lowered an inch. Loose pebbles dropped into the water, splashing in Allie's eyes.

The tunnel was unstable.

Oh, God, please, she thought. *Give me a fucking break.*

Behind her, Tess gasped with new fear. "What was that?"

"Crawl slowly," Allie murmured. "Be careful what you touch."

Everything here could be precarious: millions of tons of heaped boulders still settling and finding equilibrium overhead. All it could take was a little pressure in the wrong place. She heard ancient, brittle groans and felt the vibration against her face. More rocks splashed into the water around them, and with every splash, she knew the waterline was dangerously rising. And to her horror she heard more frenzied movement behind her, Tess kicking and pushing in all directions in blind, strait-jacketed panic: "Oh, my God. *Oh, my God—*"

"Stop thrashing. You'll kill us."

"I can't . . ."

"Slow and steady, one inch at a time."

"I can't do this."

"Yes, you can." Allie pressed her lips against rock, just barely above the lapping water. "Remember, fear is power."

"Fear is power," Tess echoed.

They kept saying it, back and forth, like a chant with squashed lungs. For a few minutes they could pretend to be friends again, sisters in arms, navigating the S-bend with their bodies pretzeled together under mammoth bedrock.

Halfway through, Allie had to ask it. "Your mom never did those things to you, did she?"

A long silence behind her. Then: "No."

"You lied about the bleach. All of it."

"Yes."

"So you could live with my family."

"There's . . . something wrong with me." Tess's whisper filled the inches between water and rock, breathy and shivering. "It's like a wire is connected wrong in my brain, or like I'm missing some important part everyone else has. I can't explain it."

Allie felt spidery fingers touch her left ankle. The faint pressure moved across her skin, a gentle motion tracing three sides. She remembered seeing Tess trace those nervous little triangles on tabletops at the dive bar on Sixth where they used to play trivia, on her Honda's steering wheel before her driver's exam, on her own thigh in algebra class. A thousand little snapshots.

"I know." Allie swallowed. "I always felt sorry for you. Your moods, your anxieties, the way you pushed people away but still couldn't stand to be alone. You were this shy, broken little thing with scaly skin that came to live in my house, and I felt like I could save you somehow." She exhaled, feeling her own trapped breath. "I guess I was afraid to leave you behind because that would mean I'd failed."

"You should've cut me loose," Tess said.

"I know."

"Why didn't you?"

"I wasn't strong enough," Allie said, closing her eyes.

But now, I am.

Because she'd lied, too.

It was already done. Minutes ago, she'd described the map inaccurately—the way out was really to the *right*, not the left. Their hand-to-hand fight on the surface would never happen, and instead they'd quietly go their separate ways on the final dive: Allie to the surface, and Tess to an unknown grave, her own cruel trick turned against her.

I'm sorry, Tess. But I can be cruel, too.

Her eyes stung with tears.

I learned it from you.

This was a goodbye, if not the goodbye Tess was expecting.

"I loved you," Tess said.

"I loved you, too."

"I peed in the water."

"It's okay," Allie said. "I'm peeing right now."

• • •

We're almost there, sesame seed.

One more deep breath, one more plunge under cold water. Then Worse Than Death will be over and Tess will be gone. We're so close to seeing the sky again.

Did I ever mention that leaving a cave is the best part?

Well, it is.

Just wait for it.

When I was nine, my dad took me to my first cave in Kentucky. It took us hours to tour just a tiny fraction of Mammoth Cave's four hundred miles, and after everything I saw—the flowstone in Great Onyx, the glittering crystals in the Star Chamber—when we finally returned to the surface I thought my eyes had been damaged somehow. The world looked wrong, colorless. All I could see were grays and blacks. The sun had become this dirty white orb floating in cloudy gray, and it took me a few stunned seconds to realize it was actually night-time. *If you're underground long enough, even the night sky can feel as bright as day. And just breathing this new air again—I could taste pine needles and tree sap and bluegrass pollen and centipede musk and campfire smoke from a mile away—I almost cried, just nine-year-old me crouched there under the moonlight gasping these juddering breaths, and my dad held my fingers in his huge hand and told me,* You can't truly appreciate the light until you've spent time in the dark. *And he was right, of course, but it was more than light and darkness. I think after hours in the tunnels my little mind was comprehending just how big the world really is. For the first time in my life I understood: there are no walls, no ceilings. Just open air. You can go anywhere. Isn't that wild? Any mountain, any city, any ocean. It's all there. You can go see it, if you're brave enough. And even now I still get that feeling every time I leave a cave, like I'm that wide-eyed little girl again gazing up at a whole life made new because this world is huge, full of beauty and terror and mystery and everything that hasn't happened yet, and I fucking love every inch of it.*

That's *what's up there. That's where we're going, sesame seed.*

I can't wait to show it to you.

And . . . I'm realizing I have another confession to make. I've been thinking about Monday, about the appointment I made.

About you.

About us.

And I want you to know I've changed my mind.

If we make it out, I'll cancel my—

Her nose slammed into rock. Cartilage crunched, and she coughed out bubbles of air. She almost swallowed a mouthful of icy water.

Disbelief flashed through her mind—then alarm.

This was wrong.

There wasn't supposed to be a dead end here. With her fingertips she searched the black water to her right and found only more hardness, more solid stone.

This is impossible, she told herself. *I'm not lost.*

I saw the map with my own eyes.

But Allie was alone now, stuck at the end of a submerged crawlspace with her lungs clenched and no space to turn around. Her mind raced with buried-alive panic, the same repeating thought accelerating—*I saw the map with my own eyes*—and she'd memorized the tunnels, turned Tess's own cruel trick against her, but somehow it was all for nothing. Allie was trapped anyway inside a ten-inch sarcophagus with nowhere to go, water filling her ears, her nose, her mouth. She wanted to scream underwater.

How was this possible?

She'd watched Tess press her flashlight to the wet paper map like a slide projector, every detail plain to see. No more mind games. Paper doesn't lie. Paper can't lie. Not even cunning, sociopathic Tess could make the map say anything other than the truth.

Unless . . .

No.

A wave of horror fell over the drowning woman.

No, no, no—

Unless Tess had knowingly held the wet paper backward. Unless the map, soaked translucent against her flashlight, had been *reversed*.

Then left would be right.

Right would be left.

And the way out would be a dead end.

44

"TESS MADE IT OUT. ALLIE DIDN'T."

Detective Washington imagines the poor woman dying alone inside a flooded crawlspace, hundreds of feet from the surface and locked into a situation not even she could overcome. Despite everything she'd done to survive that day, all her close escapes and resourceful solutions—the cave didn't care. Who lives and who dies comes down to simple physics. The positioning of your legs and arms, the orientation of your torso, your body's ability to breathe and pump blood. Oxygen, energy, space, time. There's nothing fair about it.

She opens her eyes and takes in the empty hospital room. The harsh odors of antiseptic and soap. The buzz of fluorescent lights. The dry recycled air.

"And," she says, "we *owe* it to Allie to get this right."

For a long moment the lieutenant says nothing.

It's all there. Washington has taken the puzzle apart and put it back together for him. Each person involved that day has slotted neatly into their true roles: Jacob, Ethan, Tess, and poor, heroic Allie.

Finally he exhales, a defeated crackle of static. "I think . . . I think you're right. About Tess. About everything."

And . . .

He doesn't want to say it.

And we just let her walk out the fucking door.

Tess DeWater never planned to go home and sleep, of course. That was just another lie. She'd surely known that police sluggishness had given her a valuable window of time to finish covering her tracks. She would destroy her bagged clothes before they could be seized. She would return to Jacob's mobile residence—its location still unknown—and burn every piece of evidence that might be used to connect them. It would all be ashes by the morning, every vital thread cut. Tess has spent hundreds of hours studying criminal procedure as a third-year law student. She surely knows their playbook.

"Christ. I'm sorry, Layla." She hears a faint creak, an office chair settling as he sits down. "We never should have let her out of our sight. We had her, we had the mastermind of the whole thing sitting in a room with you—"

"It's fine."

"I should've trusted you."

"I said it's *fine*."

The lieutenant stops. An uncertain pause.

"You're right. You did make a mistake." Washington allows herself to crack a vindicated smile. "But luckily, I made a mistake, too."

She touches her handheld radio.

"Due to my cognitive decline, I forgot to call off the deputies downstairs."

Within seconds of leaving the hospital's south lobby, Tess DeWater was identified and arrested by Deputies Harris and Dunn. She surrendered without incident, and by the time Detective Washington radios in to request an update, they're already halfway to the sheriff's office.

"Baker-twelve. Suspect in custody."

She lowers her handheld and grins. "Beautiful."

45

ONE HOUR LATER, THE SURVIVOR FROM THE DEVIL'S STAIRCASE HAS been photographed, fingerprinted, and seated in a soundproof interrogation room on the second floor of the Stevens County Sheriff's Department. This is now a controlled environment—no more interrupting nurses, no more distracting coughs down the hall. The walls are bare and the furniture minimalist. Instead of a cheap digital recorder, Tess's every move is now captured by two high-definition cameras and four directional microphones. She waits rigidly in a sunken chair that's bolted to the floor. She hasn't touched her bottled water. When the door creaks open, she jolts.

Detective Washington enters with a smile. "Hey, stranger."

Her face goes colorless. *You.*

"Yes, me." She sits between Tess and the door. "Remember hours ago, when I told you most killers dig the hole themselves? I just hand them—"

"The shovel," Tess says. "I remember."

When subjects are read their Miranda warning, they're often too shocked or distracted to truly listen. But Tess is different. She absorbs every word with clear-eyed awareness. On the paperwork, she signs her name with a precise swoosh. Then she sets the pen down and stares directly forward, as if challenging the detective.

"To give credit where it's due: Tess, you are one incredible liar.

Maybe the best I've ever seen. Your performance was nuanced and believable. And those details?" Washington mimes a chef's kiss. "Even I was rooting for you, and I'd suspected you were hiding something the moment I sat down in your hospital room." She scoots her unbolted chair forward. "I mean it, Tess. You're damn good at this."

The woman sits on her hands, silent.

"But I'm *better*."

Interrogation is all about psychological pressure, and that pressure requires momentum. A subject must be afforded little time to reflect or maneuver, and Tess has already proven herself to be a gifted and pathological liar. Normal tactics won't work on her. She can juggle details and handle an immense cognitive load. Her mind is agile, pin-sharp, enviably young.

No matter. Washington will break the little bitch anyway.

For Allie.

"I solved it, you know." She pats her notepad. "The whole puzzle."

Tess says nothing.

"I just got off the phone with my friends downtown. I don't believe Allie was really a secret criminal leading a double life. I don't even think she committed wire fraud." Washington scoots closer. "I think that was *you*, sweetheart."

Tess stiffens, almost imperceptibly.

There it is.

"You were stealing under Allie's nose, weren't you? Forging site metrics, lying to her advertisers, pocketing their money. Sneaky little net and gross adjustments that'll take the math nerds months to untangle. It always tore you up that your best friend was so much more successful than you, that her life was so much better than yours, that you were almost thirty and still working for her like a little pet—but you still found a way to carve out your own slice. Law school is expensive, huh? The smart parasite never kills its host, and you're the smartest. But somewhere, you made a mistake."

A muscle below Tess's eyelid tenses. She's trying to hide the flush of adrenaline.

Washington knows she's drawn blood.

"The feds were circling, and you were terrified of what would happen when Allie found out. She was never home and you ran her office, so you could have deleted the calls and emails. If you made sure to answer her apartment door, you could have even impersonated Allie and intercepted the subpoenas and target letters, too. But you were only buying time. The fuse was lit. Any day now, she would discover the truth. It was all about to crash down on you, and you'd be charged with God only knows how many felonies. You'd go to prison. Three years of law school wasted. Your future was over."

The room feels smaller now.

"So you did the only thing that might save you: you had your best friend murdered before she found out. If Allie died in a random attack from an unknown killer, you could pin everything on her. A clean break for you."

Tess is stone-still.

Truth is like the sun. You can shut it out for a time, but it ain't going away.

There's an undeniable catharsis in seeing the full picture excavated, dragged up out of the earth and exposed in harsh detail. But like so many other wins over the decades, it still feels hollow, meaningless, like too little, too late. Clearing Allie Merritt's name for her family and friends won't bring the poor woman back. It never does. The killer always gets to tell the story, and the victims are only ever trapped inside it.

Washington takes a breath and gathers herself. It's dispiriting work as always, just damages and punishments, but she'll do what she can.

For Allie.

"And when your planned murder at the Devil's Staircase fell apart, when badass Allie refused to go quietly and killed Jacob, you had to cover your ass somehow. You didn't just need Allie dead—you needed her body and her memory card to *disappear*, buried under millions of tons of earth somewhere so deep we'd never find her remains."

At least now, she doesn't have to hide her disgust any longer.

"You left your pregnant best friend to die."

46

NO.

Not yet.

Allie Merritt was underwater, wedged inside a ten-inch crawl-space, but she was *not* dead. She still had her empty water bottle. With numb fingers she popped the cap and brought the plastic to her lips. Then she pinched her nose and inhaled.

Most of it escaped as bubbles. She gagged, fighting the water leaking down her throat—but it was a final breath for her oxygen-starved lungs, a few more seconds of consciousness to solve this life-and-death problem. She knew she'd never survive trying to swim back feetfirst, but she remembered passing a gap in the ceiling five, maybe ten feet back. There might be an air pocket somewhere up there, if she could fit. It was her only chance. She braced her elbows against rock to push herself backward—and to her horror, it shifted.

The entire tunnel rearranged itself.

She felt boulders moving around her, an undertow of displaced water, loose gravel peppering her face. A heavy block slammed down beside her head. Another crushed her glowstick, and the green chemical light dimmed into ribbons of dying color.

Blackness now.

The rocks kept compacting from all sides, crushing her body even further. There was no way forward. Was there even a way back? She was so hopelessly disoriented she didn't even know which way was up. She pushed again with her elbows—delicately, this time—but she couldn't move backward. The dimensions of her body wouldn't allow it. Her right knee was pinned, her ankle trapped.

She let the water bottle float away, its air now depleted. That had been her last breath. Her mouth and nose were full of frigid water now, barely held back by the muscles of her clenched throat. She'd exhausted every option. It was over.

But . . .

A deeper part of Allie's brain knew this wasn't true. She was pushing a thought away, refusing to look at it.

Not every option was spent.

No matter how hard she pushed, her right foot held her wedged in place. It refused to budge, as surely as a square peg in a round hole. Her body's natural range of motion locked her in, because a human ankle simply cannot *bend* in that direction.

Unless . . .

Unless I make *it.*

If she broke or dislocated the bone, Allie knew, she might be able to rotate her limp foot a few more degrees and twist free.

It was desperate.

It would hurt.

It wasn't even sure to work.

God, she wished there were another option. Anything else. She couldn't reach her right foot, so she would need to use her own body weight to break her ankle. Underwater, this would be difficult, maybe even impossible. She would need to leverage her entire body and push hard—without triggering another deadly collapse. With her lungs burning and the synapses fading in her brain, she pivoted onto her knee and positioned her ankle. Every pound of Allie Merritt, everything she ever was and ever could be, concentrated on a single bone.

She pushed *hard*.

A sickening live-wire jolt exploded up her shinbone. Maybe the worst pain she'd ever felt in her life, even worse than the fer-de-lance bite. She screamed underwater, losing her last breath to a flurry of racing bubbles.

It wasn't enough. The bone hadn't broken.

I can't.

I can't do this.

I-can't-do-this-I-can't-do-this-I-can't-fucking-do-this—

She had to.

Her lungs were empty now. Out of air, out of time. She knew she had to keep trying, and she did, but every attempt was weaker than the last. Her ankle screamed with pain, the bone aching inside rubbery ligament, the skin torn to bloody hamburger.

It wasn't enough. Allie was only mauling herself, shearing off her flesh and exposing her tendons and filling the water with blood. All this agony for no purpose at all. She couldn't create enough torque to break her ankle. Not here, underwater and weightless, no matter how hard she pushed. And she was fading, sinking inside her own skull. She forced her body to try again, to subject herself to more pointless pain, but this time she couldn't.

Her muscles went limp.

Her senses faded.

Allie lost consciousness.

I'm sorry, sesame seed.

I'm so sorry.

47

IT ALL HAPPENED TWENTY-FOUR HOURS AGO. IT CAN'T BE UNDONE.

Allie's fate is out of her hands.

Even now, after a decade, Washington has never forgotten the way that grieving father's face had changed when he read the funeral home's clumsy, but well-intentioned, text message about his daughter's remains: **We have Isla here.** The shock. The widening eyes. The heart-in-throat tremor of relief. For a miraculous split second, his teenage daughter was alive again, and then she died a second time, like an unconscionably cruel joke.

God, she wishes she'd had the power to bring the poor girl back for real, in a way that wasn't fleeting or illusory.

I have something incredible to show you.

If only.

If fucking *only*.

The interview room is starting to feel smothering. It's been over an hour and the interrogation of Tess DeWater is going in circles. This sociopath, this manipulative little shape-shifter who's spent sixteen years secretly preying on the kindness of her best friend, won't surrender an inch. She already knows she's staged the crime scene at the Devil's Staircase perfectly. She hasn't left an iota of usable evidence behind. Even the *mystery hand* glove print is a dead end, as she discarded her gloves to ensure there'd never be a forensic match. A self-described worrier and control freak, she surely double-checked and triple-checked the bodies of Ethan and Jacob. In her calculations, who else remains alive to challenge her story?

"I'm telling you the truth," she repeats for what feels like the thousandth time, letting tears appear in her eyes. She's still playing her sole-survivor character, calibrated for maximum sympathy. Her breathy voice is convincingly timid and pathetic. She'll keep lying. She'll dig in, deny, double down. Washington can't help but find herself in awe of Tess's cunning, the intelligence and intent behind the performance. This shy girl with chemical burns on her back has been underestimated her entire life, and she's learned how to weaponize it. She preys on the well-meaning and compassionate. She knows exactly where to insert her hooks.

Her lip quivers. "Do I need a lawyer?"

"That's up to you."

Worse, she seems to be acclimatizing to her new situation, finding her footing, gaining confidence. She's done this all before, hasn't she? As a teenager she spent hours testifying under oath about her mother's alleged abuses. As an adult, she's an attorney in training. Now those clear eyes are scanning the soundproof room, memorizing the camera placements, sizing up her opposition. She's about to make some moves of her own.

She asks, "What am I being charged with?"

"You haven't been charged yet."

"And if you can't charge me, you'll let me go?"

"That's right."

Tess nods slowly, considering this. She's starting to sense vulnerability across the table. Eye to eye, Washington can almost read the woman's thoughts.

You don't have enough evidence, do you?

Her voice might be a meek whimper, but her thoughts are steel.

You took me in on a hunch, overriding your boss, and you gambled it all on being able to break me in this room, on scaring me into confessing.

So how's that going?

Law school doesn't teach you how to be a lawyer, but it does teach you how to think like one, and that's arguably more dangerous. This woman has spent three years studying legal procedure. She knows she's a formidable opponent.

"I thought . . ." Tess is playing dumb for the camera, but the detective knows her true intentions. "I thought you needed evidence to arrest someone without a warrant."

She's thinking, *I know you've overstepped.*

Washington nods. "That's true."

"Probable cause?"

"Yes."

"I've seen the affidavits you have to sign." Tess pretends to think. "To clear the bar for probable cause, you need specific facts to show, like, a fifty-one percent chance that the suspect committed a felony, right?"

"Something like that."

"And there are consequences to making an unlawful arrest, aren't there?"

"If it's unlawful, sure."

Tess looks across the table at the detective's handwritten notes, reviewing the details she's given thus far. An interrogator's job is to apply pressure to a suspect's narrative, but Tess is too canny to fall into the usual traps. She even seems to invite the challenge—if, she figures, Washington can even keep up.

You lonely, lost dinosaur. You missed the comet.

Tess already knows her story is airtight. Her thrilling journey of survival could land its own Lifetime movie—after escaping the carbon monoxide and reaching the surface, she'd stolen Jacob's jacket for warmth and set out to hike through the forest for help.

Faced with rain and low light, she'd taken improvised shelter under a fallen tree. Then at daybreak she'd resumed her long trek through the wilderness, ultimately reaching a highway around noon to collapse dramatically on the side of the road. The semitruck driver who'd stopped to help had feared she was dead at first, wrapped in a dead man's blood-drenched jacket, her hair plastered with twigs and dried mud, one eye burst red.

She's played the role flawlessly.

"I know the laws," she says, "and I know you only have thirty-six hours to hold me without charges."

Washington says nothing.

Tess's lips curl into a microscopic smile, too subtle for the cameras to see. "And then you'll have to let me go."

I know you're only playing a hunch, Layla.

I can still slip away.

48

"DID YOU KNOW PEOPLE USED TO INSTALL BELLS INSIDE COFFINS?"

Allie chewed on her turkey sandwich. "You're making that up."

"Really. It was a thing."

Of course their first date would be at a cemetery. But the coin must be obeyed. That was the first and only rule of the penny date, Ethan had explained, and even though it was mid-February and a crisp thirty degrees, Allie was finding it an oddly pleasant day for a picnic in a graveyard. The sky was hard blue, the foliage all skeletal sticks. She'd lost track of how many times they'd walked the same looping concrete path, their laughing breaths fogging in the air, each time passing that same headstone with a conspicuous rust-eaten gizmo.

She picked away dead leaves. "Why install a bell?"

"As someone who's already died once before, I figured you'd be an expert," Ethan said. "They were called *safety coffins*. That was ages ago, when my field was a total shit show and we cured everything with cocaine and leeches. People used to worry they'd be pronounced dead prematurely by some idiot doctor. Imagine waking up from a coma and realizing you'd been buried alive. The bell was to alert passersby that there was a living person trapped down there inside a coffin, pulling that little string for dear life."

"The origin of the phrase *saved by the bell*?"

He laughed. "Maybe."

Something about walking in circles over hundreds of dead

people prompted reflection (and Jack and Coke in the thermos didn't hurt). Allie had driven past this cemetery countless times on her way to the airport but never actually set foot in it. She'd never paid so much attention to the engravings on headstones or noticed how many husbands and wives chose to be buried together. It was oddly romantic. Reassuring, even. Her own experience with dying in Mexico had been so jarring and lonely that she'd never imagined having company when you go. She'd always traveled alone. Maybe she didn't have to.

Being a public figure is strangely isolating. Strangers may recognize your face, but the connection is strictly one way. You exist in other people's minds as a caricature of yourself, and she sometimes felt like she'd sold part of her soul the day she stopped being Alma. It sounded like the name of a 1950s housewife, but it was still hers, wasn't it? She hadn't planned to be famous or to even monetize her hobby. After high school she'd only wanted to quietly wander the world like Carmen Sandiego, seeing what was over the next hill and the next, but she was also a storyteller, and an English teacher once told her that being a storyteller is a sort of pathological emptiness—when you feel something, you're not satisfied until you've made other people feel it, too. You can't just experience it yourself. You have to *share* it.

Passing through the saddest part of the cemetery, the children's section, Ethan had softened. "My kids had better outlive me."

"You don't have kids." She was still learning about him. ". . . Right?"

"I mean someday."

"You want them?"

"You don't?"

Allie winced, like he'd grazed a nerve. "I'd be a shitty mom."

"I disagree."

"You just met me."

"I know enough." He stepped over a frozen puddle. "Actually, I knew you'd be a good mother the moment I first saw you."

She grabbed his thermos and took a mighty swig. "Bull. Shit."

They'd met last month on a multi-grotto caving trip outside Tucson.

"Before the cave," he said. "That first morning."

The groups had camped in and around an old retrofitted bus. A nifty idea, but in practice the thing stank like armpits and stale rubber. Allie had been the first to rise and claim the outdoor shower. She'd been shampooing her hair when she felt something tickle the top of her foot. Blinking away water, she'd looked down to see knuckled legs crawling over her bare skin—a hairy yellow scorpion, four inches from pincers to stinger.

"It was an Arizona Desert scorpion, right?"

She looked at him. "How do you know that?"

"I wasn't spying on you," Ethan clarified, his hands up. "I was asleep inside the bus, and your voice woke me up."

"My voice?"

"You were *talking* to it." He smiled. "You were trapped inside a little phone booth–sized shower with it, and you were naked, defenseless—"

"How do you know I was naked?"

"I'm assuming."

"Creep."

"My point is, anyone else would've screamed bloody murder or tried to smash it. But you talked to it. You told it not to be afraid. You explained that you weren't going to hurt it, that you were just catching it under a glass so you could safely move it out of the shower. You were so . . . *polite* to the venomous arachnid. And I just listened there in my sleeping bag, until I saw you scamper out of the shower with your hair wet, wrapped in a towel with a scorpion in a cup. And I remember thinking, *Whoever she is, I want to know her.*" Ethan sighed, as if he'd already said too much. "You'd be an amazing mother."

Her stomach fluttered.

For a long moment, Allie and this man she barely knew walked without speaking. His words repeated in her mind, an unexpected sentence she could neither ingest nor ignore, so she turned it over and over. *You'd be an amazing mother.*

As they walked—how many times now had they paced this same loop through the same headstones?—she felt like she was rising, like she could float away. The sensation was deep inside her stomach, both euphoric and terrifying, and she almost tugged Ethan's wrist and kissed him for the first time. Instead, she laughed. "You're full of shit."

"I meant it."

"No, your coffin bell myth." She grinned, circling him. "A bell would never save you. If you woke up buried alive, you'd suffocate long before anyone came by. Compare a human's lung capacity with the size of a coffin—that's a hundred breaths, right? You'd last an hour."

"A little longer." Ethan flashed a know-it-all smile. "Exhaled breath still has oxygen, just less of it every time. The same air can be breathed more than once."

Allie froze.

The same air can be . . .

. . . breathed more than once.

Underwater, she opened her eyes.

She knew the final breath she'd taken from her water bottle moments ago, the air that had raced past her face as tickling bubbles in the dark, had collected somewhere overhead. She craned her neck, tilted her chin up, and pressed her mouth against cold rock. With her lips she found these precious bubbles, trapped in the tunnel's highest crease.

Just traces of oxygen left.

Enough.

She sucked this final breath through her teeth. Then with a few more seconds, a few more heartbeats, Allie tensed her body and braced all her weight against her ankle, against those inches of fragile bone and tendon. This time, she thought about what her boyfriend told her in that cemetery fourteen months ago.

You'd be an amazing mother.

You'd be an amazing mother.

You'd be an amazing—

49

THE INTERROGATION ROOM IS SILENT.

Tess won't break.

Why would she? She already knows she's thought of everything. Washington imagines Tess crawling out of the Devil's Staircase sometime after midnight to finish her grim work: wiping away her fingerprints, rearranging gear, ensuring no trace of her involvement remained. She's already verified that every potential witness at the Devil's Staircase is dead, and of course, the dead can't speak.

But . . .

Well, that's the thing, isn't it?

"You're exactly right, Tess." Washington leans into her chair and finally allows her tensed muscles to relax. "If we'd arrested you without establishing probable cause, it would've violated your rights. I would've screwed up badly, maybe badly enough that my boss would get his wish and send me off to the glue factory. And to be honest, I think you wanted to see an old lady fall on her face." She sets her pen down atop her notepad, perfectly balanced. "But you never considered the alternative, did you?"

Tess stares back. She's feigning confidence, but something in her senses a new danger. A shade of doubt inflects her voice. "I . . . don't understand."

"Let's revisit that day," the detective says. "One last time."

PART IV

Ethan

50

PAIN.

White-hot pain.

But Ethan kept grinding his zip-tied wrists against rock, raking his arms up and down in the same motion, the same steady friction. His clothes were stiff with dried blood. The cloth bag stuck to his face like plastic, suffocating and damp. He drifted out of consciousness, but the sensation kept wrenching him back into his body, like the killer's knife was still there between his organs. The pain tethered him. It kept him alive.

Now after hours of effort, Ethan sensed the restraints were finally weakening, millimeters from snapping free. His heart fluttered with hope—then he heard something.

Soft, padding footsteps emerged from the cave.

Tess.

He lay still on the ground and listened to her paces as she circled unseen, sometimes close, sometimes far. Stopping to examine this and that. Wiping surfaces. Moving things around. Opening the Jeep's door, then shutting it. Tess was surveying her crime scene, confirming and reconfirming her work, the same way Ethan had seen her struggle to gather the nerve to shut her own apartment door. It was chilling, the woman's silent focus.

Then he sensed her footsteps approach him, growing louder and louder—alarmingly close, now—until they stopped inches from his right ear. He knew she was standing directly over him, watching his chest for the rise and fall of breath.

Ethan didn't exhale.

He knew Tess was only double-checking. She'd already examined his body for vital signs hours ago. The bag zip-tied around his throat was an advantage, he'd realized, because it meant Tess could only check for a pulse in his forearms. And sure enough, when she'd pressed her fingers into his wrist, Ethan had silently squeezed his arms inward—against the small rocks he'd positioned under each armpit. Pressure applied to each brachial artery, he knew, would restrict blood flow to his radial and ulnar arteries, hiding his heartbeat.

Now he sensed Tess move on. Satisfied that her work was complete and all witnesses were dead, her footsteps faded away into the forest.

Ethan waited until he was sure she was gone. Then he repositioned onto his side and resumed grinding his zip-tied wrists against rock until the restraint finally, *finally*, snapped. He pulled his arms apart. He tore an eyehole in the fabric. Then he rolled over onto his stomach and crawled uphill toward the Jeep's headlights, every slow inch of progress torturous, every motion another piercing dagger in his guts, screaming through cloth and clenched teeth. Twice, he lost consciousness. But the pain refused to let him go, and at last Ethan got there, gasping and dizzy, and with his fingernails he dragged himself up into the vehicle. Beside the dead man at the wheel he found a citizens band radio mounted to the dashboard.

With bloody fingers, he lifted the microphone.

"*Help.*"

"ETHAN RAMIREZ WAS AIRLIFTED TO PROVIDENCE PORTLAND LATE last night," Washington says. "Last I checked, he's in emergency surgery."

Tess's mouth drops open.

"Guess he's not such an airhead after all, huh? I don't even know how you'd hide your own vitals, but leave it to a physician, I guess. A few hours ago he was even conscious enough to say some very helpful things." The detective stops and smiles. "You can sense where I'm going with this, right?"

Petrified silence.

"You're clever, Tess. Work it out."

Nothing.

"Really? Weren't you paying attention?" The detective looks at her sideways. "Come on, girl. It's been right there in front of you this whole time."

Tess blinks, still not comprehending.

But it's fine. She'll get there.

"All day today, you thought you were playing me—but really, *I* was playing *you*." Washington leans forward. "You were so focused on withholding information from me, it never occurred to you that I might be withholding things, too."

The blood is draining from her skin.

"Right now, as we speak, a massive rescue effort is under way up at the Devil's Staircase. They've been working since last night, all thanks to Ethan and his radio call."

Washington opens her phone, where it all began earlier today. She scrolls through her text chain with the rescue operation's incident commander. Updates, questions, fears. Details of the grueling logistics, team injuries, setbacks.

She stops on one.

We're losing her.

"For twenty-four hours now, they've been working to save Allie's life."

• • •

"You weren't the only survivor, Tess. You only *thought* you were, and I never corrected you. Never interrupt your enemy while they're making a mistake, remember?"

Tess is too shocked to speak.

"You had no idea." Washington flashes a carnivorous grin. "While you limped for miles through the forest all night and flagged down some truck driver in the morning, while you were in an ambulance getting checked out for all your cuts and bruises and napping in your hospital bed and telling me your amazing final-girl story, the real heroes have been working their asses off. It's all over the news by now. They've got specialists coming down from Seattle, volunteers from Flour Gold pitching in with food and supplies and transportation, everyone working together to get Allie out. Bringing her oxygen bottles, clearing collapsed rocks, keeping her warm. She's managed to hold her body out of the water to avoid hypothermia. They even think she *dislocated her own ankle* to reach an air pocket so she could breathe. But getting her out is a slow and dangerous process."

The muscles in Tess's jaw tighten. Her fingernails dig into the vinyl tabletop.

The detective's text chain—**We're losing her**—stays open between them as the screen dims.

"It's been hours since my last update," she says. "And I'll be honest. It's not looking good for Allie. At this point we're all preparing ourselves for bad news. There's a strong chance she's already dead and they'll only recover her body. But I'm guessing we'll find that missing memory card with her, won't we?"

Tess looks sick.

Allie Merritt is a fighter, **a tough gal**, in the incident commander's words, but with every passing hour she's running out of steam. Every lifesaving measure buys just a bit of time.

"God, I hope they can save her. She did a hell of a thing, fighting for herself and her unborn baby, surviving everything you and Jacob threw at her. Like a lot of people right now, I'm praying for Allie. I hope I get the chance to meet her."

Tess can only stare at the dimmed screen, at those three words.

We're losing her.

Until the screen goes fully black.

"But on a lighter note, I did learn a new Finnish word today," Washington says. "Tell me, Tess—have you heard of *sisu*?"

Tess is barely listening. Her eyes are filling with tears—authentic tears, this time—and when she speaks her voice is a beaten croak, almost too faint to hear: "*I . . .*"

"What's that?"

"*I . . . want a lawyer.*"

"That's fine. I've already gotten everything I need." The detective gathers her things, shuts her padfolio, and stands up. "Thank you again, Tess, for everything you've told me today."

On her way out, she smiles wickedly.

"You were a big help."

Opening the door, Washington stops to relax her shoulders and inhale the cooling air outside. She feels like she can finally breathe again. Upon leaving a soundproof room, the world always seems to come alive with fresh ambience: the gentle hum of the ventilation, murmuring voices downstairs, gear lockers shutting. She smells hand sanitizer and stale coffee and frosted cupcakes left over from the receptionist's birthday. The cube-shaped interrogation room has come to feel oppressive, even cave-like, and as an extraordinary young woman she hopes to meet liked to say: *When you leave a cave, the entire world becomes new again.*

Behind her, Tess finds her voice.

"What does *sisu* mean?"

"Doesn't matter." Washington steps out into the hallway. "He wasn't talking about you."

The door swings shut.

Epilogue

ETHAN WAKES UP WITH A TUBE IN HIS THROAT.

To his left, a ventilator wheezes tired breaths directly into his chest. His skin prickles with needles. Through plugged nostrils he smells blood and disinfectant. His thoughts swim through an anesthetic haze, and he struggles to focus his vision, first on the fluorescent lights overhead, then on the room around him.

A shadow stands by the window.

"Hi, Ethan."

He tries to swallow but gags on hard plastic. He can feel the endotracheal tube shifting inside his chest, an uncomfortable pressure.

"My name is Layla Washington," the figure says. "I'm a detective with the Stevens County Sheriff's Department."

He tries to speak, but his vocal cords are compressed.

"You've just been through major surgery, but they tell me you're recovering. Eventually, when you're able to talk again, I'll come by and take a full statement. But only when you're rested and ready, Ethan. No rush at all. I'm just glad you're alive."

With cracked lips, he tries to mouth, *Allie*.

"I'm not here for anything procedural."

He tries again: *Allie—*

"The truth is . . ." The detective smiles, warm and knowing. "The truth is I came here because I have something incredible to show you."

Then she leans around the ventilator to hold her phone close to Ethan's face. Blinking with papery eyelids, he recognizes a text message chain. It's too blurry to read, but in the lowermost left bubble, the newest text message, he can just make out three shapes.

Three words.

He blinks again and they sharpen.

WE SAVED HER

ACKNOWLEDGMENTS

SO MANY THANKS TO MY FAMILY. TO JACLYN, THANK YOU FOR ONCE again putting up with me while I spent many hours writing this book and for always being up for visiting a cave, whether it's a lava tube by Mount Saint Helens or an underground river in Mexico. To my son, Nolan, thank you for always giving me such great company (and climbing on me, and putting stickers on me) while I wrote. Being a work-from-home dad is pretty amazing. To my parents, thank you for all your support of my writing over the years (and those research materials on caves/caving, which were a huge help!).

Thank you to my incredible editor, Jennifer Brehl, whose clear-eyed guidance helped form this story from its smallest kernel and who patiently accompanied me through its many (many, many) iterations. Major thanks to my agent, David Hale Smith; Naomi Eisenbeiss and Megan Amero; and the whole team at Inkwell Management. And a huge thank-you to my manager, Chad Snopek, who once again contributed an extremely valuable early draft read.

And, of course, thank you, reader. I'm so grateful that I get to wake up and do something that I love every day (and call it work), and it's all because of you.

ABOUT THE AUTHOR

TAYLOR ADAMS is the author of several acclaimed thrillers, including *The Last Word*, *Hairpin Bridge*, and *No Exit*. *No Exit* has been published in thirty-two languages and adapted into a Hulu Original film. Adams lives in Washington State.